Sea Horse Ranch

Natalie Keller Reinert

Natalie Keller Reinert Books

Books by Natalie Keller Reinert

The Catoctin Creek Series

The Grabbing Mane Series

The Eventing Series

The Alex & Alexander Series

The Show Barn Blues Series

The Hidden Horses of New York: A Novel

Chapter One

I put up my thumb as another truck passed, but this time it just felt like habit. The hot breath of exhaust it left behind only added to my general sticky grossness. I needed a twenty-five-minute shower and an entire bottle of body wash.

But the prospect of finding a place to bathe and rest was feeling increasingly unlikely.

How had I found myself walking up the side of a two-lane highway deep in the Florida Keys? Oh, the same way dreamy girls always got into this kind of mess.

Chasing a dream and a hot guy.

"This is always how it was going to end," I muttered to myself, watching my toes in my hot pink flip-flops as I walked carefully, one step after another, into the hard-packed white sand along the side of U.S. 1. "There was never any other outcome in play. You run away from home, you sing in a band, you sleep with the singer, and you get kicked out. At the literal end of the continent. Typical Katie."

Yeah, somewhere deep inside, I'd probably known. Of course, it would all end in tears and hitchhiking my way towards home. The only unknown had been *where* it would end.

Wasn't it just my luck that fateful spot would be at Mile Marker 0?

Another pickup truck roared past, this one hauling a small flat-bottomed boat. It bounced along on a trailer with squeaky shocks. They sure loved their boats and pickups down here in the Florida Keys. I liked them, too. Keys culture reminded me a lot of home, back up in the soggy saltwater marshes along the Gulf Coast. Sure, up in Louisiana we spiced our shrimp with Cajun seasoning and down here it came blackened with Jamaican jerk spices, but the general attitude towards life was the same: you got up, you put on your tank top and your flip-flops, and then you fished as much as was humanly possible. Finish off the day with a six-pack or three, depending on your tolerance, and sleep it all off before another big day tomorrow.

That leisurely lifestyle was the only one I'd ever known before I took off with The Bombers. It was how my mom and dad lived, and my brothers, and my uncles and my aunts and my cousins, and everyone else I knew back in St. Bart Bay. It was how I was supposed to live. So, it had come as quite the surprise to the whole lot of them when I'd taken off for New Orleans to sing back-up with some strangers I'd met online.

Well, my mom called them strangers. I'd called them friends.

Kind of sucked that she'd been right. That's the thing about moms, though, isn't it? You never want them to be right. But it seems like they usually are. At least, my mom's that way. Your mileage may vary.

The road quieted for a few minutes, no traffic in sight. It was almost calming: this empty strip of pavement marching through the sea. Water to my right, water to my left. On the right was a bright stretch of turquoise water, its gentle swells lapping against a short but serviceable white-sand beach, where a few spunky coconut palms were waving their fronds in the sea breeze. Beyond the shallow water, the Florida Straits stretched out to the horizon. No land until Cuba.

To the left, the water was deep blue, slapping gently against a grass-choked shore. Mangrove islands popped up across narrow channels, small hummocks of brush dotted with white birds. I understood water like that: not swamp, but not open sea, either. A waterlogged landscape, with islands which were more the tangled roots of trees than dry sand.

And running right up the middle: the sun-faded pavement of U.S. 1, the Overseas Highway. I stood along the roadside and gazed up the road's center line, the two colors of sea blinking on either side of me. They merged again in the distance, the shocking brightness of Caribbean turquoise swallowed up by the darker water. But I felt like I'd seen their secrets. I knew they had different beginnings, those two seas.

A rumble from behind me signaled oncoming traffic. I put out my thumb reflexively, not bothering to look over my shoulder. They weren't going to stop. No one stopped. Not the tourists in their white rental cars, heading back to Miami so they could fly home to parts north and forget their Floridays, the corresponding Jimmy Buffett playlist they'd played on repeat all holiday disappearing forever. Not the fishermen in their pickups. Not the snowbirds in their Buicks and their Cadillacs, zipping between the islands to buy groceries and pick up prescriptions.

The truck went by, a boatless model this time, although it had a big hitch on the back, and a diving flag decal on the rear window—those two were common markers of Monroe County truckdom. I was still studying the dents in the back bumper when the brake lights flashed on, and the truck pulled over onto the narrow, sandy shoulder.

Uh-oh, I thought. *I got something on the line.*

Hope it doesn't have teeth.

❧ ❧

A woman unfolded herself from the truck and walked back towards me. She looked like a typical Conch, just aging away in the sun. A turquoise tank top set off her dark tan and freckled chest, and her cut-off khaki shorts had seen their share of fish guts and motor oil, judging by the stains. She was wearing a sturdy pair of hiking sandals. In the Conch Republic, flip-flops were not required, but socks and shoes were never the correct choice. Her gray and brown hair was drawn back into a ponytail, and the strands bulged in protest, humidity fluffing it into a wild bush.

She looked kind of like my mom.

She looked the way I figured I'd look in thirty years, give or take a decade of hard living.

She also had kind, pale blue eyes which fastened on me as she stopped a short distance away. A respectful distance. She tipped her head. "You crazy, girl?"

I loosened the strap of my backpack and let it fall to the ground, rubbing at my sore shoulder. Life had been easier when both straps were working. "No, just dumb," I said ruefully.

She chuckled. "Where you headed?"

"North," I said simply. That was usually enough. A direction was all anyone offering a ride needed to know, in my opinion. And I'd been hitching since I was fifteen, which was a solid eleven years, thanks for asking, so I had a pretty informed opinion on the subject.

But the saltwater in her veins wasn't cold enough to just let me off the hook with a simple cardinal direction. "North where?"

"By northeast, judging by the road ahead," I joked, pointing up U.S. 1. The highway didn't actually turn north until it hit the mainland—or Key Largo, which a lot of the Lower Keys folks seemed to think was the mainland.

She wasn't having it. "Honey, I'm trying to find out if you've got a problem you need help with."

The word *problem* was gently stressed.

She meant a man.

"He's not my problem anymore." I smiled gamely, to let her know it was fine. My heart wasn't ripped out or anything. Just stomped on a little. It was my pride that needed worrying about. "You heard of the Saltwater and Sunsets Music Festival? Over the weekend down in Key West?"

She nodded. "Sure. Another big tourist weekend in Key West. They have a way of drawing all the drivers right past the other islands."

She sounded almost...bitter? As if she wanted some of the tourists to stay. Well, *that* wasn't the normal reaction. Now I was curious. Curious enough to hitch my bag back over my shoulder and keep talking. "I was down for that, performing. Only now I'm not in the band anymore. So I need a way home. Think you could just get me a few more miles up the road? I can camp on the beach if I don't find my way all the way to Miami."

I didn't really know what I'd do in Miami. Maybe give up, call my mom, beg for a plane ticket home. I'd rather do almost anything else. Clean toilets. Rake seaweed. Pick up garbage. Whatever it took to avoid groveling. I was prepared for something good to happen, just in case the universe wanted to go off-script for an afternoon.

"Well, if you want to keep going north, sure," the woman agreed. She looked me over again, from my sandals to my straw hat. "Or if you want to stop for a night or two and get your head back on straight, you can stay at the ranch. I find folks always feel good after they've spent some time talking to my horses."

The word *ranch* was unexpected. I would have been less surprised if she'd suggested I stay overnight in her hot-air balloon. I looked from side to side: the dark water of the bay, the turquoise of the strait. Then back and forth, up and down this narrow road, running through the narrow chunk of coral and coquina that passed for dry land in this sunken part of the world. Still didn't make sense. I asked, politely as I could, "The *ranch?*"

And that was what did it: the faded blue in her eyes positively sparkling, the smile on her face as warm and welcoming as if I'd found out the secret password. "Yes, ma'am. I run Sea Horse Ranch," she announced. "Name's Crystal Linney." She took a few steps closer and held out a calloused, sun-dotted hand. I took it.

"Katie LeBlanc," I replied, feeling the steely strength in her hand. "I'm a retired singer."

"Retired!" She looked me up and down with surprise. "Honey, you look pretty young for retirement."

"Well, it isn't by choice," I said, grinning to take the sting out. "But you know how it is. Tough world out there."

"It sure is," Crystal Linney agreed. "It sure is. That's why I try to avoid it, best as I can."

Chapter Two

Crystal took back her hand, her expression still bemused. "I don't know, though, retired? You look a little young to be using the *r* word."

I spread my hands innocently. "Sometimes you get forced out, y'know? I'm just trying to keep a positive outlook on life. Everyone wants to be retired, right?"

Crystal grinned and beckoned me to follow her as a semi-trailer blew past, scattering gravel. "Come on. Let's get out of the shoulder before one of us ends up roadkill."

Well, I'd made my choice. And while I usually liked to ride in the back of a pickup—with hitching, quick getaways can be the name of the game—I gamely climbed up into the passenger side of Crystal's truck. It was an old Chevy with a bench seat covered by a brightly colored Navajo blanket, a lot of sand and grass clippings on the rubber floor mats, and a pile of mail in the middle.

"Don't mind the mess," Crystal advised, unembarrassed. "I pick up the mail in town once a week and forget it."

"Where's town?" I put my backpack at my feet. A little grass wouldn't hurt it, not after the places that bag had already gone with me. "Key West?"

"You got it. Even though I live closer to Big Pine."

I remembered Big Pine Key from the drive south. I'd wanted to creep into the back streets behind U.S. 1, maybe find some of those elusive Key Deer that people talked so much about. But I didn't know if the locals would welcome some hitchhiker wandering their quiet neighborhoods. Back in St. Bart Bay, a vagrant got told which road to take on their way out of town, and they were watched until they were a tiny dot in the distance.

"And where's the...the ranch?" I asked, finding a hard time getting my mind around using that word out here. Crystal was pulling back onto U.S. 1, and a long bridge loomed ahead, connecting this little piece of sand with the next little piece of sand. Water spread all around us, sparkling in the southern sun. Where could there be a ranch out here?

"It's just a few miles up this way, then over a couple little bridges on the bay side." Crystal smiled to herself. "I call it Sea Horse Ranch. But we're actually on a little island called Hell and Dammit Cay."

"You're on *what?*"

"Hell and Dammit," she repeated, confirming I hadn't heard her wrong. "Funny, right? Some old cuss named it that because he kept wrecking his shrimp boat on a reef just offshore. Then some government fellas came around when they was laying out the post office codes or something, and they asked for the name, wrote it down, and that's what we got. Hell and Dammit Cay. That's *cay* like *key,* by the way. Spelled C-A-Y but not pronounced that way. Don't get it wrong, or you'll sound like a tourist."

I was almost afraid to ask Crystal anything else. So much to take in. A ranch. On an island named by an angry, mildly profane fisherman. And not for nothing, but apparently I'd been pronouncing the word *cay* wrong for like, a really long time. What else would I get wrong if I opened my mouth?

I decided I'd better just settle down and enjoy the view.

Crystal seemed fine with my silence. She pointed out places of interest as we passed them. "That there's Half-Moon Beach. Roy Ellis caught a shark off that pier once that was filled with gold jewelry. No one ever explained how a shark could eat that much jewelry." She chuckled to herself, then pointed at a low, brown building with several trucks parked in the sandy lot out front. "That's the Slutty Mermaid Saloon. It doesn't have a sign. That's to keep the tourists away. Plus, if they put up a sign with that name, the morality police would probably go nuts. We got all types down here. Puritans and prostitutes. And look there—*that's* the palm tree that my neighbor Marchant Davis tied up to when Hurricane Betty raised the water so fast, he was carried out to sea while he was still taking the sails down off his boat."

I had to admit of all that crazy, the tree thing really got me. The palm tree was all by itself on a mound of sand at least twenty feet above the water. That palm tree was probably the highest point in the Florida Keys. I could see it surviving a storm surge, its fronds fluttering gamely, but, still, I was skeptical that someone could've tied their sailboat that high above solid ground. "Oh, now, that *can't* be true."

"I saw it with my own eyes, when I rowed over to check on poor old Marchant before the water went down," Crystal informed me. "And there's a photo of it hanging behind the bar of the Slutty Mermaid. Everything here was under water."

"What about the ranch? Wasn't it underwater?"

For a moment, Crystal's easy-going expression slipped. "Well, the houses out there have stilts," she said. "And we didn't have any horses back then. Just goats. We took the goats with us up into the house and they were fine. Marchant replaced my floors, though. That floor wasn't fine, believe me. I got rid of the blame things after that. *Never again,* I said." She rested an elbow on the truck door and leaned her cheek on her hand, looking thoughtful. "We don't get many storm surges that cover the islands, though."

Then and there, I resolved I wouldn't bring up hurricanes again. The big storms were a constant threat during the long, sultry summers in St. Bart Bay, too. We mostly dealt with them by building dikes and putting houses on stilts, but only one of those options would work out in the Keys, and I didn't think horses would appreciate climbing up the stairs of a barn on stilts. They'd have to evacuate the horses to higher ground if a storm surge was forecast. Couldn't be easy trying to get out of here in a normal car, with only one road for all these islands. It would be worse with a trailer full of horses, I was sure.

Just a few dozen feet past the Slutty Mermaid, Crystal turned down a narrow road paved only in sand and some kind of pulverized stone, shimmering white in the sunlight. I'd noticed these white roads in other parts of Florida; someone at a gas station outside Daytona Beach had told me it was likely limestone rock or crushed coquina, which was a crumbling blend of fossilized shells and prehistoric sands. It had a washboard surface in a few places, and deep pools of milky colored rainwater in the occasional pothole.

We were on a wide island, no trace of the bay on either side of the road, but instead there were deep, narrow ditches lining either side. The black water in their depths hinted at disappearing bodies and creatures of unusual size. This was something else I'd noticed about Florida: it wasn't all palm trees and bikinis at all. Driving south in the band's van, taking old highways to avoid expensive toll roads, I looked out at those ditches and vast swamps and figured those, more than anything else, were what gave Florida its endless potential for crazy crime. Things could just *vanish* in Florida.

I could vanish, if I kept on hitch-hiking here. Or if Crystal turned out to be a murderer. Anything was possible. But I pushed that thought out of my head.

Palms and occasional stands of bamboos grew thick behind the ditches. Little driveways humped over the moats from time to time, and rusting mailboxes proved not everyone had to haul down to Key West to get their catalogs and bills. I tried to peer down the driveways, but mostly just saw flashes of tantalizing color through the thick foliage.

"The houses here are pretty bright," I observed, after seeing a coral-pink house through a quick break in the brush.

"Folks like to go their own way here," Crystal said. "You move out onto these islands, no homeowner's association is telling you what color to paint your house. Now, look here, this is the first bridge."

Only one lane wide, and just about twelve feet long, the little concrete bridge made a disconcerting hum when the truck passed over it. Crystal laughed at my expression. "It's a solid bridge, I swear. We call it the Humming Bridge." I could hear the capital letters in her voice. "When it *stops* making that noise, that's when we got trouble. Means something's shifted and we gotta get a county engineer to come look."

"What causes the humming?"

"Something about the rocks on either side, Marchant says."

"The guy with the boat."

"Well, we all have boats. But yeah, the hurricane boat. That's Marchant. He has the place across the road from me. Old friend of mine. The best." Crystal smiled to herself.

The island we were on now was even more intensely jungly than the last one, with only a few houses visible through thickets of palms and thickly leaved vines. I caught glimpses of coquina walls, an occasional boat resting quietly at a short pier. They didn't even seem to be bobbing on the glassy waters. "So, which island is this?" I asked.

"This is Little Bucket Key. With a *k,* this time."

"Why are some spelled like key and some like cay?" I pronounced 'cay' the wrong way on purpose this time.

"Depends on who wrote it down first," Crystal explained. "Lotta the early folks here didn't really know much spelling. At least, that's what I've been told."

We passed a mailbox with a red bucket turned over atop the post. "And that's the little bucket," Crystal said, and I didn't even question it.

This was the Keys. Nothing was too weird to be true.

"Here's the last bridge," she said, pointing ahead. Also single-lane, but somewhat longer, the bridge to Hell and Dammit Cay sat low over the blue-green channel it crossed. It wouldn't take much of a flood to cover that bridge, I thought. No wonder Marchant Davis tried to float away from the hurricane on his boat.

This bridge didn't hum. But it did seem to tremble a bit. Crystal said nothing about the gentle wobble, and I decided not to bring it up. The water was shallow when you came right down to it.

"And here's Hell and Dammit," she said proudly as the truck's tires connected with sand again and I permitted my clenched fists to relax. "A real hidden gem, we call it." She braked to give me a moment to take it in.

I looked around. The island was small, and far more cleared out than Little Bucket Key. I could see the far shore ahead of us, less than a half-mile away, though the road ended well before that. Scruffy grass covered the ground between the road's end and the rocky shore. The island seemed to be divided into quadrants, and four stilted houses rose from along the waterside. They'd been built to be identical, but I could tell their owners' distinct personalities had altered them over the years.

There were some good plantings of tropical hardwood trees and pretty flowering hedges along the road, plus some clusters of plain-Jane Sabal palms, like the ones that grew up in St. Bart Bay. If there were horses, or a ranch, I couldn't see them. I guessed the thick foliage along the roadside was blocking the view.

Closer to the bridge we'd just crossed, the shorelines on either side ran away from the road with brief, tan-colored beaches. Tall white egrets and stilt-legged sandpipers stalked the sands. From a nearby rock, a green iguana regarded me leisurely. I blinked at it for a moment. It was the largest lizard I'd ever seen: at least six feet long, from horny nose to black-tipped tail.

"Oh yeah, that's Roger," Crystal said, nonchalant.

"Hey, Roger."

The iguana slowly, deliberately, closed his eyes.

"Right," I said.

Crystal chuckled and pointed over her steering wheel. "So just ahead and to the right, behind those banyan trees, is where my fencing begins. The yellow house you can see there is mine. And on the left, in that blue house, is where Marchant lives, and then just beyond that, in the pink house, that's Stacy. You'll love Stacy," Crystal added comfortably, as if I was coming for an extended stay.

"Who lives in the fourth house?" I asked. "The sorta gray one?"

"No one," Crystal said. "That was my dad's house. It's falling apart inside. Dunno when we'll ever have enough money to fix it."

"Oh, that's too bad."

Crystal shrugged. "We got enough for us," she said.

Then the truck moved past the trees and showed me the full, startling expanse of Sea Horse Ranch, and I forgot about the abandoned house.

Chapter Three

C rystal gunned the engine, and I leaned forward, suddenly eager to see what was beyond those trees. The huge, drooping branches of the banyan trees were a sight in and of themselves; in any other situation, I could have just stood and admired those trees.

But just on the other side of their red-brown trunks, a strange little world opened up in front of us. I wouldn't have called it a ranch. I mean, I don't know what the word *ranch* conjures up for most people, but for me, it had always been wide open spaces, grasslands stretching as far as the eye could see, and probably some jagged mountain peaks in the distance. And while I knew not to expect the Rocky Mountains to be waiting for me in the middle of the Lower Keys, I still had some vague notion that Hell and Dammit Cay would end up being a lot bigger than the previous islands had been.

Let me tell you, it wasn't.

Ranch, in this case, meant a motley collection of pens, made from wooden fences running at right angles into one another whenever possible. Apparently, though, it hadn't been possible all the time, or whoever built the fences had been doing so while drunk, so there were rectangular pens, triangular pens, trapezoidal pens. The fences ran crazily together under the shade of palm trees and some scrubby island tree I couldn't name, and beneath the trees, shaking their heads and swishing their tails, stood small horses.

They were adorable, these little horses. I cooed with delight the moment I saw them, and Crystal made a small wiggle in her seat, something that looked like pride. She had every right to feel that way. The ranch might not have been a wide open vista, but the horses were absolutely beautiful. They more than made up for a lack of Rocky Mountains as a backdrop.

They were colored red and brown and golden and gray, or patched black-and-white, with their sweet little horse faces splashed with white blazes and gleaming stars and thick forelocks. All of them were turned to face us, their heads held high, their ears pricked, looking absolutely astonished at the truck's appearance, as if they'd never seen such a machine in their lives.

Behind the horses, I saw a long, low structure which must have been the barn, with a corrugated metal roof and open stall doors. Through their back windows, I could see the unrelenting blue of the sea surrounding the island. Just off to the left sat Crystal's yellow house, looking down at us from its high stilts. The house's wraparound porch gazed out over the palms and a few struggling shade trees; its wide patio doors were shaded with vertical blinds. The paint was peeling; the house looked weatherbeaten and tired, but welcoming. A few shingles flapped in the steady sea breeze.

I didn't know what to say. I'd seen hardscrabble farms before—I was from the South, for heaven's sake. We *specialized* in hardscrabble—but I hadn't expected to see such a mainland kind of settlement lifting out of the still waters of Florida Bay on this tiny island.

Crystal turned up a driveway that led to the house and parked the truck on the concrete pad beneath the house. I looked through the windshield, at the water lapping gently against the coquina rocks lining the shore just a few dozen feet away, and wondered how I was going to get out of here in a day or two. I couldn't exactly wave my hand and say, "Thanks for having me, but I must be going!" and stroll back down to the road. I was at least six miles and two bridges away from U.S. 1. It would take me until sunset to reach the highway, and no one was going to pick me up at night.

No one I'd want to pick me up, anyway.

Nope, I was stuck here.

But there were places to be stuck, I guessed. Like under some bridge along the Overseas Highway, trucks roaring overhead and the smell of rotting seaweed in my nose. Maybe I was marooned on this isolated ranch, but Crystal was nice, and the house looked comfortable, and there were horses. How mad could I be about getting stranded on a tiny island ranch populated with those beautiful horses?

This was a step up, for sure.

Crystal was getting out of the truck. "Come upstairs and drop your things," she suggested. "Then I'll introduce you to the kids."

❧❦

The view from the top was better than I'd expected. Yes, this ranch was sorely missing the sunlit vistas and green grass of my preconceived notions, but the place was pretty tidy. From the porch, I could look down at the pens and see that there was an order to the madness. They made the best use of the shade and space available, and all the horses looked comfortable and content.

Crystal's house, in contrast, was a perfect square. The outer walls seemed to be half-glass, there were so many sliding glass doors, and what with the creaking wooden porch that was always just a few feet away, the rustle of the palm fronds at foot-level, and the slap of the sea against the stones below, I could tell there would be a pleasant soundtrack to fall asleep to later tonight. Yeah, I was already okay with staying here for a while. I could use some sleep that wasn't punctuated by the snores of my former band-mates, or Justin's wandering hands right when I was drifting off.

The house's decor hadn't been updated since the early 90s, so there was a lot of pastel, some rattan furniture of grandmother vintage, and a lot of light florals which put me in mind of *The Golden Girls*—so not bad, really. The band stayed in a lot of Airbnbs while on the road and the IKEA minimalism had been getting to me. How many stark-white bedrooms with red and black trim can one girl sleep in before she starts having nightmares in faux-Swedish?

There were an equal number of horse photos and sailboat photos on slivers of wall which weren't given over to views of the sea and the island, so I was studying a picture of a younger Crystal smiling next to a flashy black-and-white pony when she emerged from the kitchen with two glasses of iced tea. "Let's go out on the porch and I'll show you the place," she suggested.

We started to the south, looking over the horses, which didn't surprise me. "These are the kids," Crystal said, waving her hand over the little farm. "Six little horses, all mustangs."

I choked on my sweet tea. "Did you say *mustangs?* Like, Spirit of the Cimarron?"

Crystal gave me a vague look.

"It's a cartoon," I explained. "A kid's movie."

"Oh, I think I know the one you mean. Yes, like mustangs from out west. I rescued them from a farm up in north Florida."

"All of them?"

"Mm-hmm. And I brought them back here to do trail rides. Well, beach rides. You know, like folks do when they go on cruises to the Caribbean. I thought that would be a fun business to try out. They did trail rides at their old place. They're real calm."

"Sure." I looked over the horses. They had gone back to eating —all of them had piles of hay, since there was little grass growing on the sandy ground. They looked pretty fat and happy. I considered what I knew about horses. They ate a lot of hay. They were sometimes surprised by things they saw every day, like squirrels or birds or a bucket moved to a new spot.

I also knew how to get on a horse and stay on, thanks to friends with horses back home, but beyond that, I found horses were kind of a mystery. Still, not seeing ribs under their coats seemed like a good sign, especially without pastures full of green grass. Crystal must have *some* idea what she was doing. "So, what happened with the beach rides? I didn't see a sign or anything. You haven't started yet?"

"Well, there was one problem with my idea. And I thought it would be easier to fix than it has been, so far." Crystal spread her arms to take in the whole of Hell and Dammit Cay, which didn't take much effort. "You see what we don't have?"

I looked around. The other houses, sitting behind their clumps of palm trees, then rocky shorelines. Just beyond the western shore, water gently swirled around that hidden reef which had caused the shrimp boat captain to lose his temper. It lapped against the coquina stones lining the island.

"There's no beach," I realized.

"There's no beach," Crystal repeated.

The enormity of her mistake made my idiotic decisions over the past year seem like tiny stumbles in comparison. "Well...um, oops," I said.

Crystal nodded and sipped at her tea.

For a moment we stood in silence, looking over the pens and the horses. This place had a strange beauty, not quite tropical, but not like the mainland, either. The earth tones of the horses and the green fronds of the palm trees complemented one another perfectly. A bougainvillea with vibrant fuchsia blooms was climbing over the nearest end of the long, low stable, and more bushes with blooms I couldn't name were dotting the house's little yard. Butterflies danced from flower to flower and caught updrafts as the sea breeze met the house, some of them so large they seemed fake.

Suddenly, I *loved* this place. I felt a rush of gratitude for Crystal for picking me up and bringing me back here to this hidden little slice of paradise. I had no idea what I was doing here, but it was miles away from dragging myself, ride by ride, to Miami and the shame of calling home for money.

When I'd told the universe I was open to possibilities, it had definitely taken me seriously.

Chapter Four

"Can you build beaches?" I wondered aloud. There was quite a bit of shoreline attached to the ranch, plus everything on the other side of the island...surely the neighbors wouldn't object to a beautification project that just included a few horses trotting by once or twice a day. Judging by the thick shrubbery and unmown grass under the neighboring houses, Marchant and Stacy weren't too fussy about appearances.

"You can, but it would cost more than I've got. Especially with the horses already here and eating." Crystal laughed and sighed at the same time, a complicated sound for a complicated emotion. "I do what I can with them—I give a few riding lessons to local kids, I trailer them to local carnivals to do pony rides. We manage. But it was a little disappointing to get them out here and realize the beaches were gone. I hadn't lived here for a while...I just didn't know it had changed."

"Wait, so there *used* to be beaches?"

"Until Hurricane Betty."

"Oh, right." I recognized the name of the storm that marooned the mysterious Marchant alongside a palm tree. "I guess the surge carried away all the sand."

"It sure did. And my dad helped Marchant put out coquina along the south and west shores so we wouldn't lose any more of the island. One of the last things he did here. This was my dad's fish-camp once upon a time. He owned the whole island. Then he built these houses, and sold one to Marchant, one to the woman who lived here before Stacy." Crystal took a long sip of her tea, looking thoughtful. "I rented this house out after he passed away. Came back sometimes and stayed in Dad's house until it got beat up in a big storm. Didn't move into this house until last year. I bought the horses before I came, but I was thinking of the old island, not the new one."

Crystal walked over to the north side of house and pointed at the water. I saw a narrow strip of yellow and gray sand. It ran along the northern shore of the island in each direction, right behind the stable. "That's the last of the beach," she said grimly. "Thing I forgot is, these islands are always changing. What's here one year might be underwater the next. Or pushed two miles downstream."

"That's the hard part," I agreed. "It's kind of like that where I'm from, too."

"You're from the shore?"

"Louisiana," I said. "Near the Gulf."

Crystal nodded. "You understand, then."

I turned, looking back over the horses in their pens. Suddenly, movement in the distance caught my eye. At the blue stilted house across the way—Marchant's, I remembered—a figure had come onto the porch. He waved a flag in the air. The motion seemed to be aimed at us.

"Is that man waving a Jolly Roger at us?" I asked, clutching my glass a little more tightly. I hoped I hadn't stumbled into some strange Florida Keys pirate adventure.

But Crystal just smiled. "Oh, good. He must have something real tasty for dinner. You up for a little company? If not, I can just fix us something on the grill here." Crystal gave me a pleading look, which suggested I choose Marchant's offer over her grilling.

"Company's good," I agreed. I was used to eating with strangers every night, anyway. What was touring with a band, if not meeting a lot of new people every day in clubs you might never return to, in cities you might never see again?

I'd thought it would be a lot more glamorous, but hey, twenty-something girls with big dreams? We weren't always that smart.

Crystal put down her glass and walked back to the sliding glass door we'd come out of. She picked up a furled flag I hadn't noticed before and snapped it into action. Below us, a few horses squealed and kicked up their legs, spooked by the rattle of fabric. It was another Jolly Roger, of course. I had a pair of pirates on my hands.

When Crystal and Marchant had finished waving their Jolly Rogers in whatever flag language they'd devised, she leaned the flag against the wall and gestured to the door. "I'm just going to head down and feed the kids first. You want to come help?"

I hesitated, not sure I was any good at helping with horses. Especially in flip-flops. And in that moment, my stomach rumbled loudly. I remembered I hadn't had anything to eat since some smoked fish dip and crackers I'd grabbed at a market just outside Key West, going on seven hours ago now.

"The sooner the kids eat, the sooner we eat," Crystal said with a wink.

"Well then, let's feed up," I agreed.

I guessed I was a ranch-hand now.

I didn't think you could feed horses while wearing sandals—someone's mom had told me that once, back in the day, but Crystal didn't seem to have a problem with it. She kept on her hiking sandals, and I flip-flopped along behind her.

It turned out that we didn't actually have to handle any horses. Crystal opened a door in the stable, then handed me a stack of buckets filled with horse feed. The buckets had names written on them; so did each stall door. So I just matched the names, snapped the buckets into place in the stalls,   and obeyed when Crystal told me to stand back. She marched out to the closest pen, opened the gate, and let the horses inside do the rest.

"They put themselves in," she explained as the first two horses went bolting past.

The horses flew into their stalls as if they were being chased by demons, snorting and huffing and sliding in the sand as they executed serious angles to get inside and eating as quickly as possible. All of them knew their own stalls; none of them made a single mistake. I was impressed. My dad's hunting dogs couldn't seem to remember their individual kennels and would all crowd into one, then beg for their dinner while standing over a single bowl, like that was how they ate every night.

"Horses are smarter than dogs," Crystal told me after I shared how different the dogs were, "because they're prey animals, and it's harder to stay alive when you're being hunted than when you're the hunter."

This seemed like an extreme version of folk wisdom, which I had previously been forced to live without, and maybe if I'd heard it before, I would have made better decisions. Like not leaving home with a handsome man in black leather who made a lot of promises I should have known he'd never keep. In the world of nightclubs and dive bars I'd unwittingly been thrust into, where I'd initially just trailed Justin with a goofy smile on my face, a young woman like me could certainly be regarded as prey.

Crystal walked back to the stable once all the horses were inside, eating. "Now, we'll just close their doors up and they'll be all set for a while. Drop the screens over each stall while you're at it, hon. Just tug on the Velcro like this—" Crystal pulled at a strap attached to a coil of black fabric above the nearest stall door, and it tumbled down, revealing itself to be a screen. "The weights on the bottom keep it close to the door."

"That's pretty clever. It keeps the bugs out?"

"Mostly. The mosquitoes here are real bloodsuckers," Crystal said. "It's probably the one really bad thing about living here." She let down another screen. "Well, that and the hurricanes."

"Are there a lot of hurricanes here?" I asked, as we went back up the stairs to get cleaned up for dinner with Marchant. "We get a lot in Louisiana, so I know what that's like."

"It's not that there's a lot, or even that they're usually that bad," Crystal explained. "It's that there's so little you can do about them. The drive is so long. When there *is* a big one and it's really time to go, that's a real bad feeling. See my trailer over there?" Crystal pointed at the shiny white rig parked just beyond the farm. It was probably the newest thing on the island. "It's a six-horse. So I can never have more than six horses. That's all I can hope to get out of here. They ain't goats. Can't take 'em upstairs."

"Have you ever evacuated them before?" I couldn't remember if the Keys had been threatened by any hurricanes in the past few years.

"Never," Crystal said, brushing dirt from between her toes on the doormat. "Hurricane Betty was years ago. We haven't had anything near that bad since. Once, when I lived on Big Pine Key, I evacuated, but the only animals I had to get out was a dog named Blue and my son's hamsters. And it didn't even flood. Waste of a drive with him hollering in the backseat."

I glanced at her when she mentioned a son, but Crystal didn't elaborate and I decided not to ask. Children could be a sore subject, I'd found. Just ask my mom.

Chapter Five

Marchant Davis lived for the color blue. His pale blue house was completely blue on the inside. Blue paint on the walls, blue carpets on the tile floors, blue sofas and blue chairs, a blue throw on the guest room bed, and a blue quilt on the master. He showed off the entire house to me with broad waves of a blue-jacketed arm and a voice swollen with pride, a captain's hat perched on his gray curls like he'd just finished navigating a cruise ship up to the dock outside his house. I liked him immediately.

"Your house is very...blue," I told him as we wrapped up the tour, standing on the porch looking over the glittering sweep of Florida Bay. The sun was sinking towards the sea, and a few streaks of pink were just appearing as clouds began to catch the changing rays. Of the two houses I'd been in so far, Marchant's would definitely win the sunset wars. A broad, uncluttered view like this would send a Key West tourist into hysterics.

"Blue's my favorite color," he said unnecessarily. "The color of the sea."

I didn't point out that the shallow water just below us was the color of pea soup. I knew what he meant. "And the sky," I suggested instead.

"And Crystal's *beautiful* eyes," Marchant sang, looking over his shoulder.

Crystal had thrown herself onto a sapphire sofa and was stroking a silken-coated Persian cat. She waved her free hand at Marchant and me. "Crazy old man. Don't believe a word he tells you, Katie."

"What's that about?" I stage-whispered to Marchant, already liking their vibe. Best friends with benefits? That would be great. An older couple living out here on this bohemian, forgotten island...why not have a little fun? Plus, the guy wore a captain's hat with an utter lack of pretentiousness. He was a hoot. I wanted Crystal and Marchant to be together so badly I could barely stand it.

"Crystal *refuses* to fall in love with me," he hissed back, waggling his thick eyebrows dangerously. "But for her, no one can compare to that rascal, Lou. He has her whole heart."

"Oh, no. Not *Lou.*" I was going to play this out as long as I could. "Why Lou?"

"Well, he's *at least* ten years younger than her, for starters," Marchant said tragically. "And he has a truly heroic tan. He looks like the God of the Sea."

"Ten years!" Crystal snorted. "He's a lot younger than that, thanks."

Marchant winked. "Lou, like his mother, does not age. He is always a perfect twenty-five years old. Like a god who has risen from the sea."

Well, damn. Now I wanted to meet Lou. "You don't say."

"I'm dead serious." Marchant crossed his heart, brass buttons and all. "But don't get your hopes up. He belongs only to Crystal."

Crystal got up and stalked over to the open porch door, the Persian cat dandled in her arms like a newborn. One paw fell dramatically over her elbow, as if the cat had fainted there. "Don't believe a word he says about Lou," Crystal informed me. "He's teasing you."

I looked back at Marchant, willing up my most hurt and pouty expression. "You *teased* me?"

He gave me a hopeful smile. "Only the part about Crystal being in love with him. I mean, she loves him, obviously, but she's not *in* love with him. That would be inappropriate."

Crystal snorted. "Just a little."

Well, that was a relief. I didn't want to have to fight off my benefactor if this guy really was a young Poseidon. "So, where is this Lou?"

Marchant turned to Crystal. "Well, Lou's Mother? Whither the prodigal son?"

Crystal huffed at us both, then turned and stalked back inside the house. I looked back at Marchant, truly blindsided. "Her *son?*"

He shrugged, but his smile seemed a little sad. "He is. But I guess she doesn't want to talk about it."

❧❦

I was afraid Crystal was genuinely mad about the whole thing, but this seemed to be a regular routine between the two of them. By the time Marchant had shuffled off to put the grouper on the grill, heavily seasoned with something he called "Dammit Salt," she was over her pique and had sent the fluffy cat off to hunt the little lizards which populated the deck.

She joined me at the western railing, where I was breathing in the scent of charcoal smoke and looking towards the sunset, watching for the green flash like a good little tourist in the Keys. "Brought you a beer," she said, holding up a glass bottle with pale yellow contents. "But then I realized I didn't ask if you drink."

"Sure I do," I said, taking the beer. "Thanks. Is that a question you have to ask a lot? I would've thought most people around here drink...beer," I added, not wanting it to sound like I was calling everyone in the Keys alcoholics.

"Oh, yeah, lotta alcoholism here," Crystal said, as if echoing my thoughts. "When it's in your family a lot, like it is mine, you learn to ask. Saves the other folks from having to explain themselves."

"That makes sense." I took a sip; the beer was light and faintly sweet, something to drink a lot of on a hot day. "On the road, I ran into a lot of people with problems, but admitting it was usually too hard, so they'd just drink to keep up with the rest." Or smoke, or snort, or whatever else was on offer. My innocence had been lost pretty quickly after I set out on my musical career. The things people were willing to do in the back of a van, or the back of a club, or off the chest of a friend, were pretty shocking.

Crystal was quiet for a moment, her gaze far away, as if she was looking past the sunset, which was a riot of gold and pink and purple. I could imagine the crush of tourists in Key West's Mallory Square right now, screaming and drunk and taking selfies with the sunset, and I felt a profound relief to be here instead, on this strange island off an island off an island, two bridges and a million miles from the Overseas Highway where they all clustered in their rental cars and tour buses.

"So, uh, is the green flash real?" I heard myself saying, and then I privately cursed myself for bringing up a tourist trap tall tale.

"It's real, all right," Crystal said, surprising me. "But you won't see it tonight."

"Why's that?" I expected an answer that was half old wives' tale, half local meteorology.

"Air's wrong," Crystal said, only partially fulfilling my prophecy.

"What's that mean?"

But Crystal just pointed over at Marchant, who was fiddling with the grill down at ground level. "The fish is almost done. And you'll want to eat it while it's hot. Save yourself some beer. Even if you like spicy, you're going to be crying when you taste that Dammit Salt."

I was a girl reared on Crystal Hot Sauce and Cajun spices, so that sounded promising. Still, I made sure there was a decent level of beer left in my bottle when Marchant arrived on the deck, placing a big platter of blackened fish on the picnic table.

Crystal went inside and emerged with a bowl of salad, a bottle of ranch dressing, and a big loaf of some rustic-looking bread. One look at that hunk of bread and my mouth was watering. I was a sucker for carbs, and I hadn't had any in weeks. Justin liked me in hot pants and tight shirts up on stage, but it was awfully hard to keep a sleek figure when you spent most of the day in a van. The only way I'd been able to stay slim was to put up with a very exhausting no-carb flu on my way to perfect ketosis. But honestly? I hated every minute of my high-protein diet. "Bring on the flab," I told the bread, reaching for a slice as soon as Crystal finished cutting into it.

"Are you talking to your bread?" she asked, eyebrows lifted.

"You don't?" Marchant countered before I could find an excuse. "I made that bread from scratch. The least you could do is say hello."

"Marchant has a sourdough starter he's been keeping since before Hurricane Betty," Crystal explained.

"Did you take it on your boat with you?" I was even more excited now that I knew it was sourdough.

"You better believe it," Marchant assured me. "This sourdough is named Louisa, and she is like a daughter to me."

"A delicious daughter?" Crystal took a heap of grouper and slid it onto my plate. Dark seasoning had been scorched right onto the pale flesh. It looked incredible and smelled even better. "You need to lay off the weird parental jokes, Marchant. That's two too many for me"

"I'm sorry," Marchant told her. "That was ungallant of me, before. Very unseaworthy joke."

"Against all maritime law," I added, before forking a heaping helping of grouper into my mouth. I nearly choked on the tastes of charcoal and pepper filling my mouth. I felt like I'd taken a bite of bonfire.

"Another beer?" Crystal asked, getting up from the table. "I'll bring us all some. And maybe some milk," she added, with a last concerned look at me. I guessed my face was turning red.

Marchant didn't seem to notice anything was wrong. "So, what on earth brings you to the loneliest little island in all the Keys, my dear? No one comes here by accident."

"I can imagine." I was having trouble speaking, what with the blistering action in my mouth right now. I swallowed everything left in my beer bottle. It helped in more ways than one. "I was just leaving for up north, but then Crystal gave me a ride here."

"Up north? But why? Did the Keys treat you badly? Oh wait." Inspiration struck Marchant. "You went to *Key West*."

"Well, yes."

"There's your first mistake."

"A true tourist move," Crystal agreed, bringing out several clinking bottles. "But she's learning. Our Katie is a quick study."

I wondered how I'd become *our Katie* so quickly. Were they adopting me? Was this my new family? What if they were a cult? And why hadn't that occurred to me before?

I looked around. The sun had set, and the sky was shifting from pink to indigo. The sea was dark, and the tiki torches Marchant had lit to scare away the mosquitoes were snapping cheerfully in the ever-present breeze. In the distance, the barn where the horses were eating their supper hay was a shadowy reminder of this island's truly unique charm. And the two people sitting at this table with me were gazing at me with fond eyes.

If this was a cult, sign me up.

"But I must know more," Marchant insisted. "Please. I have given you grouper a la Hell and Dammit Cay. Give me a story in return."

I swallowed another smoldering bite of the blackened grouper, gasped, and drank more beer. With this much alcohol lubricating my tongue, there was no way telling this story would be painful. Right?

Chapter Six

"I don't even know where to begin," I said eventually.

"At the beginning," Marchant suggested, somewhat predictably.

"Or at the end," Crystal said wryly. "You were walking up U.S. 1 hitchhiking without even turning around to see what kind of crazy person might be driving up behind you."

"You were *what?*" Marchant gasped in tones of horror.

"Well, I've been hitching for a while, and I hadn't been murdered yet," I admitted with a shrug. "So far, the system was working. I trusted the system."

"So you were hitchhiking from Key West to…" Marchant swirled his beer like it would help him think. "Up north, you said."

"Up north," I confirmed.

"Back home?"

"No. Home is Louisiana." *Home is admitting you failed.* "I figured I'd get to Miami. Maybe go home. Or I don't know, maybe a city, someplace with more prospects. Baltimore, Philadelphia…" My voice trailed off at the looks on their faces, thinking if I actually said *New York* or *Boston,* they might drop dead of horror. "I just figured if I didn't go home to Louisiana, I'd better try for a fresh start, where nobody knew my name." I laughed at the phrasing. It had been accidental, but apt. "Nobody knowing my name was kind of the problem to begin with. The reason why I left home."

Crystal nodded like she knew what I meant, which was impossible, but reassuring. Marchant looked utterly befuddled, which made more sense.

"I was a singer," I explained. "Sort of. I was a back-up singer with a couple of duets with the lead singer, and one song of my own."

Marchant's face brightened. "A singer! Then you might know —"

"No," Crystal said, putting her hand on his. "She doesn't." She smiled at me kindly, letting me know she was saving us all some long, drawn-out conversation about someone Marchant knew in show business. Now *that* I understood.

Marchant gave her a quizzical glance, but subsided. "You must get that all the time," he said to me apologetically.

"Sort of." I smiled to show it was no problem. "I really don't know anyone who is anyone, though. The Bombers weren't exactly a big band." And now they were even smaller.

Down one person, anyway. In terms of listenership, fandom? Probably about the same. Not nothing, but not bringing home any gold records for the wall, either. Justin didn't even have a stalker. His complaint, not mine.

"Anyway, long story short, things went sour, the band didn't play well for a few gigs, we went to Saltwater and Sunshine, got booed offstage, and then I was asked to leave the band."

"You were kicked out?" Marchant's eyes were piteous, as if *he* had been the one who was dumped and left jobless in Key West.

"I was asked to leave," I repeated, but now I grinned, to take the edge off. "With a certain amount of kicking out in the phrasing."

Crystal gave my arm a sympathetic squeeze. "Men are dogs," she advised me.

"It's true," Marchant said. "I've always said so."

"We don't allow men on Hell and Dammit," Crystal said. "Except for very brief visits."

I glanced at Marchant and lifted my eyebrows.

"Oh, he's grandfathered in. But we keep a close eye on him. Marchant, where is Stacy, by the way? You didn't invite her to dinner?"

"Stacy went to Miami," Marchant said in dire tones, much as he might have said, *Stacy went to her watery grave.*

"Oh, that sister of hers." Crystal cast her eyes heavenward, shaking her head. "I'd cut that woman off." She caught my quizzical expression. "Stacy's sister is a mooch and a half. But that's Stacy's story to tell. She'll probably share it with you sometime. When she's gotten to know you."

Again, I got the feeling that these people had already adopted me, signed some papers I didn't know about. And I couldn't really muster up any way to feel mad about it.

We ate in comfortable silence for the next few moments. There was more to my story, but the important bits had been told: I had been there, and now I was here, and they had the gist of why. Including, I thought suddenly, the fact that no one was waiting for me. It should have made me uncomfortable, but instead I just went on alternating between bites of fish, hunks of bread, and deep drafts of beer.

A new thought wafted into my brain: this was the life. When people said *this is the life,* this was what they meant. This deck, this company, this breeze, this food. Which meant everyone else was wrong, because I was the only one here, living it. Well, and Marchant and Crystal.

Then, cutting through the silent dusk like a sonic boom, came a sound which did not belong. A rumble which made me swivel in my chair, peering into the darkness. But of course, the thick barrier of banyan trees was there by the road, blocking a view of the bridge. I glanced back at my dining companions.

Crystal and Marchant were looking at one another. "Stacy?" Marchant asked.

Crystal shook her head. "I'd know that truck anywhere," she said softly. "That's Lou."

❧❧❧❧❧ ❦❦❦❦❦

Marchant nearly spilled his beer. I watched him put the bottle down with trembling fingers, trying to hide the incident from us. I glanced at Crystal, wondering if she'd responded the same way.

But Crystal wasn't upset. She was transcendent—as much as a woman with the complexion of old leather could be, anyway. She rose from the table. "I have to go down and meet him."

"He'll come over here," Marchant suggested. "Soon as he sees the house is empty, he'll know where to find you."

"He's my son and I'm going to meet him," Crystal said, and she disappeared down the stairs. I could hear her sandals slapping on the concrete pad beneath the house, and then she must have been out in the sandy driveway, because I lost the sound.

I looked back at Marchant. "Um?" I smiled nervously. "What's going to happen?"

Marchant smiled wearily in return. He lifted his beer again and clinked it against mine. "We'll drink to a homecoming. Lou has been gone seven months this time. It's the longest he's ever left."

"He—leaves—a lot?"

"He sure does. And it breaks Crystal's heart every time. She just wants him to stay."

I got *that*. "My mom was the same way when I left home. She used to call me every day. She was so upset that I went on the road."

Marchant peered at me. "Well, I'll bet she was. Young girl like you, heading off to who knows where. You shouldn't be out there hitching, y'know. I don't want to preach to you, but you do too much of that in Florida, and you're going to wind up feeding someone's favorite gator."

I stared at him. The firelight sent twisted shadows over his face, and for just a moment, Marchant changed from a kindly old man to frightening local psycho. Then moonlight broke through a patch of passing cloud, softening the sharp edges of his profile, and he was the eccentric seafarer again, smiling idly at me.

It was unnerving. Things had shifted so quickly. Five minutes ago, I'd been eating dinner with the funniest pair of old islanders I could ever hope for. Now everything felt unsettled and weird. I decided to soothe my soul with another piece of sourdough bread. At least Louisa would never let me down.

A quarter of an hour passed, with no sign of Crystal or the mysterious Lou. Marchant pointed out a pod of dolphins passing by the island, their fins sharp and black in the moonlit waters. They were beautiful, and made me think of freedom, and soft, slippery, smooth things, and my mother, who loved dolphins so much she had a different pair of dolphin earrings for every day of the week. I resolved to send her a text tonight and let her know where I was. *Safe and sound, Mom, on Hell and Dammit Cay.*

We'd finished the bread and started new bottles of beer when footsteps began to make their way up the stairs. I turned, my beer arrested at my lips, half-terrified and half-fascinated to see who would arrive.

Crystal appeared first, a new Crystal with shining eyes and full, happy lips. With the torchlight glowing against her frizzy curls, she looked like a sea witch rising from the tides. Or maybe that was all the beer.

And behind her, a man, a full head taller than her, with a head of thick black hair and a beard that wrapped him from ear to ear like a wooly collar. He had shoulders twice as wide as his slight mother, and his red and black plaid shirt was more lumberjack than islander. At least he was wearing cut-offs and flip-flops, or I'd have thought he was just another northerner.

"Lou!" Marchant rose from the table unsteadily, and pushed himself around its corner, overturning empty bottles, which clinked musically as they rolled together. "I can't believe it. Look at you! Where did you get that *beard?*"

Lou's smile was dazzling, splitting that black beard and turning up the corners of his deep blue eyes. I caught my breath at that smile. Good lord, Crystal had produced *this?* Well done, Crystal. What an accomplishment. She should get a medal.

Content to ogle Lou from afar, I sat tight in my patio chair and let the older people make a fuss over him, showering the newcomer with praise and kisses and hugs. Crystal was so overwhelmed by Marchant's reaction to seeing Lou, she went straight back into welcome mode, acting as if she'd just seen Lou for the first time, instead of having gone over to greet him at her house. It was cute. At first.

But as the minutes passed and the love-fest didn't end, I started to wonder if something might be...not wrong, exactly, but not quite right.

I was used to eccentrics. I came from a small coastal town where fishermen climbed into their little boats and chugged out into the marshes to sit alone all day and drink beer, coming home with strange stories conjured up by their loneliness and the alcohol. As a kid we knew about voodoo women in the cypress swamps, although the closest we ever got to an actual voodoo woman was Carli Boudreaux's terrifying Aunt Kimmie, who lived in a rotting shotgun shack at the end of a long wooded drive and sold love potions to teenagers. If the love potions rarely worked and tasted oddly of flat Mountain Dew, that was beside the point. We'd heard the stories, and Aunt Kimmie definitely fit the bill. And who else would live in that tangle of jungle vines and Spanish moss, but a voodoo woman?

Anyway, something about the line where land became sea seemed to attract the different in people, or maybe it just accentuated the different in some people. So it was no surprise, really, to land here on an island ranch, where a woman planned to offer beach rides with no beach, where a landlubber captain served me flaming hot grouper and made a plain filet for his Persian cat, and where a prodigal son had just returned in what I could only assume was a *very* large truck, judging by the noise it had made crossing the bridge...and I wasn't uncomfortable, so much as, I wanted in on the joke. I wanted to know why Lou's return was such a big deal. I wanted to know why they seemed to be so crazy about him. Seven months wasn't *that* long. I'd been gone from home a year, and there was no way I'd get this kind of reception if I wandered back to the house in St. Bart Bay.

Maybe it was just that he was clearly an only child, whereas I had sisters to take up my parents' time and attention. Or maybe there was something else about Lou, something secret.

They were looking my way now—Lou had caught sight of me early on, but he hadn't been able to escape their grasp. Now he was crossing the deck, and I stood up, feeling a tiny tremor in my outstretched hand.

"This is Katie," Crystal told him, "and she's staying with us."

I noticed the lack of a time definer...not *for a while,* not *for a few days,* not *tonight.* Just *staying with us.* Then I forgot everything, because Lou had taken my hand in his and the hard warmth of his palm was taxing my senses in a very distracting way.

"I'm Lou," he said in a rich baritone, with just a hint of gravel roughening the edges. "But you probably guessed that already."

"I had an idea," I deadpanned.

He was still holding my hand. I looked up at his face, and suddenly, something about the shape of his eyes, the curve of his eyebrows, seemed oddly familiar.

"Have we met?" I asked.

His smile slipped slightly, and he relinquished my hand. I took back my fingers and shoved them into my back pocket, as if I could hold on to some of his heat. "I don't think so," he said. "But I get that a lot. I must have a very generic face."

I laughed nervously. He did *not* have a generic face. "Didn't mean to call you out on that," I said, going with the bit.

"It's fine." Lou glanced back at Marchant. "Hey man, you think I could grab a beer from your fridge? I'm parched."

"I'll get it," Marchant assured him, bolting back into the house like he was being timed on the assignment.

Lou settled down into the chair next to me. He plucked at the foil on the table, searching for more fish. "Ah, here we go." He forked a filet onto a paper plate, then shoveled a mouthful into his mouth.

I almost gasped, but I choked it back and settled for watching him carefully. The pepper would hit the back of his tongue and close his throat in three...two...one...

Nothing happened. Lou took another bite, then another. Marchant was taking forever with the beers, but Lou didn't seem affected by the Dammit Salt at all. He finally noticed my gaze and smirked at me. "I was raised on this stuff. But it's hard on mainlanders."

"How do you know I'm a mainlander?" Honestly, I felt a little insulted by getting the tourist honorific just because I wasn't from the Keys. I was still a Gulf Coast girl. I was just as handy with a skiff in seagrass as any of them. "How do you know I'm not from somewhere else in the Keys?"

Lou's gaze raked me from head to toe. The smirk remained firmly intact. "You have *up all night in a Key West bar* all over you. Except for the flip-flops and the dirty feet, which I admit is very local."

"I was in Key West for work," I sniffed. "Some of us have to earn a living." Was I really arguing with Crystal's son? Crystal's feral, gorgeous son? I needed to get some sleep. "And my feet are dirty because I was helping your mother feed the horses."

"Is that so?" Lou's expression grew marginally less mocking. "I didn't know you were a horse girl." He didn't use the term with any of the derision I might have expected.

I wasn't a horse girl, but I was friends with some. "I know my way around a feed room," I retorted. "Enough to help out."

He forked up some more grouper. "Well, my mom needs the help," he said around a mouthful. "So I'm glad you're here."

There it was again: the implication that I hadn't just come for the night. Maybe I'd been kidnapped to be a permanent ranch hand. Maybe I'd never be allowed to leave Hell and Dammit Cay.

There were worse things, I supposed, and I smiled as I took a beer from the panting Marchant.

❧❧❧❧❧ ❧❧❧❧❧

Crystal offered to take me back to the house after a while. The moon was high in the sky by then, and I was yawning despite the good company. Marchant was telling stories of his seafaring life, the kind of yarns only a very rum-soaked islander could fully believe, a lot of them featuring large sharks, ferocious hurricanes, and undercover boats belonging to either the FBI, the CIA, the Marines, or the Cuban secret police.

"And then the one-eyed fella says, we'll dump the bodies in Cuba as a message," Marchant was saying as I stood up to leave, feeling a bit unsteady on my feet. Well, I was going on twenty-four hours without sleep and probably four beers too many, so it was no wonder my legs didn't want to work properly. I bobbled as the porch seemed to sink below my feet, and suddenly Lou was there, his hands clutching beneath my arms.

All at once, I was acutely aware that I hadn't showered in some time and I had accumulated quite a lot of sweat today. "I'm fine," I protested, batting at him weakly. "Just lost my balance."

"I'll just be helping you back to the house," he informed me. "Mom, I'll take her home if you want to finish your drink."

I half-expected Crystal to protest, since she'd been so overwhelmed by Lou's surprise return, but she just leaned back in her patio chair. "Well, cheers, babydoll," she said, an endearment which apparently applied to both of us, and then she turned back to Marchant.

I managed to shrug myself free from Lou's grasp, feeling an unwelcome tingle of adrenaline as I did so. Damn, that man had muscles. What was he doing while he was out on the road, being all prodigal son? He definitely wasn't commuting to some office. I doubted an off-rack suit jacket would even button around a chest like that.

After a bleary moment of silence, I realized Lou was looking down at me with some amusement. He asked, "You want to walk on your own? Or should I just scoop you up and carry you?"

"I'm a little tired, I'm not pass-out drunk," I replied snippily. "I'm fine on my own."

"Okay, slugger," he agreed, starting for the staircase, "but I'm going to go down the stairs first, just in case you trip. You can fall against me instead of hitting the ground head-first and breaking your skull open."

I eyeballed his broad shoulders. He was just as burly from the back as the front. "I'm not sure hitting your chest would be much improvement over the concrete."

Lou glanced back at me and grinned. "I promise I'll give you a softer landing than the pavement would."

That *grin!* Devilish, those white teeth in that thatch of black beard. He might have just come back from the mainland, but Lou's vibe was all pirate. I kind of wished he'd scoop me up in his strong arms and sweep me away, back to his ship, back to his truck, back to his mother's house—I wasn't picky. But he started down the stairs ahead of me. With a resigned sigh, I followed.

My flip-flops slapped against the wooden steps, sounding weak against the thumps from his hiking boots. I felt like Lou had come from another world, from another climate, in his plaid and denim and heavy brown boots. Compared to the tank tops and flip-flops of everyone else in the Keys, he looked like an apparition from a colder, crueler world.

The one I would have to head back to, eventually. What a depressing thought. Suddenly, the cities I'd been daydreaming about as an alternative to St. Bart Bay didn't seem so appealing. Who would trade this secret island and all its potential for the concrete of the city?

I caught up with him at the foot of the stairs, and we walked in silence across the thin grass of Marchant's yard and the gritty shell road separating the island in two. I heard the interested rumblings of horses in the stable beyond the pens, wondering if the humans they heard walking were coming over to feed them. For a moment

I thought it would be fun to go pet some horses and while we were at it, I'd ask Lou to tell me everything—who he was, why he'd been gone—but Lou turned his feet towards the house, passing the sandy path to the stable without a single glance. Okay. We weren't playing with horses tonight.

Upstairs, moonlight glinted off the sliding glass doors, and the yellow house seemed to glow a cool blue. I could hear water slapping the narrow strand of sand below. The wind had picked up a little, blowing from the north, from across the great, sleepy sweep of Florida Bay.

I leaned on the railing, happy for something solid after climbing the stairs. But Lou walked around to the north side of the house, where the land dropped off quickly and there was nothing to see but moonlight on rippling water, all the way to the horizon.

I'd thought he was supposed to be showing me to my room, giving me a towel, host-stuff I was sure Crystal would have handled, but since it was past mosquito hours and the breeze felt so good against my skin, and because I still wanted answers and because, I guess, I was just drawn to him, I followed the sound of his footsteps. We leaned against the railing, side by side, and I let my gaze seek out the emptiness of the sea.

"I missed these nights," Lou said eventually. "The days can get old, but the nights never do."

I understood *that* sentiment. It was part of the reason I was—used to be—a singer. Because at night, when the bands were setting up, and the bars were coming to life, that was when *I* felt alive, too. I had yet to find such a good use for daylight, although I supposed I'd miss it if it was gone. "So, are you a night owl, too?"

He chuckled. "When I can be. When I get away, you know? It's hard to be a night owl here. Not much to do but stand out here and think."

"You mean, in the Keys? Or at your mother's house?"

"Yeah," Lou replied, his rueful smile glimmering in the moonlight. "Both."

In the middle-distance, something large leapt free of the bay. It shimmied in the moonlight and vanished underwater again, almost before I could register what had happened. I blinked, wondering if I'd imagined it.

Lou whistled. "You see that?"

"Um, was that a sea monster?" I ventured.

"Close. A marlin." Lou straightened, stretched his back. "Long day in that truck. I wish Mom had gotten that hot tub she kept promising me."

Damn, I wished she had, too. Now I had to deal with the mental image of Lou in a hot tub, his broad chest rising from the bubbles. I swallowed and changed the subject. "Where did you drive here from?"

"Illinois. I was in Chicago, working on some projects."

The word *projects* was suspiciously at odds with the lumberjack motif he presented. 'Project' was generally a word for creatives, in my experience. My Uncle Charley didn't call a roofing contract a *project*. He called it a job. "Mind if I ask what you do?"

Lou turned to me and studied my face for a moment. I tried to imagine what he was thinking, but his brows kept his eyes in shadow. Finally, he cracked another smile. At least it seemed like he liked what he saw in me.

"I'm a fraud," he said eventually, turning back to the sea. "A shyster."

I started to protest at that, but Lou pushed back from the railing and gestured toward the sliding glass doors behind us. "Guest room's through there," he said, his voice suddenly brusque. "And towels in the closet. Lock the second bathroom door—it opens into the living room."

And then he walked around the corner of the house, and was gone.

Chapter Seven

It's easier to sleep by the sea. At least, it is for me. I suppose everyone is different. But I wonder how *anyone* couldn't sleep at least a little more soundly with the purring sound of water outside—and in a more abstract way, simply with the feeling of water nearby.

I'd been a fitful sleeper on the road, sometimes missing entire nights of sleep—well, mornings and afternoons, if we're being strict about how we measure our days, because evenings and late nights were given to work. Even if the band didn't have a gig wherever we'd finally stopped driving for the day, our rhythms were completely out of sync with the outside world. The sun sank, but our bodies were just getting started—especially after all the boredom-napping in the van. So we usually sat up until the wee hours, drinking cheap beer in cheap hotel rooms that were really a waste of the money, considering all the use we got out of those beds.

Hotel rooms are set up for night sleepers. They're for normal people who only need a bed after sunset and won't need it again after ten a.m. It would be great if there was a chain of roadside motels just for the night owls of the population, with a check-in time of midnight and a check-out time of five p.m. I would have gotten a lot of value out of a place like that, as would just about every other musician I met out there, driving the interstates from college town to college town, trying to drum up a little support for a career that was more of a wish than a sure thing.

Now, confronted with a real bedtime, I yawned convincingly. I gave myself a pep talk. I hadn't had a nap today. I hadn't really slept in over a day. I could do this. I could sleep in this guest room, with the water slapping the rocks below.

I pulled back the pink duvet atop the queen-sized bed, noting the paler pink sheets beneath, and pushed down on the squeaky springs of the mattress. About what I'd expect, about what I'd gotten used to: a bed which pre-dated pillow tops or memory foam. It fit in with the room, which had been decorated in the same early 90s pastels as the rest of the house. Those squeaky coils went along with the pale dresser and arched mirror on the opposite wall, the two bedside tables of curving bamboo, topped with glass and pink ceramic lamps, and the washed-out watercolor of a roseate spoonbill lifting one long leg delicately above a clump of seagrass.

I liked the room, all of it. Well, I could have done without the tile floors, which were cold and a little clammy beneath my bare feet. But I understood that in a sandy place, some comforts must be abandoned.

I slipped between the sheets and sighed at the coolness. Thank goodness for being clean and cool and cozy in bed. My shower had been life-changing, knocking off layers of sweat and dirt I hadn't even realized I'd accumulated since the last one—when had that been? Oh, right...in the scummy back rooms of the Slip Knot Inn, two days ago. About an hour before our late-night gig.

So, about an hour and ten minutes before everything changed.

I glanced at the glaring red numerals on the old alarm clock next to the bed. 1:04. The house was quiet. Wherever Lou was, he wasn't making any noise. Crystal wasn't back yet. I wondered how late she stayed out, how early she got up, if she stayed over with Marchant. I was rooting for those kids.

Maybe it was inevitable that my thoughts slid back to Lou. After all, he was definitely on the other side of that wall *right there,* the one with the big mirror that was currently reflecting my toes under the rumpled-up duvet. The house's floor-plan was pretty simple: bedrooms on three corners, living room and kitchen on the fourth. There was nowhere else he could be—and I knew he'd gone to bed, because I'd peeked through the second bathroom door before I'd locked it, and the other rooms were dark.

So this mountain of a mystery man was separated from me by just a few inches of dry-wall and a few layers of pink paint...and how was I supposed to sleep knowing that? I told myself I would be up all night wondering who he really was, then I turned out my light, and I immediately fell asleep.

Being awake for a day and a half'll do that to ya.

The scent of coffee woke me.

Now, that's really a luxury. I could be carried from my bed on the waves of a coffee scent. Like a cartoon hobo smelling a ludicrously pink baked ham. In an ideal world, I would simply push back the covers and let myself be transported on the little wavy scent thingies. What would you call those? I pondered the question, but 'thingies' was the best I could come up with as I begrudgingly pulled on a relatively fresh tank top and wriggled into a pair of cut-offs. They felt too tight this morning. Maybe Louisa the sourdough starter was already working her magic on my thighs.

I glanced into the bathroom cautiously, found it empty (this sharing the guest bath with the living room situation was a little unnerving) and carefully locked the door before I cleaned up. I didn't put on makeup in the morning, but I thought my face looked acceptable. My green eyes were usually bold enough to make up for fantastic cheekbones or a perfect nose. When my unruly red-brown hair was contained in a bun, I deemed myself tidy enough to be seen in public. At least by Crystal. I wasn't so sure about Lou. For him, I thought I'd like a few layers of makeup between us.

Crystal looked up from the little bistro table in the kitchen, where she was turning the pages of a newspaper and drinking coffee. "Good morning, sleepyhead," she sang. "Did you sleep well?"

She looked remarkably fresh for a woman who hadn't yet been home at one o'clock in the morning.

"I did, thank you." I hesitated in the kitchen, not sure which of the white cabinets hid the coffee mugs.

"Top, to the right of the sink." She pointed with her paper.

"Thank you." I pulled down a mug with a bright illustration advertising the 35th Annual Underwater Music Festival. "Well, this sounds...interesting."

Crystal took in the mug I was waving. "Oh, it's a hoot. We dress up in costumes and go out on boats for the day. I'm always after Lou to join one of the underwater bands, but he says no."

That was interesting. "Is Lou a musician?" I asked, pouring coffee. Once again, I tried to place his face, this time through the filter of roughly a thousand music blogs and magazines I'd perused over the past few years. He really did remind me of someone.

"Hmm?"

I looked back at Crystal. She was gazing at her newspaper with intensity. Was she...did she just pretend she hadn't heard me?

"Where's the newspaper from?" I asked, rather than testing out my theory. "Surely no one delivers out here."

"Oh, I went up to the Slutty Mermaid and picked up some cinnamon buns. They're in the fridge. Grabbed the paper while I was there."

Cinnamon buns! Lou could be a secret musician all he wanted. I would be devouring cinnamon buns and not worrying about anyone else's business, thanks. I put down my coffee and tugged the cardboard box out of the fridge, salivating at the scent before I could even get the lid open.

The cinnamon buns were beauts. I put one in the microwave for a few seconds—Crystal's suggestion—then sat down across from her. The bistro table rocked gently until Crystal put her foot on the pedestal base. "Always does that," she said idly, flipping the paper over. "Ought to get Marchant to fix it."

I took a bite and barely suppressed a moan. Oh, Slutty Mermaid, you dirty, dirty thing, you! The food on this island was absolutely insane. First the red-hot delight of grouper rubbed with Dammit Salt, then these perfect pastries for breakfast the next morning? Forget the real world. I was never leaving this magical place. Also, I couldn't *wait* for lunch.

"Where's Lou?" I ventured once I'd recovered from that first perfect bite, wondering how many cinnamon buns I could get through without him finding out. Not that his opinion of my pastry consumption mattered, of course.

Crystal lowered the paper slightly and gave me a smirk. "Don't ever expect to see that boy before noon." She went back to reading.

I glanced at the headlines on the backside of the paper: *Deputy busts two men on lobster violations. Officials plan Conch Republic Birthday Celebration.* Yup, nothing too unusual there. Just your usual fishing town/fictional Independence Day stories. But what a lot of fun it was to consider these kinds of stories newspaper-worthy. I liked the Florida Keys.

I'd definitely felt a stirring of connection here, from the moment the land had narrowed on either side of U.S. 1 and the water began to shimmer into view. I recognized country like this. I came from a waterlogged place. And I'd just spend the past year touring around inland, dry, even rocky places where I'd been starving for open water, even though I hadn't realized what was missing until we'd started crossing bridges on the Overseas Highway.

Justin, on the other hand, hadn't seemed to care for it here. He'd rolled his eyes after the third or fourth bridge. "How much longer?" he'd asked, over and over. Finally, our drummer Vinnie had thrown a bag of potato chips at his head and told him to take his bitching to the back of the van until we reached the end of the highway.

Which was unfortunate, because that's where I was sitting, pressed up against the window, looking out at the Caribbean-blue waters.

I felt my toes curl against the cold tiles as I remembered the way Justin had thrown himself into the center seat, his thighs pressing up against mine. I'd tried to shrink against the window. There wasn't any heat there, not anymore, not for either of us. He was as sick of me as I was of him. We'd started off as young lovers in search of some great destiny, but I was pretty sure the monotony of the road and the endless stream of bars and nightclubs had killed off whatever promise our relationship had held—which, let's be real, probably hadn't been much to begin with. We were hanging onto each other for our own reasons; Justin because he was a jealous bastard who didn't want anyone else to have me, and me because I knew if we broke up, he'd push me out of the band.

And I wanted to be a singer. Back-up in The Bombers was the best—the only—opportunity I'd ever gotten. So Justin could be the biggest asshole in the world, which he was on the regular, and still I stayed.

He'd ripped open the bag of chips from Vinnie and held it under my nose, shaking it so the smell of them wafted into my face. The stench was awful—no matter how much I complained, these idiot guys I was traveling with refused to understand that some snacks simply didn't belong in close quarters on long trips, and sour cream and cheddar chips fell into that category. Possibly *led* that category. "Dude, get those *out* of my face," I'd snapped, pushing them away.

Some of the chips spilled, and Justin's face twisted with anger. He had a rubber face, which was incredible for grandstanding on stage. Justin could make a Mick Jagger sneer with one side of his face and bring his eyebrows together in a Brandon Flowers bid for sincerity with the other. He had a face built for paparazzi shots and *Rolling Stone* photoshoots. Since those were both on his bucket list, he exercised those muscles. A lot.

But I was just as tired of his incredible rubber expressions as I was the rest of him. "Please just save your snarls for the stage," I retorted, looking back out the window, searching for more blue water. Couldn't he see I was enjoying the ride?

Maybe that had been the problem, I thought now. I sipped at my coffee, considering the likelihood that Justin had just wanted to ruin the drive for me, because I was happy, and he wasn't.

Well, he'd pretty much succeeded.

Crystal pushed a section of paper over to me. "Done with Local if you want it," she said companionably.

I flipped through the pages. *The Arts Scene* was granted the back page. The second day of the Saltwater and Sunsets Music Festival had garnered a few inches of space. I let my eyes flick through the text, looking for any mention of the band. Maybe the Saturday night gig had been a disaster, but the Sunday afternoon spot could have been something.

Even without me.

Especially without me, if Saturday was anything to go by. God, things had happened so suddenly. Things had been normal, not our best gig, not our worst, and then the crowd decided they wanted me off the stage, and they'd gotten what they wanted. The booing, the jeering, the thrown beer cans: I'd had to run for it. Without me, the band must be doing better.

But there was nothing here about their performance.

What an incredible diss. Maybe the reporter hadn't even seen them. Maybe he'd used their set as an opportunity to hit the Port-a-

Potties, or grab a Coke. Or he'd heard that the night before, The Bombers had let their female singer get booed off the stage and hadn't stood up for her, and he'd decided he didn't have time for a band like that.

I liked that particular explanation. They deserved a diss for letting me get trashed like that, ambushed out of nowhere. And Justin deserved to be unnoticed, for telling me I wasn't going back onstage. For saying, "You had an okay run, but it's time to move on."

For kicking me out at the literal end of the road.

Good, let them get dissed.

The reporter *did* mention a half-dozen other bands of our size, the kind of bands that were in the small print on festival posters. I knew these people, had performed with them in the sparse crowds, and hung out in the wings watching bigger bands wow our crowds. We had traveled the country in the same shapeless loops, living the same vampiric lives.

Cody West and the Stranglers, Mervyn's Motorcycle Gang, The Vitals: I knew all of them. They got good press in the few lines the reporter granted to the fine-print bands, which was nice for them. Cody's band was described as "bombastic"; the all-female crew of Mervyn's Motorcycle Gang were granted "a killer sound"; Johnny from The Vitals was labeled "one to watch." I nodded gently over the words, feeling a little burst of pride in the growth of my friends. The Bombers might have bombed. But some people had succeeded this weekend. It could be done.

I glanced up at Crystal, who met my eyes over her section of paper. She lifted her thin eyebrows questioningly. "Yes, ma'am?" she asked.

"Could I learn about the horses today?" I asked. I didn't know what came next in life, but for now, I just wanted to keep moving.

"Yes, ma'am," Crystal agreed, smiling. "Lots of work to do today." She turned her head, looking pointedly at Lou's bedroom door. "And I don't expect we'll get much help from the men around here, either."

I chuckled. "Well, I'm used to that."

Chapter Eight

"**S**o, these are the kids."

Crystal stopped by the closest pen and waved her arm, taking in all the tiny glory of Sea Horse Ranch. The horse in the pen looked up at us with furry ears pricked. I'd gotten to see them last night, but they'd been in a hurry—all about that dinner. Now I could investigate the horses at leisure, as they nosed through the hay in their pens. This one was particularly pretty: small and compact, like the others, but with a splashy coat of bright, foxy red and white. The horse's forelock fell over her eyes, red and luxuriant. People paid fortunes for wigs that weren't half as nice.

"This is Ruby." Crystal introduced us by waving a baby carrot by the fence, which was all the impetus the horse needed to come over for a quick visit. "She's kind of our matriarch. All their ages are just guesses, but Ruby acts like the queen, so we think of her as the oldest."

"She's stunning." I took a carrot and held it out, letting Ruby reach her upper lip out to scoop it from my fingers. "I have a friend back home with a horse this color."

"A paint," Crystal said with satisfaction. "Officially she's called a sorrel tobiano, but around here, we just call spotted horses paints. It's easier."

"Sure," I agreed. My friend Missy had called her horse a paint, too. Sometimes I heard her arguing with her horse-girl friends about horse colorings, throwing around words like *homozygous* and *dilute* and *sabino*. The arguments about which were which could get pretty heated, too. Crystal's way was simpler, which made sense, knowing Crystal. "Sounds good to me," I said, and Crystal smiled.

We walked around the pens, where the horses lived in pairs—to keep down arguments over hay, Crystal explained. Reggie and Trinket, Bart and Patty, and Ruby's companion, Jasmine: they were all cheerful, round-bodied, long-maned horses who were so small, we were able to look each other in the eyes without my needing to crane my neck. A big difference from Missy's giant horse, who was intimidating and knew it.

"I like their size," I said finally, as we gave Patty her carrot. The mustang mare had a gorgeous coat which seemed to shift in color with her height, starting with smoky black legs and ending in a navy-tinged ripple across her back. Crystal said her color was called blue roan. "They're not too big. I find big horses kind of scary."

"This is the size a horse should be," Crystal said firmly. "Especially if you're just riding them for fun. Or on the beach. You don't mind getting on in your swimsuit, and if you fall off in the water, you can get back on without a stepladder."

I took my fingers back before Patty ate them. "So, do you ride them?"

"Yup. Usually a couple of them every day. Keeps them in shape, keeps their manners really good. Mustangs are real smart, so they don't have to be reminded of what to do very often. They just have to be reminded that when we say something, we mean it."

"But they're beginner-safe, right? They must be. Because you use them for parties and stuff."

"Of course." Crystal waved a hand. "Totally beginner-safe. You want to ride one?"

"Oh..." I hadn't actually thought about riding a horse. I was up for petting them, maybe brushing them, the way I'd done with Missy's horses. Riding? I had a vision of myself tumbling into the water behind the stable and the horse galloping away, disappearing into the vastness of the bay. Possibly laughing at me. "I don't know about that. I'm not much of a rider. I just got on my friend Missy's horse now and then."

Crystal put her hands on her hips and regarded me. She was wearing threadbare cut-offs and a t-shirt from the Islamorada Arts Festival. The artwork included a watercolor marlin thrashing across her side, reminding me of the monstrous fish I'd seen while standing on the porch with Lou last night. I glanced over my shoulder almost involuntarily, wondering if he was up yet, maybe watching me from the living room's glass doors. But it wasn't even ten o'clock yet. There was no way he'd be up, let alone see me out here. If I was going to get on a horse and make a fool of myself, I better do it before Lou was on the prowl.

Crystal made her decision. "I'll put you on Bart. He's so quiet, I let toddlers ride him at the K-Mart parking lot carnival a couple weeks ago. Bart's a daydreamer."

That sounded appealing. I, too, was a daydreamer. Maybe Bart and I could just space out together. "Okay. Deal."

Then I glanced down at my feet. I'd put on a pair of sneakers, which had been riding in the bottom of my backpack like an anchor. Missy always made me wear her old riding boots when I climbed on her horse. But Crystal had no such concerns. She picked up a halter and lead-rope hanging by the pen's gate, ducked through the fence, and marched right over to Bart—all in her ratty flip-flops. Once he was haltered, she walked him to the gate, unhooked it, and led him out. Then she thrust the lead-rope into my hands. "You hold him while I go get Jasmine. She needs some exercise, too. We'll go on a little ride together."

I found myself clutching the fat cotton lead-rope, feeling kind of freaked out by how quickly things were moving. I had wanted to *meet* the horses, maybe learn to brush the horses or clean up after them, not ride them. Bart stood still, gazing at me with dark, liquid eyes. His ears flicked forward as he waited to see what came next. When he realized I wasn't taking him anywhere fast, he swiveled his ears to follow Crystal's motions as she walked across the pen to catch Jasmine. With a sigh, he adjusted his weight, resting one hind leg.

"Settling in for the long haul?" I asked him. I reached out one cautious hand and gave him a rub beneath his long forelock. The hair, mottled black and white with a few blonde streaks, felt coarse and strong and smooth all at once. "I like your style. I also enjoy doing as little as possible."

"You two bonding?" Crystal called. "Good job!"

"But unfortunately," I continued in the same private tone, "we are in the presence of unbounded energy."

Bart sighed, his nostrils rippling.

"Same, buddy."

It wasn't that bad, of course. Crystal was fun and generous. I could deal with a little excess energy, as long as it didn't end with me falling off a horse. As she led Jasmine up to the stable, I followed with Bart. The view was great. Jasmine was a black and white paint, as patchy as a cow, but twice as classy. Her tail was white beneath, with a black cascade falling over the top. It swung sassily with every step.

"Sassy's the right word," Crystal laughed when I described the mare's tail. "I usually keep Jasmine for myself, unless someone swears they're a real experienced rider. She has her own opinions about the way we should do things."

"Like how?" I accepted the offer of a five-gallon bucket filled with horse brushes and started rubbing Bart with a round curry comb, trying to avoid his sensitive spots the way Missy had shown me on her horse.

"Well, like if the water is rough, say. Jasmine doesn't like waves. She would rather they don't break against her legs. So to avoid them, she'll jump them."

"She jumps the waves?" I giggled, imagining a horse hopping a steady stream of rollers. "She must look like a kangaroo out there."

"She can," Crystal agreed, laughing along with me. "But after a few jumps, a lot of riders tend to lose their balance and then they end up in the water."

"Yikes. Not so funny."

"Well, it's refreshing, anyway. No one comes to the Keys because they want to stay dry all the time."

This was perfect logic to Crystal, and I supposed she had a point.

With saddles and bridles on the horses (made of nylon, because saltwater would eat traditional leather, Crystal explained) we were ready for our ride. "You can use that step-stool to mount," Crystal offered, pointing to a plastic stool next to the stable. She held Bart for me while I got up the courage to put my sneaker into the plastic stirrup and haul myself aboard. But honestly, I don't think Bart was going anywhere. By the time I'd managed, panting and gasping and sweating, to get settled in the saddle, he had closed his eyes and gone to sleep. I thought I even heard a snore.

Bart was definitely my type of horse.

Crystal was up on Jasmine almost as soon as she'd handed me Bart's reins, and before I could get used to the rolling gait beneath me—Bart seemed to have a very different step from Missy's tall Quarter Horse—we were strolling off across the scruffy lawn, heading down the short driveway, and turning onto Hell and Dammit Cay's lone shell-paved road.

"We can ride anywheres we want," Crystal explained. "Marchant and Stacy don't care. Not much grass to ruin," she added, which was a fact: the lawns surrounding the houses were shrubby and sunburned, and any grass which managed to grow on this little lump of coral and sand was barely more than stubble.

"So where do you take people when they come out for a ride? I assume sometimes folks get out here?"

"Real rarely, but now and then." Crystal reined Jasmine back a little; the mare was dancing now, tugging at the bit. "She wants to go get in the water today, I guess. Yeah, I take any guests on a loop around Hell and Dammit, and then we can cross between the islands and do a little half-loop of Little Bucket. Some fool ten or twenty years back wanted to put an eco-resort on Little Bucket and he scooped out some beach from the mangroves then, so we use that for our riding along the water. We come back the same way and it adds up to almost an hour. Plus a half hour to get ready and take pictures, so it's worth their time."

"That doesn't sound bad," I agreed. "I mean, how much riding can people do if they're not used to it, anyway? It makes a person sore."

"Well, wait and see what you think," Crystal said with a little sigh. "If we had a decent, long stretch of beach, we could get in some running and really give these folks a show."

"Running?"

"Y'know, galloping."

I put my hands a little more firmly against the reassuring bulk of the saddle. I didn't want to think about galloping. This walk was plenty, thanks.

We had circled around the abandoned house and were letting the horses find their way down to the water below Crystal's house when I heard a door slam overhead. Crystal's horse skittered sideways a bit, and I tensed, waiting for Bart to react, but he just put his head down and plodded forward. "That's a good boy," I told him, thankful he hadn't unseated me.

Crystal was looking up at the house. "Good morning, Lou!" she called, waving one hand.

I looked up, and saw Lou leaning over the patio railing, shirtless. Hair tousled. Arm swinging in a lazy wave. Shirtless. Muscles rippling. I was embarrassed by the little gasp that escaped me, but that was nothing compared to the next moment, when suddenly Bart wasn't underneath me anymore, and my mouth was full of sand.

Chapter Nine

I picked myself up as quickly as I possibly could, spitting out sharp-edged Florida sand. My ears were ringing and my hands were tingling, but I hadn't broken anything. Just my pride, thanks. I looked around and saw that nothing had changed in the roughly twenty-five seconds I'd been out of the saddle, except that Bart was now grazing the stubbled grass at the edge of the road. Crystal, still seated on Jasmine, had her hand to her mouth—I suspected to hide her surprised laughter—and Lou was still standing above us on the deck.

Of course. Of course, I fell off in front of Lou.

"Well, I'm up," I said to the world at large.

Crystal's laughter finally escaped her hand, and Lou joined in.

Shaking my head, I walked over to Bart and picked up his reins. The horse went on snuffling through the sparse grass, ignoring me.

"I'm sorry," Crystal gasped, recovering herself. "That was just so fast! I barely saw what happened. Are you okay?"

"I'm fine." I eyeballed the stirrup, wondering if I could mount without the help of the ladder. Bart wasn't very big, but then again, I wasn't very limber.

Lou felt like he needed in on the action. Leaning over the patio railing, he called, "He just stepped really quickly to the left and *thump,* you were hanging in midair for half a second and then you were on the ground. It was amazing."

"I'm glad it was at least visually spectacular," I replied, trying to be a good sport.

"Hang on," Lou said. "I'll come down and help you back into the saddle."

"Oh no, that's not necess—"

But Lou was already pelting down the stairs, his sandals slapping against the wooden steps. Bart picked up his head and looked towards the sound, suddenly interested. He was probably hoping Lou was going to come ride him instead of me, the clumsy stranger from parts north. I couldn't blame him.

And just how was Lou going to help me back into the saddle? I had a sudden vision of him scooping his arms beneath me and flinging me up onto Bart's back. Equal parts exciting and embarrassing—I couldn't let that happen. I hopped on one leg, trying to get my foot close to the stirrup, but it wasn't happening.

"Just wait," Lou said, coming around the corner of the staircase. "I'm right here."

Resigned, I watched him approach. At least the view was rewarding. Shirtless Lou had been impressive when he was twenty feet above me on the deck, and he was considerably more so at eye level. I brushed anxiously at sand, real or imagined, on my face as he approached. I tried to paste a bland smile on my face as I waited, but the thoughts burning in my mind were anything but vanilla, and included such beauts as: *Does he sleep in the nude?* and *Could those shorts slip down any farther on those hips?*

Don't judge me. I just fell off a horse. I was not in my right mind.

Okay, maybe I was, but seriously, Lou was clad only in a pair of shapeless old khaki shorts which should have looked ratty and tired but instead just gave him an air of suntanned saltwater cowboy—a subgenre of men I hadn't previously known I was attracted to. When he bent in front of me and cupped his hands at my left knee, I got a glimpse of tanned neck and black hair, curling at the ends. *Someone needs a haircut,* I thought, trying to ignore the tingle in my extremities. Yeah, Lou needed a haircut. And I needed an ice bath.

"Put your knee in my hands and I'll toss you up," he suggested, in case I hadn't gotten the hint. So I forced my limbs to listen to my brain, and even managed to do a decent hop when Lou counted me to three. He pushed up, I jumped, and it worked... eventually. Once I was back in the saddle, I looked down at him to say thanks—but found I was only above his eye level by an inch or two. Lou was tall, and Bart was short.

And wiggly. The horse shoved towards Lou, who laughed and pushed Bart's big block of a head away. "I didn't bring any cookies down with me, buddy," he told the horse. He ruffled his hand through Bart's multicolored forelock and gave me an apologetic grin that would have made my knees tremble if a pair of chunky plastic stirrups hadn't been holding me in place. "The horses know I'm usually good for a couple of cookies."

"Like, horse cookies?"

"Nah. The good kind. From Publix. Sandwich cookies."

"Sandwich cookies! What's your favorite kind?"

"Chocolate and vanilla," Lou said. "And yes, I lick the cream out of the middle first."

What? I was going to die. "Maybe we need to go on a Publix run," I suggested, feeling weak.

"Too far to ride," Lou informed me, his grin turning to a smirk. "If you want cookies, you're going to have to get back in the pickup truck and drive there."

"But it's a stick." I sighed as pathetically as possible. "I can only drive automatic." I leaned forward a little, my fingers resting lightly on the saddle horn, waiting for Lou to reply that he'd be happy to teach me how to handle a stick shift.

"Oh well," Lou said, shrugging and turning away. "No cookies for you until someone feels like going to town."

That was it? I wanted to yell *hey, wait!* or maybe just send Bart over to stomp on his bare toes, but the horse had gone back to chewing the scrubby grass, and my voice seemed to be completely off-limits to my brain again. It was probably for the best, I figured, as I tapped my sneakers patiently against Bart's tough sides. Push my luck with Lou, and I stood to lose my spot in the guest bedroom.

And I wasn't ready to leave.

❧❧❧ ❧❧❧

We let the horses wander around the island for another half-hour or so, until the Florida sun was high in the sky, and I was beginning to feel about as cooked as I had on the side of U.S. 1 the day before. Crystal finally noticed my pink cheeks and nudged Jasmine with her bare heels (apparently riding in flip-flops wasn't done, so she'd gone barefoot) until we were standing in the shade of the barn's overhang. She hopped down from her horse and, after a moment of steeling myself for impact, I did too.

The ground was closer than I realized. Bart blinked at me as I let go of his mane and slouched against his shoulder. "Sorry," I told him. "Last time I hit the ground, it felt farther away."

"Less impulsion," Crystal informed me, grinning. With the glare of the sun white-hot behind her, all I could see were her teeth. The effect was a little unnerving, like a tanned Cheshire cat. "Well, all in all, you did okay with riding. That one little fall didn't mean much. Tomorrow, we can try going over to Little Bucket and splashing around in the water. Should be fun for you. As long as the weather don't act up."

I watched her work as she started to untack, then followed her lead, making sure I was unbuckling the same straps on Bart's bridle that she was unbuckling on Jasmine's. Horse bridles were complicated, I'd always found. More stayed put together than came apart, and the whole thing came off in one piece, like magic. "Are we expecting the weather to start changing?" I asked. "I thought Florida in April was always this sunny. This is spring break season, right?"

"Well, it's changeable. Maybe a little more unpredictable than summer. Sometimes in spring, storms can come in from the north, shake things up for a few hours. You're not afraid of storms, though, right?"

I considered myself pretty good in a storm, actually. "No, we get rough weather up in Louisiana all the time. Hurricanes, waterspouts, hail." I heard my boasting and stopped. They got all that here, too. Staying cool and collected through a little tropical weather was not going to make me special in the Keys. "The only thing I really hate is a blizzard."

Crystal laughed at that. "Well, not much fear of them."

"Lou must not mind them."

She glanced at me over her horse's back. "Why do you say that?"

"He was in Chicago, during the winter. That's blizzard central, right?"

Crystal shrugged. "Lou don't always notice his surroundings. He spends a lot of time indoors. More than anyone else in my family. I don't know where he gets it from."

I filed this information away for later contemplation. At least I could confidently get messy outside without worrying about Lou coming out and seeing me covered in sweat and grime.

After we'd put the horses back into their pens, I kind of hoped we'd head upstairs and find some lunch, but Crystal puttered around the horse pens for a while instead, picking up fallen palm fronds and topping off the water in the troughs. I tried to help, but I was fostering a fear of large spiders, and also some concern that Roger might have some relatives taking a shady nap under one of the fronds.

It wasn't that I was *afraid* of iguanas...I just didn't want to be *surprised* by one. After all, Lou might not be outside, but he was still just a few dozen feet away, and with a bird's-eye view of the fun below. And there was no telling what kind of shriek I might emit, or what kind of face I might make, should I run into a six-foot lizard without proper warning. Whatever happened, there was no chance any of my reactions would be good for my self-esteem. And I needed all the positive self-love vibes I could muster for the next time I saw Lou. No one who made my insides quiver as much as he did could be good for me, but I was plenty eager to find out more about him.

And make the best impression possible.

"Well, the place looks pretty clean," Crystal said finally, putting her hands to her back and surveying the property with satisfaction. "If we get any visitors before this weekend, I think we'll be ready. Even if it does storm tomorrow."

"So it's really going to storm?" I felt like we hadn't gotten this all out in the open yet.

"Weather radio says so. But who really knows?" Crystal seemed content to let the weather do whatever it wanted. I guessed if you had no plans, you had no reason to worry about the weather. "I just want it sunny and dry on Saturday. Got a group coming. Need it nice and calm for them to ride." A little worry slipped into her expression, lines stretching from her forehead to her nose.

"What kinda group?" I asked. "Like, a beach ride?"

"Mm-hmm. We don't get many groups, like I told ya, but when we do, we roll out the red carpet. Try to make a real good impression. These folks this weekend will pay for all our horses' feed for the next month." Crystal brightened a little as an idea popped into her head. "What I ought to do is go up and ask Lou to take pictures for them. He's good with a camera. Takes real nice portraits. We always take cell phone pics for the folks who come out, but with Lou's help, we can add souvenir photos. And get some to put up on the website, too." She glanced in my direction. "Maybe I'll have him practice on you. You up for a little photo shoot this afternoon?"

I felt the pink returning to my cheeks, and it wasn't the sun causing it this time. "Oh, I don't photograph very well," I demurred, while imagining myself posing provocatively against the backdrop of the turquoise sea, Lou exclaiming that he'd found his muse at last. Because that was a thing amateur photographers said. Thanks, Hollywood. Thanks for the realistic expectations. "I'd probably break his camera."

Crystal laughed. "Hah! That's what Marchant says, and that's what *I* say, but we're old wrinkled islanders. You're a pretty thing who hasn't let the sun ruin her skin yet. Speaking of, you look a little burned. Let's get you inside before you crisp up. And I'll make us some lunch."

My stomach grumbled in happy anticipation as we jogged up the stairs, Crystal's flip-flops slapping the wood with every step. As we reached the deck, the sliding glass door to the living room was flung open, and the scent of frying bacon hit my nose like a wave of pure endorphins. I took a deep breath and said, "Oh, *boy.*"

From the open doorway, Lou grinned and waved a spatula. He was wearing an apron over his cut-offs and old t-shirt, patterned with rainbow-colored seahorses. Domestic god, too? Pitter-patter, little heart. "Lunch is coming right up, ladies," he sang. "Do we like BLTs?"

"We love them," I informed Lou, more enthusiastically than I intended. He grinned and went back to his pan.

I looked at Crystal. "He can cook?"

She grinned. "Not bad, right?"

⁕⁕⁕⁕⁕⁕⁕ ⁕⁕⁕⁕⁕⁕

The answer was yes, Lou could definitely cook. The man appeared to be precariously close to perfection. Certainly, in terms of looks and domestic skills, he was the whole package. Of course, there was that whole issue with him basically telling me he was a con artist. And there was the weird vibe when he'd first arrived back on the island—as if Crystal had never expected to see her son again. What kind of guy did that to his mother? Especially a mother as cool and chill as Crystal? Lou had his secrets, and I wanted to uncover them all. Otherwise, he seemed like half a jerk, half a picture-perfect nice guy, and that was just confusing.

Either way, he had my full attention. I felt like I'd stumbled out of a terrible long-term relationship just in time to find a fabulous fling...or more.

If I could get him to pay attention to me. I disappeared into my bathroom long enough to change into clean clothes and wipe the dirt from my face and arms, hoping I could give a better impression over lunch.

But Lou seemed to be all about his mother. He served her himself, making sure she sat down at the table before he placed her filled plate before her. (I scooped up a handful of chips and grabbed a sandwich from the platter on the counter for myself.) As she ate, he sat next to her and asked her about the horses. He refilled her sweet tea as soon as the glass got low. He smiled and twinkled and was basically the most doting son anyone could ever hope for. I found I was jealous of Crystal, and not just because I wanted her son's eyes on me. I wanted a son who would treat me like this, too! Someday, anyway.

Eventually, she begged off from all the attention, saying she needed a nap after last night's late bedtime. She toddled off to take a shower and climb between cool sheets. The idea was appealing, but the sun was so bright outside, with the light reflecting off the sea and shining right back into the house, that I felt drawn back towards the outdoors. This didn't feel like the kind of afternoon a person should sleep through.

Lou tipped back his chair on its back legs and gazed at me lazily from across the table. "You're not going to take a nap?" he asked, his smile slightly mocking. "After all that excitement falling off poor Bart? I think you scared him."

"I think I might go back outside," I admitted, ignoring the reminder of my lack of riding skills. "I know there's not really a beach here, but that water sure is calling my name. It's so clear and blue, it hardly looks real."

"You want to go swimming? Or maybe snorkeling?"

"Nah, I just need to get my feet wet," I corrected him. "I'm not much of a snorkeler." The last thing I needed was Lou watching me splutter and snort seawater through a snorkel.

"Are you sure? A lotta folks think that's the best part of being here. Clear water and plenty of marine life. You don't want to see all the fishes?"

The sarcastic note in his voice was subtle, but it was there. "Are you making fun of me for *not* wanting to see fish, or making fun of the people who *do* want to see fish?"

His smile curled up at the ends. "A little of both, I guess."

"You make fun of everyone, don't you?"

Still with the wicked smile. "What gave me away?" he asked.

"You just have a smart-ass way about you," I told him, with a smirk of my own. "Trust me, I've known enough smart-asses to spot them at a hundred paces. I attract them."

"You do, do you?"

Oh *no*. Why did I say that? "I mean—stop laughing! You know what I meant." My cheeks were turning pink. The sunburn was probably making all my blushing worse. So this was a hidden danger of a beach romance, the one the novels didn't tell you about: enhanced embarrassment potential from flushed cheeks!

"You're right, I *do* know," Lou said, pushing back from the table. "But what can I say? I'm a smart-ass. I can't react any other way, or you'll be disappointed."

"I guess you're right," I sighed. "You're just difficult by nature."

Lou snorted as he started clearing the table. I hopped up to help him. We filled the dishwasher together, then I went over to the sliding glass door overlooking the Gulf side of the house, gazing out over the glimmering waters. I really needed to get out there, splash in that beautiful sea. Feel some sand between my toes. Not between my teeth, the way I had when I'd fallen off Bart.

"It's better over on Little Bucket Island," Lou said from behind me.

"What is?" I watched an egret pick his way along the rocks lining the shore, long white neck jutting out as the bird watched for fish in the clear water below.

"The good beach. Get into your swimsuit and I'll walk you over."

"But that's not our beach," I said, turning around. "I've been wondering about how Crystal takes the horses over there, but I figured at least that was quick. Hanging out on the beach seems way riskier. Wouldn't we be trespassing?"

"Maybe you'd think so, but this is Florida." Lou grinned. "No such thing as a private beach. They're all public land."

Well, in that case, I could hardly say no.

"Give me just one minute." I held up a finger, then dashed into the guest bedroom. If we were going to go to the beach, and I kept my face out of the water, maybe things were looking up for the Lou and Katie experiment. I had the perfect two-piece for the occasion. I just had to find it.

I was digging through my backpack when I noticed my phone sitting on the dresser. I must have left it here earlier when I'd changed out of my dirty clothes. It wasn't like me to leave my phone just anywhere, but the conversation and company at lunch had been good enough that I hadn't noticed. I picked it up, thinking I'd just check quickly for notifications. I doubted anyone would be reaching out to me, though.

I was wrong. There was a message.

And it was from Justin.

Chapter Ten

I read the text message three times before the words all made sense together, and even then I couldn't believe what I was seeing. But it was from Justin, alright—the message even had his usual lack of caps and correct punctuation.

> hey babe where are you! van is leaving key west at
> four, driving all night, next show in gainesville. let
> me know if we need to pick u up or if youre coming
> back to motel

What? I nearly screamed at the phone. He couldn't be serious. He could *not be serious*.

Did Justin really think nothing had really happened? Like Saturday night, he hadn't told me to find my way home? The crowd had spoken, he'd said. They couldn't handle boos at a music festival. It wasn't going to work out. Blah blah blah. And I'd done what he'd said. I'd left.

They should have been gone already, too. They should have left yesterday. They'd stayed an extra day—but no one had thought to look for me until today. So yeah, hard to believe that he'd wanted me to stay, and I'd just misunderstood him. Maybe Justin had really had a change of heart, but two nights had gone by before he'd decided to wonder where his girlfriend had gone.

"No, sir," I muttered. "You do not deserve me back."

Not that easily, anyway.

My career, on the other hand, was worth thinking about. Even if I never forgave Justin—and I wasn't really planning on it—I should pause before I gave up my spot in The Bombers. Maybe they weren't much, maybe they weren't topping any charts, but they were a decent band. We'd been saving for studio time in the fall. With an album out next year, we'd have more chance of making it up the next rung of the indie music ladder. Space in music blogs. Maybe a spin on some college radio station, or the satellite radio channels. And even if I was just a back-up singer, it was a start. At every club, every gig, there was a chance I'd meet someone who thought I really had something, someone who would help me produce my own music or give me a shot on a song they thought my voice would be perfect for.

Maybe it was a long shot, but the chance existed.

If I stayed here, my chances went from little to none.

"No better place to think about it than the beach," I told myself. The water always helped me get my thoughts in order.

So I put down the phone without answering the text and went back to my rummaging, finally pulling out both halves of my two-piece. It was still new and untried, because most of the places we stayed on the road didn't have a pool, much less beach access. I shimmied out of my shorts and top, and slithered back into the bathing suit. White, with red polka dots, it was almost vintage, almost decadent, and all flirty. I looked at myself in the mirror, eyeing the sharp points of my hips and shoulders. Maybe low-carb didn't look that great on me. This bikini was made for a fashion trend which had celebrated fuller figures.

Well, I'd had bread in the past three meals, so if I kept it up for a few more days, I'd have some curves to fill out this cute design. Hah! After a year of trying to eat healthy on the road, a nearly impossible task, I was giving it all up while staying in a beach house —the ultimate irony. I could just imagine what Justin would say if he saw me eating a Pop-Tart or something else junky from the bin of snacks they kept in the band van. He'd feign so much horrified surprise, he'd probably choke on it.

Maybe that was what he deserved.

There was a rap at the door, and I called, "Come in," without really thinking about it. Lou stepped inside and then stopped short, his eyes raking over my half-clad figure.

"Whoa," he said.

I approved of that reaction. "I haven't worn this before," I replied. "You like it?"

"I—uh—yes. Love polka dots, obviously." Lou recovered himself neatly. "Anything with a nice dot really pulls an outfit together."

"Perfect, I'm convinced." I tugged a loose cotton sundress on over top. "This is just for the walk. How far is it? I mean, how long will it take to get there?" I had a decision to make, and about two hours in which to make it. I hoped the walk to the beach and a little splashing in the surf would help me make up my mind: go back to the road, or stick around Sea Horse Ranch a little while longer. It was going to be a tough choice. Maybe Lou would help me make it. I eyed him speculatively.

"Ten minutes, at most." Lou was still giving me a pretty thorough once-over, even with my cover-up in place. "I grabbed us some towels."

"Lead the way," I said, waving him out of my room. *The* room, I mean. The guest bedroom, not *my* bedroom. I was already feeling a little too comfortable here, I guess.

⁓⁓⁓ ⁓⁓⁓

We walked down the single-lane road that cut through the center of Hell and Dammit, white fragments of shell and coral crunching beneath our flip-flops, a fine dust settling around our toes. The horses watched us as we passed. One of them actually whinnied, as if she wanted us to come over and visit.

"That's Trinket," Lou said. "She likes me best. I always ride her when I'm home, so she's probably wondering why I'm walking right past her now. Did you miss me, Trinket?"

"Are you usually gone for a long time?" I asked, sensing an opportunity to learn more about Lou.

He ran his hand along Trinket's long forelock before setting off again. "Well, not *too* long. A few months or so at a time, then I come back for a month or two, then I head out again. I might stick around for a while this time, though. Not so much going on back up north. And it's nice here in spring and summer. Hot, but it's hot everywhere. Might as well be hot on an island with a breeze, right?"

"And you're still going to keep it a secret, what you were up to?" I gave him a sidelong smile. "Mr. Con Man?"

"It's a big secret," Lou laughed. "You don't even wanna know. I might incriminate you just by telling you."

The smile on his face told me he was teasing me, but I still wanted to know. In fact, I was pretty sure I couldn't leave Hell and Dammit Cay without getting the goods on Lou. He fascinated me: mystery, rugged good looks, and a man who obviously loved his mother. Who could resist him?

We crossed the bridge to Little Bucket Key, the water swirling underneath the low roadway and splashing against the rocks on either shore. Without the weight of the truck, I didn't notice any trembling. Roger was sitting on the Little Bucket side, sunning himself on a chunk of coquina along the side of the road. His long green tail dangled in the sand.

"Hello, Roger," I said. "I guess you're allowed to cross the bridge?"

The iguana blinked at me.

"You know his name? Look at you, a local already." Lou gave me an approving look. "So, how long are you staying? Because my mother will never kick you out. You know that, right?"

"Well, that's what I have to think about," I admitted. "I have a text on my phone which needs answering. And I have until—well, depending on whether someone will give me a ride up to U.S. 1, I have until about four o'clock to decide how I'll answer."

Lou was quiet for a few minutes. He turned off the road at a little path cut through some thick, jungly foliage, and I figured his silence was just because he was concentrating on keeping to the best parts of the footpath, stepping over roots and pushing aside tangles of vine. Lizards skittered from beneath our feet, and there were flashes of wings in the leaves overhead as birds hopped to higher branches. Shallow pools of water glimmered in the shadows, with delicate white orchids opening around their banks. I spotted a few wooden huts as well, which must have been part of the abandoned eco-resort Crystal had mentioned. They were being swallowed up by the jungle. The pathway was lush and exotic with plants which the resort owner must have placed here, and I was almost sorry when the sunlight pierced the vines ahead.

Then I saw the beach.

No more than two dozen feet wide, this wasn't a beach for tourists. There wasn't room for striped pop-up cabanas or chaise lounges. This was just a long, narrow strand of white sand, with turquoise water lapping gently against its slight slope. It was wild, populated only by animals. Sandpipers poked their long beaks into little clumps of seaweed, and there were waving ruffles in the water which looked suspiciously like seagrass just under the surface. Fish jumped from the water, snatching at insects before falling back with little splashes.

The colors of the water and sand, the sudden coolness of the salt breeze, and the wild beauty of the running seabirds all brought home to me what a truly remarkable place I'd stumbled into. Few people would ever see this island. I was lucky.

Lou turned around. "You like it?"

"It's incredible," I told him. "But there aren't any houses? I thought people lived here. I saw houses on the way in yesterday."

"See where the beach wraps around the corner of the island?" He pointed. "That's where the houses begin. This little corner was supposed to be some kind of yoga or meditation retreat, but the investors ran out of money. Probably just an owner up north sitting on the deed now, waiting for it to appreciate." Lou shook his head, his expression almost regretful. "It probably will, really soon."

"You think? It's pretty remote out here."

"Nothing's sacred in Florida. No bond that won't be severed, in the name of beachfront real estate." He looked out at the water, his expression suddenly remote.

Several questions popped into my head. But I knew he wouldn't answer them, so I shelved them. Another day, perhaps. If I stayed.

Was I staying?

I needed to figure this out, before the clock ran out and made up my mind for me. In a couple of hours, my music career was going to drive up U.S. 1 in a battered van, with or without me.

Lou tossed some old beach towels on the sand and placed a few chunks of coquina on the corners to keep the breeze from sending them flying. He pulled off his shirt—a sight which certainly had me riveted—and sat down on a towel. I took a moment to admire his broad shoulders and the definition of his pecs.

Lou raised his eyebrows at my inspection. "Well?" he asked, waving towards the water. "I was promised splashing. And polka dots."

"I didn't realize I was putting on a show." I cocked my hip.

"You knew exactly what you were doing when you bought that bikini," Lou teased.

"I just thought it was cute!" I tugged off the sundress, anyway. The breeze kissed my skin, little tickling ripples across my belly and thighs and shoulders. "Oh, that feels good," I remarked, stretching my arms over my head and giving a little twirl. "Is it really only April? It feels like summer."

"It was snowing in Chicago when I left," Lou mused, still watching me with frank admiration. "I think I'm done with the north for good, to be perfectly honest."

"I'd like to be," I admitted. "On days like this, I'm for sure done with it. You know, I was thinking about going up to New York."

Lou shivered theatrically. "Bone-chilling."

"But a lot of potential for someone in music."

He lifted his eyebrows. "You didn't say you were in music."

"Didn't I?" Now I had a little mystery. "Anyway, the sun feels amazing, just reflecting off the water."

"Put your feet in," Lou suggested. "See if it's cold."

"I doubt this water is ever really cold," I snorted, but I was still cautious as I walked across the firm, warm sand by the water's edge. The lapping waves looked almost teal in color, but as I pushed my toes into the foam and looked down into the water, it was crystal clear—like looking into a swimming pool.

"Chilly," I said. "But not cold."

"That's what passes for cold here," Lou remarked. "I'll be staying out today, thanks."

"Nooo, get in!" Ankle-deep in the cool water, I spun around to face him and put my hands on my hips. "Come on, I don't want to play in the water by myself!"

"I'm four whole feet away," Lou told me, amused. "You don't even have to raise your voice to talk to me. Pretend I'm in the water. And tell me about your big decision."

"I have to do some splashing first." I kicked one foot experimentally, bringing sparkling drops of water into the air.

"Fine." Lou laid back on the towel and closed his eyes. "You splash. I'll nap."

I let him pretend to snooze while I wandered through the water, flicking my toes through the seagrass and watching tiny silver fish scatter. Before too long, I was knee-deep and several dozen feet from shore, while the quiet waters rose and fell gently against my legs.

The quiet, and the peace, and the light: it was all so heavenly. I did a long, slow twirl, taking in the infinite blues surrounding me, considering my future.

I didn't know how I'd ended up here, but it seemed crazy to leave it so soon. And yet—being a singer had always been my dream, and being a back-up singer had been my job. Apparently, it *still* was my job. If I let Justin and the rest of the band drive north this afternoon without me, it would be over, and where would that leave my ultimate dream, of fronting my own band someday, of being a professional singer myself?

All this time I'd been traveling with The Bombers, I had been just waiting, just holding out, for the prospect of meeting the right people, the ones who would want to create *with* me, instead of handing me lines to sing and telling me where to stand, when to dance, when to slip offstage and start dumping platters of green room treats into my biggest purse before the club manager noticed. I'd been so sure my origin story was just getting started. Discovery was imminent, right? It had to be, when I was surrounded by so many industry insiders.

I'd put up with so much. Was it really time to walk away?

And then, supposing I did let Justin leave me here—what happened? I didn't have a back-up plan. There was no second place finish here. If I didn't make it as a singer, who would I be? How long could I hide out on Hell and Dammit Cay, masquerading as a ranch-hand?

I stared out at the horizon, suddenly wishing we were on the Atlantic side of the Keys, where the distances were greater. The endless ocean felt more grand for this kind of decision than the tame, charted waters of the Gulf. I was gazing northwest—in a way, I was looking towards home, towards the quiet marshlands and small town life I'd left behind. How would I be better off in a place called Hell and Dammit Cay than I had been in St. Bart Bay? And how would I ever get out of here when I finally had my fill of peace and quiet?

This place was a beautiful diversion, but that was all it was.

I sighed. The realization was both disappointing and reassuring. I could go back to the real world. Get on with my dreams. Remember Sea Horse Ranch as a little mystery in my past. Maybe I'd come back someday, when I was a success, a household name, on my own little retreat from the world of fame and fortune I was bound to create for myself.

I turned back towards land just as Lou sat up. Hoo-boy, that man made my heart thump. I felt a thrill run right through me as I watched his muscles ripple and contract as he squinted across the water to see me.

And I realized then that Lou was a problem. Because he made me want to stay. When I saw his gaze focusing on me, I wanted to stay. I wanted to get to know Lou, and help Crystal, and listen to Marchant's stories, and maybe even meet the mysterious Stacy, who was still up in Miami.

But I couldn't do any of that and still achieve my dreams. My life was on the road, for better or worse.

So, it was time to leave.

As I left the water, I threw back my shoulders and tossed back my hair, unable to prevent myself from preening just a little, putting on the mermaid act. It wasn't really fair of me, not when I was leaving, but I had Lou's full attention for just a few seconds. I wanted to savor it.

Chapter Eleven

Lou grumbled a little when I asked to go back to the house, but he folded up the towels and stuffed them back into his bag without asking why we were leaving so soon. He walked in silence alongside me, and we were crossing back over the short bridge to Hell and Dammit Cay before he said anything.

"So, where are you heading? When you leave here?"

"Gainesville," I admitted with a sigh, remembering Justin's text. "You know it?"

"Of course I know it. The University of Florida. It's a college town in the middle of nowhere." He turned, folding his arms across his chest, as if he was planning on stopping me from passing. But he was standing between me and the rest of Hell and Dammit, not me and the rest of the world.

"Well, I guess tomorrow night I'll be singing back-up in a half-empty bar in a college town in the middle of nowhere. How's that for a forwarding address?"

"Depressing."

I glanced at him, wondering why he cared. Lou leaned against the coquina rock near the bridge, where Roger was once again standing with his head held high. I watched Lou reach out one hand, his movement slow and measured, before he tickled the giant iguana under his chin. The iguana blinked at him, but didn't move. I drew back in surprise, and a little fear—that was a *big* lizard. "Wait, people can touch Roger? I just assumed that was a no-go."

"Only I can," Lou boasted. "He'd run away from *you.*"

I suddenly felt completely jealous, even though I'd never had any interest in touching an iguana before this point. What was Lou, the lizard whisperer? "I bet I could touch Roger if I wanted to," I countered.

"Oh yeah? Try it."

"No. I don't want to." I folded my arms across my chest and took a step backwards, just in case my hands got any crazy impulses and reached for him. The idea of touching those scales was giving me the heebie-jeebies. "I'm not a lizard kind of girl, anyway."

"Scared of a lizard?" Lou's smile was infuriating. "A little old lizard like *Roger?*"

I measured the iguana with my eyes. "He must be four feet long!"

"I saw a lizard on Big Pine Key that was six foot from nose to tail."

I snort at that. "No, you didn't."

"Wanna bet?"

"Only if you can take me to Big Pine Key and show me this dinosaur."

His smile turned down. "Well, I can't. Because you're leaving."

"That's right." For a moment, I'd forgotten—kind of crazy, really. Getting back to the band should be the only thing on my mind. But...I let my eyes rove over Lou as he turned back to the iguana. With the palm trees rustling overhead, the salt tang in the air, and a guy like that standing across from me, the atmosphere wasn't exactly conducive to remembering the real world.

Well, the islands can be like that. How many people go to the Caribbean and lose themselves for a week, thinking they'll never return to reality? But almost all of them do, because reality is where everything *is*.

Still, Lou was here, even if it was only temporarily and I wasn't happy about leaving him behind. Maybe I should give him a shot at convincing me to stick around. "You don't seem to think I should leave," I said, keeping my voice light. "You think I should hang out in the Keys a while longer?"

"I certainly don't think you should get in a van with a bunch of guys and drive to Gainesville," Lou said pointedly. "Whatever else you do is up to you, but that, in particular, feels like a poor decision."

"They're my *band*. I've driven all over the country with them."

"But they didn't even know you hitchhiked out of town. They had no idea you were out on the road alone. You've been here two days. You could have been dead, and no one thought to check on you. What kind of people are they?"

Well gosh, when you put it like *that*.

I looked away from Lou, as if an excuse for my bandmates' behavior would present itself, but I saw only the sapphire sea, the azure sky, the fluffy cotton-ball clouds, the horses in their pens, pulling at hay. And, of course, Lou and Roger, somehow waiting at the end of my circling gaze, like my own bizarre true north.

"I'm a singer," I admitted finally, coming back to the heart of the matter. "I sing in a band. And I can't do that here."

"You might be surprised." Lou's voice was a surly growl. He pushed away from the rock while Roger watched him unblinkingly, his lizard tongue tasting the air. I waited for him to say something else, but Lou just turned on his heel and walked up the road, leaving a shimmer of white dust in his wake.

For a moment, I wished I had somewhere else to go, but we were heading in the same direction.

For the moment.

As we approached the house, I saw Crystal was up from her nap, sitting on the shady side of the deck, swathed in a caftan. She'd set the coffeepot on the patio table and was working her way through a cup.

"Hey there, kids," she said as we came up the stairs. "Cup of coffee?"

Lou mumbled something and went into the house, sliding the door shut behind him.

Crystal looked at me curiously.

"I'm leaving," I said. "I don't know if that's what has him in a mood."

Crystal sighed. "You're *leaving*?"

She looked disappointed when I explained the band wanted me back, but took my decision with better grace than Lou had. "You can always come back and stay," she assured me. "You know where we are now."

Lou came back onto the patio, carrying a glass of iced tea. "You told her?" he asked me. "Mama, can you believe this girl?"

Crystal smiled weakly. "Will you give her a ride back up to the highway? I have a little headache. Too much nap, I guess."

"Sure thing, Mama," he agreed, his voice gentler now. He flicked his eyes to me. "See you downstairs. Three forty-five," he said, in his normal tone. And he stomped back into the house. I watched him disappear into his room, closing the door behind him.

It was frustrating, knowing I probably had a decent shot with this guy, who seemed genuine and caring beneath his sarcastic veneer, and I was giving it up to go back to Justin and his indifference.

Sad, the way things turned out sometimes.

At exactly three forty-four, I picked up my packed backpack, slipped my feet back into my sneakers, and went down the stairs. Crystal waved to me from her deck chair, but she didn't get up, and I didn't expect her to. We'd had a good twenty-four hours together, and it was over now. Hey, better to have loved and lost, right?

Leaning against his big red truck, Lou watched me approach. He had a surly expression on his face. I wondered if it was because he had to drive to the highway, or because he was sorry I was leaving. But judging by the silence as I climbed into the passenger side, I wasn't going to find out.

So I looked out the window as we passed the horse pens, crossed the bridge, and drove past the upside-down bucket on the mailbox post. I watched the stilt-walking houses in their pinks and plums and yellows disappear behind the palms, and listened to the strange chorus as we crossed the Humming Bridge. And then we were back on Cutlass Cay, which almost passed for mainland now, it was so wide and long compared to Hell and Dammit. Lou pulled into the parking lot of the low, unmarked building which I knew housed the Slutty Mermaid, and I felt a twinge of sadness that I had this insider information which I wouldn't get to use ever again.

Tourists would pass this restaurant for years to come, never knowing the best cinnamon rolls in the world were made inside its plain walls, and I would be out in the world, thinking about them.

There was the real tragedy: that tomorrow morning, I wouldn't be eating one of those cinnamon rolls.

With the truck in park and the windows rolled down, we watched the U.S. 1 traffic tear by. White rental cars, trucks hauling skiffs, rattling old station wagons, delivery vans. It was crazy how much commerce was centered on Key West, how many miles of near-emptiness had to be crossed so that one island, blessed by distance and moderate size, could be a playground for so many. The traffic buzzed through Cutlass Cay without pause, no one knowing what waited down the gleaming white back-road which led to Little Bucket and Hell and Dammit. The lives I'd left back there were secrets hidden just off the busiest road in the county.

Another secret, like the Slutty Mermaid's true identity, which seemed wasteful to have but not to hold.

Lou watched the cars without comment until the quiet between us was like a roaring gale in my ears. I wanted him to say something, tell me to stay, tell me I was making a huge mistake. But of course, he didn't. We barely knew each other. It was crazy to hope for a grand gesture from a near-stranger. Lou wouldn't even tell me what he did for a living. He wasn't about to beg me to stay on his tiny island, living in his house with him and his mother.

I remembered something my mother had told me once, after a botched date I'd set a lot of store on. I'd come into the house and wiped away a few tears, but she just led me into the kitchen. "Girl, you're going to have to make your own fairy tale," she'd said, shaking her head and putting a cup of tea in front of me. "The stories are about two people, but they're written by just one. Never forget that."

For a moment, I thought about that one person, writing the love story for two. Then I glanced over at Lou. His face was set and still beneath his black beard. As if he felt my eyes on him, he turned his head slightly, lifted his brows questioningly.

I swallowed. I wanted to know his side of the story, and it didn't matter now if I made him mad by pushing for his secret. "You never told me what you did in Chicago," I said.

A faint smile lifted his lips as he regarded me. "By day, or by night? I'll tell you *one*."

I'd been asking about his day-job, because I'd thought that was the big secret. But he had a nighttime hustle as well? My heart beat a little faster. I couldn't resist. "Night," I said impulsively.

"Are you sure?" His eyes crinkled with mischief.

"I'm sure."

"You can't tell anyone."

"Who would I tell?"

"You might be surprised who you want to tell."

Now I was leaning towards him, my eyes round with curiosity. "You have to tell me! You said you would!"

"Okay." He took a breath, as if it really was a huge secret, as if he couldn't believe he was going to tell me. "I front a band called Silvery Star."

I stared at him, my mouth falling open from shock. "No."

He nodded slowly.

"No. You are such a liar." I made myself laugh so I wouldn't look so gullible. As if Lou was the secret genius behind the cult indie band whose trippy beats had been propping up club playlists for the past year. I heard Silvery Star's *Ferocious Heart* at every gig we played. And now Lou wanted me to think he was their frontman?

Well, it was the perfect lie. *Anyone* could be the frontman of Silvery Star, because no one knew who they were. They'd gone viral just off their recordings, without ever playing a live show. Their secrecy was probably fifty percent of their marketing. The rest? Really good tunes.

Lou was grinning at me, so I smacked him on the arm. "You are *such* a liar! Tell me the truth."

Lou tipped his head back against the truck's headrest. The seat was too short for him, and the angle made his chin point towards the roof. He looked...defeated? Like he didn't know why he'd said that, and he didn't know why I wouldn't believe him.

The expression made me realize he might be telling the truth.

"Wait..." I leaned towards him, as if proximity would give the game away. "Are you—serious?"

Yes, it was crazy. But then again, *someone* had to front Silvery Star. The band existed. And Marchant had said something about Lou being a musician...hadn't he? Or had I dreamed all that up? Suddenly, last night seemed as unlikely as anything else Lou could tell me. All of Hell and Dammit Cay seemed unlikely. Where had I really been for the past twenty-four hours? Maybe I'd been hit by a car and I was in a coma right now, wasting away in some white-lit hospital ward.

I shook my head, hard, until the vision floated away. Sometimes being physical was the only way to get rid of my awful flights of fancy.

"I'm serious," Lou said. "Dead serious."

"How could this be?" I look around, as if a record executive might be waiting outside the truck with a stack of contracts and his latest royalty check. "You have to explain."

"We did the first few recordings as a way to blow off steam after work," Lou said, still looking at—or past?—the roof of the truck. "We—my buddy and me—we just started playing around with instruments, layering everything on his computer. We hit a sound we liked, and we started uploading tracks. It was a hobby, nothing more. Then that guy from the *Strange Music* blog got hold of it somehow and posted the links and boom...streaming everywhere. So we made an album and uploaded that, too. And it just—*hit*."

"But why didn't you claim it? If you could be a famous musician, why wouldn't you jump on that?"

His eyes never left the sagging liner of the truck's ceiling. "Being famous would ruin everything," Lou mumbled. "It's not what I want. And anyway—" He sat upright, shook his head. "It was a one-off. We're not producing anything else together. He's got other stuff going on."

I wanted to ask if *Lou* had other stuff going on, because his buddy wasn't the only person in the world who could produce music with him. But then a car door slammed next to us, making us both jump. I turned slowly, expecting to see the band's van, unwilling to accept that our time together was really over. But it was only a few minutes past four, too soon for them to have made it up to Cutlass Cay, and instead, I saw a long, yellow Cadillac idling next to our truck. A willowy woman of indeterminate age had gotten out of it, and folded her long arms across her slight chest. She was a tall Black woman, with long, braided hair gleaming with twists of purple and blue. The wide-brimmed yellow hat shielding her eyes, the same color as her vintage car, hid her expression from us.

"Who's this?" I whispered, almost afraid the apparition would vanish if we gave her away.

Lou glanced across at me, and a smile briefly reappeared on his face.

"Oh, boy. That's Stacy," he said. "Now you're in for it."

Chapter Twelve

Stacy waited until we were both out of the truck and standing in front of her, waiting like supplicants for her blessing, before she said anything. Her hat covered nearly all of her face; the long sleeves of her white shirt and her billowing yellow harem pants covered the rest of her. Only her toes, each nail carefully enameled in royal purple, were allowed to see the sun, peeping out from leather sandals.

Then she tipped back her hat and revealed dark-rimmed eyes, startlingly green, with wide arching brows on a high and regal forehead. Stacy looked like a queen.

I felt very small and shabby, with my messy ponytail straggling down my neck, wearing cropped jeans and a tank top. But at least she couldn't see my six-week-old pedicure under my dirty sneakers? Small blessings.

"Lou, what have I told you about hanging out with nice girls along the highway?" Stacy's voice was low and authoritative, with a tantalizing trace of smoke at the end of her question. I instantly wondered if she and Lou were a thing, and quivered with jealousy. She was too old for him, but Stacy carried herself with a royal majesty which would allow her to poo-poo societal conflicts she didn't care for, like a twenty-year age difference.

But Lou's laugh was anything but uneasy, making that theory unlikely. "Only do it when my mom's not home," he recited. "I know, I know. But it's for a good cause. Katie here is going back to the mainland with her band. She's a singer. I'm just keeping her company until they get here."

"The mainland, huh." Stacy swept her gaze over me. "What's so great about that place? I was just in Miami. I hope to God I never go back."

"Stacy is an *artist.*" Lou enunciated the title with theatrical flair. "She probably had a gallery opening in South Beach. The *horror.*"

"I don't see *you* putting yourself out there." Stacy snorted inelegantly. "Sitting at home with your mother again, Lou? Always on the retreat, my boy. This girl and I have something in common. She and I are both out in the world, selling our wares, giving away pieces of ourselves like we're common whores."

I choked on a protest, and Stacy turned kind eyes on me. "I don't mean you're a *literal* whore, darling," she said reassuringly. "I'm speaking purely about emotions, here. I put mine on my canvas, you put yours into songs. Right?"

I wished she was right. And someday, she would be. That was why I was here, right? Waiting to go back to the mainland, where my shot was. "Right," I agreed at last. It was easier than explaining the truth about my real place in the musical community.

"Lou doesn't know anything about that kind of life," Stacy confided. "All he does is sell—"

"That's enough making fun of Lou!" he interjected, hands between us. "Maybe it's best you're leaving, Katie. You get along with Stacy way too well."

"Maybe she *should* stay with me," Stacy smirked. "Keep you on your toes, Lou."

"I don't want to be on my toes. I want to be left alone."

"Such a grump! How is your mother?"

"The same as when you went to Miami, I assume. Nothing changes out there."

Stacy crossed her arms again. "How about the issues with the bank?"

Lou glanced at me. "The same," he said guardedly. "I looked last night."

"You're being selfish," Stacy told him. "My offer stands. Let me help."

"There are other ways. We just haven't figured them out yet."

This was all clearly not meant for me. I started looking back out at the road, edging away a little so they wouldn't feel like I was butting into a private conversation. But Stacy noticed immediately. "There's no need to stand in traffic," she chided me. "I'll stop arguing with Lou. It's just an old habit of mine. I've known him since he was a little boy in Spiderman underwear."

"Stacy!" To my delight, pink was creeping into Lou's tanned cheeks. "Come on. The less said about my Spiderman underwear, the better."

Stacy eyed him. "So you're still wearing them, huh?"

I was about to jump into this line of chat when gravel crunching under tires startled all three of us. I looked up, and my heart made an odd little flopping motion. It was weird—as if I hadn't wanted this moment to arrive at all. And then I felt a brief pulse of hope.

Maybe this wasn't them. Maybe it was *another* nondescript, battered white van that needed to stop at the Slutty Mermaid?

But it was Justin who slid open the side door, wincing as it squealed on its rusty runners, and it was Tom and Mac who were sitting in the front seats, grinning at me through the windshield. I knew from his absence that Vinny was somewhere inside, probably passed out asleep on the middle seats, snoring. I remembered the way he'd snored all the way from Key Largo to Key West just a few days ago. The memory didn't make me want to leap back into the van.

Justin grinned down at me. It was a smile that used to melt my heart—and other parts of me—all the way down to my shoes. And he looked good. There was no doubt about that. In a world of all-nighters and endless roads, Justin was a man who could sleep anywhere, looked fabulous in a rumpled suit, and had a five o'clock shadow more trim than the most put-together Hollywood star's perfect beard. His tawny hair and long, elegant features seemed perfect for the fame he hadn't found yet, and in a lot of ways, everyone in the band was just waiting for Justin's charisma and looks to propel The Bombers into the big-time. Sure, our music was pretty good, we always thought, but *Justin* was the real key to success. His charisma, his cheekbones, the way he looked in a skinny-cut suit.

Justin believed it, too, and trust me when I say the confidence showed. It was practically dragging me into the van, back into his non-committal arms. I wondered why I thought anything would change. When I climbed back into that van, I was Justin's girlfriend again. The girl he put on the stage to sing back-up, the girl who waited for him back at the motel while he caroused with whoever caught his eye at the show.

I'd followed him this far; why did I think I could stand up to his charisma now?

"You getting into the van or what, Katie?" he called now, as I stood there, watching my life get smaller when it should have been expanding.

He's your only shot, I reminded myself.

I hiked my backpack up on my shoulder and glanced back at Stacy and Lou. Well, mostly at Lou, if we're being perfectly honest here. Dark-bearded, full-shouldered, tan, rugged Lou couldn't have been more different from the elegant rock-star-in-waiting hanging out of that van door. From, you know, my *boyfriend.*

Lou's gaze was flicking between me and Justin, and I could tell he didn't like what he saw. The knowledge gave me a little rush of power—*Lou likes me, after all*—along with a corresponding downturn to my mouth, because dammit, Lou liked me, after all. And I really liked Lou. And his mom. And Marchant. And the horses. And gosh, it had only been about six minutes since we'd met, but I thought I liked Stacy, too.

And she was the one who spoke up. Stacy looked over at Justin, then back to me. She said, "Don't go with them, Katie."

Stacy's words were delivered with the cool confidence I already expected from this woman. Stacy would never say anything she didn't completely believe to be her truth. And right now, her truth was that I, a person she'd just met, should give up my life's work and stay on the side of the road with her.

"Why not?" I asked. "What else will I do? That's my *job.*"

I didn't mention my boyfriend.

"It's not the right move," Stacy said simply. "Can't you feel it? I feel it. They're the wrong energy for you."

"Today, Katie! It's a long haul to Gainesville!" Justin's voice was already impatient.

I turned my head and regarded my beautiful jerk of a boyfriend. "Just a minute, please," I called. Justin made a face, but subsided, turning to say something cutting and funny to Mac.

I walked past Stacy and Lou, and looked across the gleaming lanes of U.S. 1. On the other side of the Overseas Highway, the white crescent of Half-Moon Beach beckoned. The water, a patchwork of turquoise and teal and the deepest of azures, lapped against the sand with gentle, curling waves. As I gazed across the shining sea, two dorsal fins cut the surface.

Dolphins? Sharks? Marlin? It was too far away for me to tell. But they reminded me there was a world out here that was impossibly beautiful and beguiling, and people who were warm and welcoming. I wouldn't find these scenes on the road ahead. And the asphalt would lead me straight back to the mundanity of the real world. If I wanted to be an artist, shouldn't I indulge myself, just once, in pleasure and beauty and the natural world?

It was a good argument, if I did say so myself.

I turned back to Lou and Stacy. Lou's eyes were dark and hooded beneath his brows, watching me warily. Stacy just looked expectant, as if she knew the dolphins had finished the argument she'd started.

"I want to stay," I said.

"Of course you do," Stacy told me, nodding.

Lou didn't say anything, but his body seemed to relax, and his blue eyes glittered as he looked past me to the wide Atlantic. I watched him for a moment, aware of Justin's growing impatience behind me, but ready to find out if there was something lurking between me and this mystery man of Hell and Dammit Cay.

Justin shoved aside to let me climb into the van next to him, but I kept my feet on the ground. "I'm not coming," I told him.

He scowled. "You can't just stay here because the water's a pretty color, Katie. Get in the van. We have a *gig.*"

"And you told me to get out just two days ago," I reminded him. "Did you forget?"

"I was mad," Justin growled. He lowered his head closer to mine, trying to keep from being overheard by the rest of the band, who were unabashedly leaning back to eavesdrop. "We got *booed.* You got booed. They were chanting *'Katie get off the stage'*— remember that?"

I bit my lip and prayed for serenity before saying, "It didn't *start* that way. The gig was going just fine. I don't know who started that chant, but it could have been personal." It *had* to have been personal, but I had no idea who would have started it. I didn't know anyone in Key West, and I had no enemies on the road. Well, there were a few women who coveted Justin, but...would they go this far?

"Still, we were booed," Justin persisted. "What did you expect me to do?"

I don't know, not dump me at the end of the continent? Aloud, I countered, "Booed by a bunch of drunks at a music festival, when we weren't even close to headlining. What did you expect? We'd be hailed as the next big thing? We're not exactly Silvery Star," I added, unconsciously dragging up the viral band sensation that Lou had recently claimed to front. *Could* that be true? I was still going to have to make him prove it. Maybe he could show me the email he used to upload music or something. I shook my head, trying to get my brain back on track. It was entirely too focused on Lou.

"I know we aren't," Justin hissed. "But still, we should be past the point where people want you off the stage. Admit you came in wrong and hit the wrong notes, or don't, I don't care—just don't let it happen again and we don't have a problem. Okay? Now, will you please get in the van?"

I shook my head, suddenly resolute—suddenly *certain.* What a great feeling. I wish I had it more often. And the certainty was this: it was time to cut Justin out of my life. Justin wasn't my future—I'd had it all wrong. Whatever my chances of becoming a singer were, he wasn't the answer to making my dreams come true. Come on, he'd had a year. How much more time could you give a guy? "No. I'm sorry. Or wait—no, I'm not sorry, either. Goodbye." I raised my voice. "Bye, boys!"

Mac's bearded face appeared over the passenger seat headrest. "You're really not coming?" He had the grace to look disappointed.

"I'm really not coming."

Tom leaned around the driver's seat. "What are you going to do?"

"Stay here," I said. I shrugged, looking around. "Work at the Sea Horse Ranch. Get a really good tan. Maybe I'll work on my own songs. Anything I want to do, really."

I didn't get a chance to hear what Tom or Mac thought about that decision, because Justin slammed the van door shut, just inches from my nose. There was instantly a rise of heated voices, and I felt a little cozy inside, knowing the other guys in the band were at least fighting for me. They could have done some of that fighting sooner, instead of letting me wander up U.S. 1 on my own, but better late than never.

Still, it didn't matter. I stepped away from the van, leaving them to argue. I knew that in a few minutes, Justin would prevail and they'd get back on the road without me, off to chase down that next gig, that next shot at making the big-time, without me. It was fine. My feelings wouldn't be hurt. Well, they were a *little* hurt by Justin—but I'd already known by now he'd always pick himself first. I'd gotten used to it. I'd get over the insult.

Pretty quickly, actually, considering the people I was picking over him. Stacy's face was warm with approval as I walked back to the Hell and Dammit Cay contingent. Slouching next to her, Lou watched me closely, an unreadable expression on his face. I stopped just in front of them, and Lou reached out, gently unhooking my backpack from my shoulder. The gesture made my heart stutter. I looked at my heavy bag, hefted so easily in his hand. Justin never carried my bag.

"Nice work," Stacy told me warmly. "Excellent use of backbone."

I smiled at her, feeling a little bashful. "Thank you," I replied. "I surprised myself a little."

"Let's get you back to the island," Lou said. "My mom's going to be thrilled you decided to stay."

"How about you?" I asked daringly.

Lou's mouth tipped up in a grudging smile. "I'm not mad about it."

Behind us, gravel crunched beneath tires as the band's van pulled out, rejoining the stream of cars heading north. The weekend was over, the tourists were heading home, and The Bombers were leaving for good—but I was staying here, in the salty air of the Florida Keys.

And though I had no idea what would happen next, I was excited to find out.

Chapter Thirteen

When I got back to Hell and Dammit Cay, the first thing that happened (aside from Crystal singing a happy song and dancing around me, and Marchant waving the pirate flag over the balcony to invite us to dinner) was Stacy's request that I come over for a chat.

Maybe "request" was the wrong word. This was more of a summons. Stacy had an incredible presence to her. When she stood to leave Crystal's and head back to her own house, she turned to me and said, "I'll see you in half an hour for a cup of tea and a chat," I just nodded and replied, "Yes, I'll be there," without even considering there might be another option, like suggesting an alternate time or even venue for this audience.

Lou thought it was funny. "You must have a crush on Stacy. All she has to do is snap her fingers and pop! There you go!"

"Pop?" I asked, raising my eyebrows. "Snap her fingers and *pop?*"

He gave me a glare, but I could see from his cheeks that he was hiding a smile. "Pop," he repeated, doubling down. "That's the noise your fingers make when you snap them, obviously."

"Of course," I snorted, and went to leave my backpack on the bed in the guest room. My room, I supposed, for real. Crystal said to unpack and settle in, that I could stay for as long as I wanted provided I didn't mind helping with the ranch—and of course I didn't mind. Who would mind helping out with those adorable little ponies down there? It was a lovely room, even with—especially with—the dated bamboo and wicker furniture, the pale eighties artwork on the wall. The light from the water dancing on the ceiling. The pinkish glow on everything.

But it was also really close to Lou's room. I looked at the wall we shared, half-hidden behind the dresser and its matching arched mirror. He'd be on the other side of it every night. And I'd be over here, *very* aware of his presence.

I had to be careful with Lou. The attraction between us was mutual, no doubt about that. But if it was just something physical, well, when that burned out, I'd have worn out my welcome on this island pretty quickly. And now that I'd decided to stay and see what Sea Horse Ranch had to offer me, I wasn't in a hurry to mess it up. This could be a retreat from the world that opened up my brain and let me find my own musical genius, right? The genius I knew was in there. Had to be in there.

So I left my bag unpacked at first and instead headed to Stacy's house for that tea and chat she'd demanded. Maybe the answer was waiting for me in our conversation. Stacy saw things. I was sure she'd already noticed the looks Lou and I shared. She'd probably have something to say about that.

Ready for some wisdom from an elder soul, I walked across the thin grass of Crystal's yard and over the crunching white shells of the road, curious about what was waiting for me. I paused at the coquina posts set to either side of Stacy's driveway, taking in her corner of the island. Her house was perched close to the water, where a dozen or so tall Sabal palms lifted themselves to the roof line, their trunks occasionally jogging to one side for a few inches before righting themselves and heading sunwards again. Hurricanes will do that to a palm tree. Not for the first time, I wondered how often big storms hit here.

Stacy's house loomed on its white stilts behind the clustered pompoms of the palm tree heads. It was painted a faded pink and surrounded by the same wide porch as Marchant and Crystal's houses. As an artist, light must be so important to her, I thought. But as I approached the house, I could see curtains hanging around the glass porch doors. So maybe Stacy liked to control her environment more than the other residents of the island, who were happy to leave their vertical blinds pulled back all the time.

I climbed the stairs and found Stacy sitting in her living room, waiting for me with a serene expression. The sliding glass doors were open, heavy curtains of navy blue drawn back and drifting gently back and forth in the sea breeze. Stacy lounged on a bottle-green couch just inside, a burgundy brocade dressing gown split open over her thighs, a tea kettle draped in a knitted cozy on the shining coffee table at her side. The table was set with two cups, two saucers, a plate of butter cookies, and a bottle of champagne in a silver ice bucket. I raised my eyebrows at it all.

The scene was one of messy nobility, like a tea party after an all-night ball which got very out of hand.

"Come in," she sang out. "Welcome to my gallery."

I stepped through the curtains and into the room, feeling like I had really entered some sort of gallery. There was art on every flat surface, every medium, every school. On the walls, mosaics of mermaids vied with reproductions of Dutch masters and bright watercolors of sunsets, which had probably come from sidewalk vendors in Key West. The shelves were heaped with bronze and stone and marble: busts, animals, trees, random shapes. A Persian carpet stretched luxuriously over the floor's wide ceramic tiles, masking their beige plainness with a geometric pattern of lines and flowers.

The room was chaotic, but it worked. After a moment of staring, I realized it was because the colors all blended into one another. It was like someone had swirled up a giant paint set.

Stacy grinned. "Do you like it?"

"I do," I said. "This is...incredible."

"Marchant says it gives him a headache," Stacy confided, pouring tea into the two cups. "And Crystal says it depends on her mood, whether she likes it or not. I don't invite them over very often; they're more comfortable in their own spaces. I go to them."

I didn't ask what Lou thought of Stacy's gallery, but I had a feeling he liked it. He might even have been complicit in its creation.

"Sit and have some tea," Stacy encouraged, patting the cushion next to her. "This is my ritual. First we drink tea, for the caffeine, and then champagne, for the fun."

"Seems sensible," I agreed, taking my seat. "And it's after five, anyway."

Stacy glanced at me, one eyebrow lifting.

"The whole five o'clock drinking rule? 'It's five o'clock somewhere?'"

She shook her head, a small smile mocking me. "That's not a rule here."

"Of course not." I doctored up my tea with plenty of sugar. "We're well outside civilization here."

"And that's the way we like it." She kicked up one foot on the coffee table. Her purple pedicure gleamed in a golden pool of sunlight. "We don't need a reason to party. Although, trust me, getting home from Miami is reason enough to celebrate. I wouldn't mind visiting a nearby city once in a while, but it's unfortunate *that* sprawling eyesore is the welcome we get to the mainland. My agent forced me to do a show at a gallery downtown. My agent is my sister. She has no taste. That's ironic for an artist's agent, isn't it? Downtown, in glass and steel. She couldn't even have the grace to set me up in South Beach, where at least there's some history, some architecture, some *water* to look at." Stacy groaned to give me an adequate picture of what she had to put up with.

"Did you at least have a good opening?" I asked. I sipped at my tea. *Hot.* Or my lips were sunburned. Or both. I put the cup down again.

"Pretty good. I sold some paintings." Stacy waved the sales away with a slosh of her teacup. "Equine art always has an audience. Rich people love surrounding themselves with horses; it makes them feel connected to *actual* aristocracy. If you want to make money in art, paint horses."

"You paint horses?" I gave the chaos of artwork around us another glance. "I don't see horses in your collection."

"I don't even *look* at other people's renderings of horses," Stacy said with satisfaction. "I look at the horses out the window, and then I paint them. That's all the influence I want."

"Wow. That would be like, if I never listened to music in my genre."

"Maybe you shouldn't! Go into your next musical journey with a clear head." Stacy nodded at me. "If you want to make punk, listen to classical. Or vice versa. But don't let anyone else affect the dreams inside your mind."

This was getting more esoteric than I liked. I mean, I enjoy a good horoscope as much as the next person, and I always tried to parse out some meaning from my fortune cookies, but I wasn't really big on the whole spirit-moving-me shenanigan a lot of artists enjoyed so much. I thought about things, I enjoyed expressing them through song. But it wasn't a spiritual experience. Thinking in music was just who I was. I didn't know how to do things any other way.

"Sure," I said finally. "Worth a thought."

"Oh, you don't have to. The process is what matters. If your process works for you, tune me out. I don't know everything, and I don't know your mind." Stacy drained her teacup. "What I do know is that *those horses* have to stay."

"Those—Crystal's horses, you mean?"

Stacy nodded. "I need them on the island."

"And are they going somewhere? That I don't know about?"

"Everyone's going somewhere." Stacy worked the cork from the champagne bottle and tipped it over her empty teacup. "Crystal's on her last legs, financially. She's never been in good shape, but I've been talking to Lou about it for the past six months. He was working on some plan to make money for the place, but I guess it backfired. Lou's a sweet boy. He tries very hard. But I don't think he's the business genius he thinks he is. I've offered to help as best I can, but he keeps pushing me back, thinking he can do it." Stacy sighed. "I don't think he can do it."

I didn't know what to say. Sea Horse Ranch was supposed to be my fresh start, my saving grace. Not a financial disaster about to sink under the waves.

"So, now you know," Stacy went on. "Crystal needs help or she's going to have to sell the horses. And that can't happen." She took a swig of bubbly and gazed out the door, towards the horse pens in the distance. "Even if I never sold another painting, I want to open my curtains every day and look at those horses. Their lines. Their curves. Their expressions and their manes and the graceful way they move. Painting that motion and spirit is my life's work. Do you know what it's like to have found your life's work?"

She subsided for a moment, retreating into her own thoughts. I took the opportunity to finish my own cup of tea, swallowing the dregs of sugar in the bottom, and she served me from the champagne bottle.

"You're here to help Crystal save the Sea Horse Ranch," Stacy said at last. "And *that's* why we're drinking champagne. You wanted a celebration? You've got one. You're the celebration."

I had no idea what Stacy thought I could do. But when she held up her glass for a toast, I held up mine, as well.

Sure. I could be their superhero. It was as good a job as anything else, I supposed.

"So, you think I should stay on with Crystal for a while," I said after a few minutes of contemplation and champagne. "Live in her house, and all that."

"I do think that," Stacy replied. "Unless you think it's a bad idea?" She lifted one brow. "With Lou there? Maybe you don't want to be too close to him."

"I wouldn't say I don't *want* to be..." I hazarded a grin, and she returned the favor.

"I thought as much. I like the energy there. Lou is...Lou is lost. He needs a reason to stay. When he gets bored, he leaves. When he thinks he could do better with his life, he leaves. When he thinks he could make more money—you see where I'm going with this. And when he leaves, he gets himself into trouble. Lou looks for father figures, I think. And he chooses the wrong men."

"Men like his actual father?" I guess, even though no one has mentioned Lou's father before.

She nodded. "Arnie wasn't exactly reliable. And his business choices were rarely above-board, which always concerns me when Lou hits the road for one of his attempts to make money for his mother."

Well, that checks out with Lou, telling me he was a fraud. But it's worrisome. "He said something that gave me the impression... not everything he's been doing is legal."

Stacy sighed. "I don't know what he did this time, but he's hiding from something. I could tell the moment I saw him this afternoon. He made a mistake back on the mainland. If you want to pry that out of him, well, be my guest. But I don't know how much he'll give you."

I know what I'd like for him to give me. Not helpful, Katie. Focus. "He's already told me one secret," I admitted. "I'm not sure why he thought he should, honestly. He barely knows me."

"That's what I mean, when I say I like your energy together. He wants to confide in you. Pretty unusual, for Lou." Stacy nodded. "Pretty unusual," she repeated. "Maybe you can figure him out. Someone has to."

"Well, why?" I put my teacup down, and Stacy leaned forward, topping me off. "Why does he have to be figured out?" Maybe Lou was at his best as an enigmatic mystery. Maybe that was how his creativity thrived. I'd met all types on the road. The creative process was a mysterious thing. "You never know where someone gets their energy."

"You think I don't know that?" Stacy laughed, and I remembered I was in the presence of an artist. She knew all about isolation and mystery. "Because Lou's done something he's ashamed of," Stacy continued. "And it has to do with all of us. I want to know what it is. I'm trusting you to figure him out, Katie. And help him get on track. So we can get Sea Horse Ranch back on track."

Great, I thought, draining my champagne in one swig. Get close to the island's prodigal son and figure out his deep, dark secret. Then, save a tiny island farm from financial ruin! That wasn't a tall order *at all*.

Chapter Fourteen

Dinner that night was another pile of grouper filets grilled up and served on Marchant's porch, blackened and spicy with Dammit Salt and washed down with plenty of beer. I had no complaints about this repeat menu, or the company, or the setting: on the deck under a darkening sky, clouds spreading over us from north to south. By nine o'clock, dusk long gone, the thick layer of stratus overhead had blocked out the stars. Looked like the change in weather was really coming.

I was full of food by then. Crystal had contributed baked sweet potatoes with cinnamon butter, and Stacy revealed that she cooked a fine pan of cornbread—the jalapenos were a surprise, their bite combining with the robust spice of the Dammit Salt to ensure many beers were required.

Tipsy and full of spicy food, I arranged myself in a cotton hammock on a quiet side of Marchant's deck and looked up at the thickening clouds, which were moving quickly on some mission of their own. I considered taking a little cat-nap. There was no sign of the fun letting up on the other side of the house, so it wouldn't be an early night, and today had been long. Marchant was strumming a ukulele and Stacy was begging him to stop, while I could hear dishes stacking in the sink inside. Crystal must be clearing up, I thought. I should go inside and help.

I closed my eyes. I'd get up in just a minute.

The hammock swayed gently. The wind must be picking up, I thought. Maybe it would rain. I should really get up. So sleepy, though. The hammock swayed more violently. I thought I might fall out, and I opened my eyes quickly, starting at the sight awaiting me.

Lou was grinning down at me. I stared at his handsome face and for a moment, I felt a brightness behind my chest: a lifting, joyful sensation. His smile was enough to send my heart racing, but not in the nervous, I'm-not-good-enough way that Justin's seemed to. Lou actually liked me. I wasn't sure Justin ever had.

Then he shook the hammock again, and his laughing face was more like a mischievous boy's than that of a mysterious man with a hold on my heart.

I clutched at the ropes on either side and screeched, "Stop it, you're going to make me fall out!"

"No, you won't, just sit in the middle—"

"I'm not some kind of hammock native like you Keys types!" I snapped, genuinely freaking out as the hammock lurched from side to side. "Now quit!"

Lou immediately took his hands off the hammock and put them behind his back. "Sorry. Won't happen again."

"Thank you." I loosened my grip on the ropes. "I'm sorry I yelled."

"No problem." He was already over it. "Hey, what did Stacy want earlier?"

"What?" I blinked at the question. Maybe that was the real reason he'd woken me up, though. Not to play, just to get answers. "Stacy? She only wanted to talk to me a little, that's all. Get to know me." No reason to share Stacy's concerns about the ranch. Or about him.

"Did she offer you a room in her house?"

I frowned at him. "What makes you ask that?"

The truth was, I'd kind of expected her to do that, too. I'd had a feeling, for just a moment, that she didn't want me to share the wall with Lou. But I'd read her wrong. She wanted me living practically on top of him while I sussed out whatever was going on with his mysterious life outside Hell and Dammit.

Lou shrugged, looking out to sea as if the conversation didn't matter. "She doesn't like living alone. I thought back to the Slutty Mermaid parking lot that she was sizing you up. Maybe you could be her little art assistant."

"I'm already your mother's little ranch assistant, remember?" I took a deep breath and popped myself up from the hammock. I wobbled a little as I tried to find my feet and was gratified to find Lou's hand on my arm, steadying me. His touch was reassuring, and I turned to cast him a flirtatious smile. "But do you think I should move in with her? I could ask her if she wants a roommate. Maybe I could commute across the island, all ten feet of it."

"If you want to." Lou's fingers were warm on my skin, his fingertips calloused in a familiar way which I couldn't quite place. "It's your life."

"Well, first, I'd like to know if I'd be missed." Standing up, it was harder to think, as if all the beer in my system had suddenly swum up to my brain. "Would you miss me if I moved out?"

"Oh, I'd miss you." Lou's voice was low, a purr to my ears. His fingers rubbed mine for just a moment, and the callouses pulled along my skin.

"Guitar," I blurted, realizing where I'd felt those callouses before.

He raised his brows. "Guitar?"

"You're a musician." He had mentioned laying down tracks on a laptop, but Silvery Star wasn't just synths. "I mean, you *play* music. I mean—" The words weren't coming out right. I was flustered, standing so close to him, his fingers touching my skin, heat spreading to every corner of my body. His eyes were reflecting the flames from the torches, making things even more confusing. I just wanted to tip my chin up and kiss him, hard.

He was smiling down at me. "Yes. A musician. We talked about this. How drunk are you?"

"No—I mean, I forgot, for a minute. I swear I'm not drunk. There's been a lot to take in the past few days. A lot of change for me." Justin's fingers—that was where I knew that rough-edged touch from. But Justin's grip had never felt as tender as Lou's. His eyes had never seemed to spark at me with such promise. Still. Falling out of love with one rock-star wannabe and into it with another? At least Silvery Star was successful. I laughed softly at myself, shaking my head as I said, "I must have a thing for guys with guitars."

Lou's sigh was as big as the north wind rolling over the bay. "Well, keep in mind that I also play keyboards, the trumpet, and drums."

"Is that meant to impress me or warn me off?"

His gaze was impossible to judge in the darkness. "You decide."

I let him guide me back over to the populated side of the deck and allowed him to place a bottle of water in my hand. Stacy was sitting on a low sofa, and she moved over, patting the seat next to her. I slid down to join her, hydrating cautiously. It would be awful to dribble water down my front while the artistic Stacy was looking at me. But she was talking quietly with Crystal, and left me alone to sober up in my own way. Lou settled down into a deck chair nearby, his face half-hidden in the shadows, a beer bottle in one hand. It was all I could to keep from staring at him, entranced by his dark beard and hooded eyes. I knew I was going to be impossibly weird for as long as I was inebriated. *Mental note: don't get drunk in front of Lou again.*

Eventually, Marchant put aside his ukulele and gazed out to sea, studying the clouds as they went on tumbling over one another, hurrying to blanket the island in thicker layers. The humidity was almost overpowering. "I do believe it's going to blow up a storm tonight," he declared. "The palm trees are starting to rattle. Any of you see any lightning out there, yet?"

"The weather radio will be happy to tell you if it's going to storm," Lou reminded him. "A whole group of scientists does this stuff for you and then they stick it out on the airwaves, free of charge."

"Scientists!" Marchant scoffed. "Look. You can tell by the feathering in those clouds. High winds and cold air in the heavens. Prepping for a storm."

"Weather radio's right inside."

"The clouds are lowering to the north, that means rain," Marchant persisted.

"I'll get the weather radio."

Marchant smiled indulgently as Lou pushed himself up and went into the house. "Live here long enough, you don't need the weather radio," he chided, shaking his head. "The signs are all right there in front of you."

"Hasn't Lou always lived down here?" I asked. "How long do you need?"

"At least five decades," Marchant said, and gave me a wink.

"Oh, it's not that hard to tell the weather," Crystal tutted. "Any old fool could see it's windy and cloudy. Florida weather's real simple," she added, glancing at me. "In the summer, it rains a lot, but not for real long. In the winter, it doesn't rain a lot, but if it does, it settles in for a soaker. That's about it. And when there's a lot of cold air hitting a lot of hot air, we get waterspouts. You feel a real cold wind all of a sudden, you better look out. There, that's the weather."

"I've seen a waterspout," I offered. "Before a tropical storm, back when I was in high school. It came on shore and wrecked Bernard Hogan's tackle shop. Tore the awning right off." I noticed my old accent coming back into my words. Must be the beer. And the company.

Lou came back through the slider with a small weather radio in one hand, joining the conversation again as if he hadn't left it. "Sometimes in the summer you'll see a waterspout every day," he offered. "I've lost count of how many I've seen."

"That sounds...bad."

"They're usually not very serious," he said. "And far away. You can see pretty far here, don't forget. Now listen, Igor is going to tell us the weather."

"Igor? *You* call the weather radio guy Igor, too?" Every house back home with a fishing boat in the front yard had a weather radio, and everyone called the computer voice which recited the weather and the marine report 'Igor.' I'd thought it was a hometown quirk.

"Everyone calls him Igor," Lou said. "You can look that up online. It's because his AI voice makes him sound like he has an accent." He hit the radio button, and we all listened attentively, as if at a concert, to the weather forecast.

Igor confirmed for us that it was, indeed, going to rain. Quite a lot. And there was a chance of a waterspout.

Marchant nodded, satisfied. "What did I tell you?"

"If there's a waterspout, I want to see it," I said.

"I'll come and get you," Lou offered. "I wasn't going to go downstairs at all tomorrow, but if you're working outside and I spot one from the house, I'll make an exception."

I beamed at him.

"He stays inside when it rains," Crystal interjected. "Lou melts in the rain."

"I *work,*" Lou corrected her. "I do have work to do, Mother." He took the radio back inside.

Stacy laughed. "Touchy boy."

"He's so secretive," Crystal complained. "Who knows what he's doing these days?"

I thought I knew what he'd be working on tomorrow, but I definitely wasn't at liberty to say. I finished my water instead, the plastic bottle crinkling as I sucked it dry. Stacy glanced my way and passed me another. "I guess you have an early start tomorrow," she said.

"Do I?" I glanced from Stacy to Crystal, who was grinning. "Did I miss something?"

"Well, tomorrow we really get to work on the ranch," Crystal informed me. "Yesterday you were still my guest, but today you decided to move in, right?"

I considered the implications of this statement. Ranch-hand. It was happening. Was I okay with this? I heard Lou moving in the house, putting away the radio, taking something out of the fridge. *Yes.* "Right," I said. "I'm all moved in."

"Perfect," Crystal said happily. "Because we have to ride everyone tomorrow. We have a bachelorette party booked for a ride and photos in a few days, and all the horses have to be reminded of their jobs. We can't have them getting silly with a paying customer on their backs."

"No," I agreed, wondering how I'd just been promoted to sea horse wrangler. "Can't have that."

Lou leaned out of the sliding glass door and touched me gently on the shoulder. I looked up at him, my heart in my throat. He could say anything, and I'd agree—that's how silly I was over this guy.

"Yeehaw," he said softly. "Welcome to the ranch."

Chapter Fifteen

The storm hit late in the night—or early in the morning, depending on your personal clock. For me, anything before five o'clock in the morning was still late night, although all the sun, beer, and big dinners on Hell and Dammit were helping me fall asleep much earlier than I was accustomed to.

But even the deepest sleep wouldn't let me ignore the sounds wrapping themselves around my bedroom. A low throbbing roar, the heavy splash of water on glass, a wailing which peaked at a shriek. At first I just stared into the darkness, looking for any speck of light to reach my retinas, my fingers clutching the blankets like a child woken from a nightmare. I was *afraid*.

Then I realized everything I was hearing was just a storm. A violent storm, but nothing supernatural or impossible to understand. I threw back the covers and got up, trying to look outside. But even when I pushed aside the vertical blinds hanging in front of the sliding doors, there was no way to see through the thick screen of rain. Beyond the glass, there might as well been a yawning abyss. The wind rose to a spectral howl and slammed a sheet of rain against the door, right in front of my face, and I retreated across the cold tiles to my bed.

And fell right back asleep.

When I woke up again, night was gone and things were calmer. Gray, drizzling, breezy. Now when I looked out, I saw a creased sheet of dark water where the lovely tropical sea had been the day before. Even the Keys got the blues.

Coffee and toast scents were wafting beneath my door, so I checked the time—-past eight o'clock already. The house was cooler this morning, the tiled floor sticky and chilly with humidity. Kind of disgusting, really. I was reminded of some particularly gross motel rooms I'd stayed in while on the road with The Bombers. But such was life along the water. I tugged on some socks and shuffled out of my bedroom.

In the kitchen, Crystal was bent over the sink, peeling a hard-boiled egg into the garbage disposal. She was dressed in what I was starting to believe was her daily uniform: worn cut-offs, a sagging tank top. The equivalent of a house-dress from the last century. But she'd been outside already; she had mud on her knees and there were discarded rubber boots leaning against the sliding glass door. A dripping raincoat hung over the back of a chair, dragged over to the door to keep the worst of the water on the doormat.

She grimaced at me in greeting as she dropped more eggshell into the sink. "Wet morning. And one thing this house always needed was a mudroom. I always make a mess coming in from feeding the kids."

"It's gross out, huh?" I was relieved she'd already fed the horses. "Nice day to stay inside and catch up on some reading."

Crystal shrugged. "We'll still be able to ride this afternoon. It's letting up. Just a few more heavy storms to go. Did you hear the water last night? There's foam and seaweed all over the rocks this morning. We'll have to do some clean-up."

"Oh, is that what that sound was? That sort of roaring noise?"

"Yup. We must have gotten a *big* storm." Crystal's eyebrows came together, and she picked up the weather radio sitting by the kitchen window. "I think this thing's batteries are dead, or it shoulda woke us up."

"Are you saying we could have been struck dead by a waterspout last night?"

"It's a tornado as soon as it reaches land," Lou contributed cheerfully.

I jumped, wheeling around, only to see him waving from the living room couch. "I didn't even see you in there. Turn a light on, why don't you?"

"I like it dark."

I rolled my eyes. "Of course you do."

"Don't mind him," Crystal said absently. She took the weather radio to the kitchen table and plugged it into a socket under the window. "He gets grumpy when it rains. And then he gets embarrassed that he's grumpy. And then he gets grumpier."

"No, I like the rain," Lou said, flicking through his phone. "Makes a nice change from all that pesky sun."

"Isn't this the *Sunshine State?*" I countered, sitting at the table. "Your sunny native land?"

Lou wrinkled his nose. "Too much of a good thing, if you ask me."

"I guess you miss all those gray winter days in Chicago." For some reason, this felt like something I should argue about. Maybe I should just drink some coffee and wake up properly before I said anything else.

"Too much of a good thing, times two. Also? Ice. No bueno. I'm glad I left Chicago."

"So why are you grumpy, if it's not the rain?"

"Who says I'm grumpy?" Lou looked up from his phone. The blue light lit his face, picking out all the craggy cliffs of his nose and cheeks and brow. "I'm not grumpy. I'm just sitting in the dark."

The peaks and valleys of his shadowy face were hypnotizing. I wanted to walk across that damp tile floor and climb onto that sofa next to him and kiss his beautiful mouth and slide my hands under his shirt and—

"Have an egg and some toast," Crystal said, putting a plate in front of me. "And then we'll see if any of my muck boots fit you."

Eggs and toast and muck boots. Reality, baby. The daydreams of a shirtless Lou would have to wait.

***

The third pair of muck boots we tried were the ones that fit me. Coincidentally, they were also the pair with the most duct tape over holes and cracks. In fact, they were almost entirely held together with duct tape. They looked messy, but the tape held out the water. I splashed through plenty of deep puddles as I brought Reggie back to the barn and started knocking the mud and grit off him with a stiff brush.

"He won't come perfectly clean without a hose bath," Crystal called through the slats of the stall wall. She was next door, grooming Trinket. "But as long as there's no mud on him where the saddle and girth goes, we're all set."

"You hear that?" I muttered to Reggie. "You don't have to be perfectly clean. Just kinda clean."

Reggie tipped back an ear, listening to my voice. He was a pretty little horse, oddly colored with a pale and reddish coat, dark red mane and tail with some blonde streaks, and interesting bars of the same dark red striping the top halves of his legs. Crystal said he was a red dun. "Some kind of Spanish coloring that mustangs can have," she elaborated.

By the time we were up in our saddles, the rain had let up, although the clouds were still a menacingly dark color in the northwest. My phone, snug in my back pocket, had been pinging weather alerts for the past hour. Special marine warnings and severe thunderstorm warnings and gale warnings, even a tornado warning —but they were all for the Middle Keys and Upper Keys. Looking at that sky, though, I wondered if our turn was coming up.

"Maybe we shouldn't ride too far," I suggested, nodding my head at the black belt of cloud over the slate-colored bay.

"Just around our island today," Crystal agreed. "We'll go to Little Bucket and do the tourist circuit tomorrow. That's the reminder the horses need. Then they'll be all ready for our guests."

I wheeled Reggie alongside Trinket, trying to remember what kind of party was coming to the island. But I'd had too much change in the past few days. My brain was out of business. "Remind about our guests," I said to Crystal, as our little horses stepped in tandem. "Church group? Rotary club?"

"A bachelorette party. Well, not the whole party," Crystal added, as I made a snorting, choking sound that made both horses tip back their ears in alarm. "Just a stop on their way to Key West. Nice-sounding group. The Lowel—no, the Lowan—no, the *Lewandowski* party. Yeah. Long name, but I'm pretty sure that's it."

"Second marriage?" I asked hopefully. Maybe they'd be staid grandmas, not crazy twenty-something woo girls. I was not in the mood for that kind of energy in my newfound paradise. I also didn't want any bikini-clad party animals anywhere near Lou. No, these would be geriatrics with blue hair and canes. They probably couldn't even get on the horses. They'd just pet them. "I know the Keys are popular with senior citizens."

Crystal shook her head. "Oh no, they're a bunch of kids, if you ask me. I got their ages for the insurance forms ahead of time. All around your age. I think the bride is twenty-five. Too young to get married, if you ask me."

"When's the right age to get married?" I was momentarily distracted by the potential delight of getting life advice from Crystal.

"Forty-five," Crystal said grimly, and then she laughed. "At the *soonest*. And preferably with a shotgun."

"Not a fan of holy matrimony, I take it." I wondered if she'd been married to Lou's father. The no-good guy.

"It ain't for me." Crystal ran a hand along Trinket's dark mane. "But then, I ain't everyone."

We turned the horses down the road, then down Stacy's driveway, and let them walk through the thin grass, heading for the shoreline. Stacy's house sat at the northwest corner of the island, standing bravely in its thicket of Sabal palms as that threatening bank of cloud slowly drew closer. As I watched the approaching storm, trying to time its arrival, a thin finger of lightning slipped from sky to sea. There was no sound for a whole minute, then a low, barely perceptible rumble seemed to shake the surrounding air. I wouldn't even have called it thunder, just the idea of thunder.

Before the tremble in the air was fully gone, Reggie snorted and shied, nearly throwing me from his back. I grabbed hold of the saddle horn with one hand, hearing myself shriek as I tried to haul back on the reins with my free hand. For a moment, all I saw was sky and palm and flying mane. Then he put his hooves back on the ground and blew out through his nostrils.

I was still on his back.

I sucked in a much-needed breath and shrugged some tension from my shoulders. *Wow.*

"You sure stayed in that saddle good," Crystal called.

Reggie walked meekly back to Trinket, who was looking at him with a disappointed expression.

"That surprised me," I told Crystal. "What'd he do that for?"

She glanced at Reggie's pricked ears, then back at the storm cloud. "You know, I think we might be in for something real nasty. Reggie always knows when there's a big storm coming."

"Oh, really? You didn't tell me he was a *weather* mustang." That sounded like something we could use to make money. We could go on TV and let Reggie predict the weather for fun and profit.

"I think it's more like he has real sensitive hearing, and faraway thunder spooks him when other horses don't notice. But he does seem to get more prickly, the more dangerous the storm."

Another flicker of distant lightning flashed. I tensed, my hands in Reggie's straw-and-strawberry mane, and waited for the thunder to reach us. After a long interval, the air seemed to tremble with a sound I couldn't quite hear, and Reggie snorted, backing up several steps with quick, anxious strides.

"Damn, look at him," Crystal said. "Well, hang on tight in case he bounces again. We still got a few minutes. Let's at least get them around the island once before we head inside."

"How big a storm you thinking?" I asked, taking a careful grip of the saddle horn as I nudged Reggie alongside Trinket.

"Oh, you know spring storms," Crystal said vaguely. "Just a good reason for us to stay inside. Lou will like the company."

"You think?" I imagined keeping Lou company. It would be better without his mother in the house. "Maybe Marchant would like some, too."

Crystal glanced at me, eyebrows arched. "Marchant? He don't even get out of bed if it's raining." She chuckled. "Lazy son of a bitch."

I sighed to myself. I guessed I wasn't going to get Lou alone in the house anytime soon. But...at least we'd be trapped up there together? A guy his age didn't want to sit and talk to his mom all day.

Right?

Chapter Sixteen

By the time we splashed back to the house and trundled up the stairs, the sounds had grown loud again. The wind was rattling in the palm fronds, loosening whatever hadn't been knocked down the night before, and there were crashes as the dislodged fronds finally came free of their trees and plummeted to earth. Waves were pushing steadily against the northern shore, and gusts whistled between the supports of the house. And the thunder was long, low, and steady. The sky? Forget it. A deep and forbidding charcoal color, turning the day into night as the storm accelerated across the sea.

"This is kind of scary," I admitted as we tugged off our boots outside the kitchen slider.

Crystal looked at me from beneath her brows and winked. One boot came off, then the other. "This is just Florida," she told me. "Don't let her scare ya off."

I started to follow her into the house, but suddenly Lou was in the way, blocking my path with his broad chest. He was dressed in *his* uniform: stretched and sagging t-shirt, saltwater-stained cut-offs, and a pair of leather flip-flops. I drew back a little, annoyed that a guy could look this good with such a total lack of effort. I was covered in mud and horsehair, and there was no way I was making an equally good impression on him right now.

He held up a pair of flip-flops, the yellow and blue ones that had been in my backpack. My 'nice' flip-flops. "Put these on and come around the other side of the deck with me."

"What are you doing with my good—"

"Come on! This is worth seeing."

I snatched the sandals and stabbed my toes into them. Lou was already heading around the side of the house. I scampered after him, half wishing for one of those safety harnesses workers wear in high places. The wind wanted to pick me up and throw me off the deck.

I saw it as soon as we turned the corner. Northeast of the island, on the leading edge of that cloak of darkness spreading across the water, a long and eerily white finger stretched from cloud to sea. A mist rose up around its base, as if the gods were conjuring a spell to disrupt the waters.

I took a deep breath and leaned back against the house. "A waterspout," I gasped.

"Sure is," Lou agreed. He was leaning on the deck railings casually, as if the wind wasn't howling in our ears, as if the world wasn't losing every scrap of light as the clouds hustled up to overtake the house. He just gazed at the waterspout, which was only a few miles away, if that, a graceful rope of white standing between the black of the oncoming storm and the flat gray of the sea beyond. "You like it?"

"You talk like you made it," I snorted, recovering myself enough to get my defensive snark back.

"Maybe I did." Lou shrugged his wide shoulders. "Maybe I knew you wanted to see one." He glanced back at me, a knowing grin on his face.

I gave in and smiled back. "You must give severe weather systems to all the girls."

"Just you. You're special."

He was still grinning, or I would have allowed myself to melt a little. But I had to be on my guard if I was going to stay here. No matter. This was just mild teasing between a ranch-hand and the boss's son. Normal stuff for my normal new life. I could keep from acting on it, getting myself mixed up in a physical relationship which would just burn out before I was ready to leave.

If a person could ever be ready to leave this island.

A few cold rain drops slapped against my face, and then I heard a strange hammering sound, as if a million construction crews had suddenly descended on Hell and Dammit. I looked left to try to find the sound, reluctantly tearing my eyes from Lou, from the departing whirlwind, and that's when I saw the rain coming like a charging cavalry across the water.

"Holy crap," I breathed, elegant as ever.

"Here it comes," Lou laughed, and I turned to run. I stopped at the corner of the house, my feet just inches from the slider and the safe, dry indoors, but I was shocked to find Lou wasn't coming after me. Instead, he turned his face up to the onslaught of rain, and as the wall of water hit him, his clothes were soaked through in an instant.

Lou just kept on laughing.

Crystal had showered off the mud and was sitting cross-legged on the couch, frowning over a sheaf of papers. She barely glanced up as I staggered inside and sat down at the kitchen table, trying to process what I'd just seen outside. But when Lou came in, soaked to the skin, she flung down her papers and looked severe.

"What have I told you about standing out there in the rain?"

Thunder rumbled around the house, shaking the floor.

Lou held up his hands. "Not to do it?"

"And yet here you are, dripping all over the tiles."

"What harm does it do?"

A flash of lightning made us all blink. Crystal lifted an empty hand as if to say: *Exhibit A.*

Lou shrugged. "Turns out I missed the crazy Florida weather. It isn't like this in Chicago."

"No one told you to go to Chicago," Crystal grumbled.

"Mom!"

"Sorry, sorry." Crystal shoved the papers into a manila envelope and tossed it onto the coffee table. "I forget I'm not allowed to mention Chicago to you, ever."

I felt like I was interfering with some ongoing family argument, so I retreated to my bedroom, leaving the door open a crack. Just in case...something. I didn't know. It was a really scary storm, okay?

I used a washcloth to mop off the worst of the mud and sat in the middle of my bed, waiting for the lightning to pass so I could shower. The house was creaking in the wind, maybe even wobbling a little, and I wished for some mindless television to block out the storm's power. I had to settle for my phone, though, which meant that I was looking at things I shouldn't.

Like my old band's Facebook page.

I didn't need to check, obviously. I knew that last night they'd played a last-minute gig in Gainesville. I knew next week's schedule, and the big festivals on the roster for the coming summer. Not the *big* big festivals, of course, but there were some decent slots booked. A Thursday afternoon set at a large mid-Atlantic music festival in July. A coveted Saturday spot at a smaller weekend festival put on by a Phoenix radio station. Some food festival slots Justin wasn't proud of, but which always paid some bills and put gas in the van—these were 'live to fight another day' type of paychecks.

What was really important wasn't *where* the band was heading after they'd played in Gainesville last night. It was *who* would go with them. There were female vocals in most of the songs, and I had one song of my own. It wasn't technically their song; but who was going to stop them from playing it? The song was popular, and, unfortunately, my crack legal team wasn't returning my calls. Probably because they didn't exist.

Justin would have to get someone else on the road to sing back-up with him, maybe even take on the lead vocals for my song, if it stayed on the set-list. Who would it be? Almost certainly, she'd be someone we both knew from long nights propping up bars while we waited for our sets, wearily applauding through the other bands on the night's billing. There was a community of bands on the same circuit. We traveled together, we played the same clubs, we opened for each other. Occasionally, we stepped in and helped one another. A borrowed drummer here, a back-up singer there.

One or two nights with a new singer in my place, I had always lived with. Everyone had to take a sick day once in a while. Sore throats and colds weren't good for singing. I'd taken the night off and given my mic to people like Gina from Cackling Vampires or Daisy from The Flying Seven before, without fear they'd out-perform me and steal my spot.

But this was a permanent absence. Justin would find someone to replace me full-time.

There'd be someone else in my seat in the van. Someone else singing into my mic. Someone else sweet-talking the motel overnight clerk into comping us an empty room when our booking had been 'mistakenly' canceled—poor musician shorthand for not making a reservation at all because the credit card was maxed out and the last three gigs hadn't paid up yet. Women were always better at getting around hard-nosed night auditors than men were.

And where else would this new woman replace me?

It wasn't hard to guess. Justin wasn't good at separating work from pleasure. And our great romance, the two muses serenading one another from across the stage every night, was just a myth. I'd seen him throw plenty of promising winks at hot girls in the front row; I'd seen him corner a bartender after a show with that wicked dimple of his flashing; I'd seen him pretend to fend off the advances of the occasional groupie behind a club before meeting her down the block and swaggering into her backseat. Justin hadn't been faithful to me for more than a month or two, if he'd even managed that.

We *had* been almost happy for a while, despite all that. Well, I had been almost happy. I wasn't sure Justin had true happiness in him. One thing was for sure, he wasn't interested in sparking that feeling in anyone else. Justin was all about Justin.

Whoever he put in my place wouldn't find any comfort there. The knowledge made me feel a little better about myself, although I still felt bad for her, whoever she was.

Thunder crashed around the house again, rattling the windows in their panes, and I resisted the urge to dive under the duvet. Not that I was scared of a storm, but seriously, it was just so *close*. Being sixteen feet in the air shouldn't make a thunderstorm scarier, but it does, okay?

I needed something to calm myself. Something that wasn't a social media post of Justin's face smiling against the blue water off the Overseas Highway, a pic taken somewhere east of here, as he held up a sandwich from a roadside diner. After they'd left me with Stacy and Lou, they'd stopped somewhere for dinner and taken pictures clowning around in the blinding-white parking lot, their black motorcycle boots coated with the dust of crushed shells and sand. After they snapped these pics, they'd have driven through the night, arriving in Gainesville late, or maybe sleeping at a rest area for a few hours.

I'd never know which, and I felt a little pang of sadness which had nothing to do with wishing I'd gone with them, and everything to do with simply feeling excluded. I'd been in a band, and now I wasn't.

Forget it, Katie. You can do this on your own.

I put my earbuds into my ears and flipped to my music app.

I tapped on favorites. There, at the top, was the music I'd been spending the most time with over the past month.

Silvery Star.

What a strange, strange coincidence.

I leaned back against my pillows and closed my eyes, ready to be taken away. Silvery Star's signature sound was layered synths, steady hypnotic beats, and the clever interweaving of traditional instruments, from strings to piano to brass to guitar. And of course, now I knew Lou could play most of those instruments, which added a layer of intimacy. Most of the tracks had lyrics, spoken or chanted or sung by a husky, deep voice—which I *also* now knew had to be Lou's.

Trust me, that knowledge made the music that much more entrancing...and I was absolutely dying to hear him growl those lyrics in person. Could I convince him to give me a live performance? I glanced at my door, mentally measuring how far away he was. Fourteen feet? Twelve? In a concert hall or a club, that would be scream-worthy. Bra-throwing-distance, not that I'd ever done it.

I considered throwing my bra at Lou. I pictured him on a stage, three feet above me and mugging a mic, his lips pressed against the mesh as he sang directly to me. The fantasy wasn't as easy as it should have been. I was still having trouble making the connection between recording artist Lou and the grinning, dripping-wet Lou I'd left in the living room.

Truthfully, it should have been strange, listening to him make love to his mic like that, channeled into my ears through the magic of hi-def recording. But I didn't see how this honey-on-gravel voice meshed with the guy I knew, the one cracking jokes with his mom and the neighbors.

Or the one who had gone through my bag and found my flip-flops so I could come see a waterspout without getting splinters.

Wait a minute—he'd been in my bag!

I sat upright and pulled my earbuds out, tossing them on the duvet. If Lou had been fumbling around in my backpack, he might have found—

No, it was here. The rubber band still firmly around it.

I pressed the little black book to my chest and sat down, wondering what was wrong with me. Why would I assume Lou would go through my things? Or worse, steal my lyrics notebook?

Why would I assume Lou was just like Justin?

Chapter Seventeen

I eventually fell asleep on top of my duvet, slowly lulled by the rain and wind and the departing thunder. When I woke up a few hours later, sore and disheveled, my lyric book underneath my right shoulder and my face red from pressing into the pillow, daylight was dancing across the room and Lou was peering around my door.

"Wake up, sleepyhead. Crystal needs us to take care of the horses."

I scrambled up, pushing my notebook beneath my pillows. "Did I sleep all day?"

"It's only four o'clock. You could have gone longer."

"Oh, man. I'll be up all night." Naps were *not* good for me if I was going to change from my nocturnal existence to a more conventional, daylight-first human. "I don't even know why I fell asleep."

"Rainy days will do that to you." Lou's voice was gently amused. "You didn't eat any lunch. Do you want a snack before we go out?"

My stomach growled in reply. Lou laughed while I blushed.

We sat at the kitchen table and ate crackers and hummus. The house was flung open, all the sliding doors and windows pushed open to let in a cool breeze. It wafted around the house like a curious stranger, stirring the pages on the papers and magazines scattered around the living room. We were silent as we ate, just taking in the views and breathing in the salty air.

"I don't know how you ever leave here," I said eventually. "It's so beautiful."

Lou shrugged. "Sometimes a guy wants to earn some money."

"But if you're a musician, you can make that money anywhere. You don't have to go to Chicago to record."

"That's not the only thing I was doing in Chicago."

"I know, I *know,* you were up there making deals and doing bad things." I grinned at him.

"Very bad things." He grinned back. "I like to keep my mom fed, you know. I send back money. It's like the olden days. I go off to the city to keep the farm funded."

"That's very noble of you."

"Well, would you give this place up?" Lou's voice was gruff.

"Why not stay and improve the place instead? I mean, Crystal has a party coming, and that's without the beach, so clearly the ranch can pull in money. She needed help, so she had to hire *me.*" I laughed self-deprecatingly. "I'm hardly qualified, though."

"That bachelorette party isn't going to pay many bills," Lou replied. "We'd need to do ten of them a week to get ahead. I don't think improvements are going to make Sea Ranch self-sufficient. Maybe if we had a beach—but until I can make enough money to buy the sand and get it spread, we're still going to have to borrow the little strand on Little Bucket Key."

"I just hope no one remembers they own that land and decides to do something with it," I mused.

Lou looked down at the hummus and didn't reply.

I noted his silence, filing it away. Lou was worried about that, too. I glanced around the room and saw the manila folder Crystal had left on the coffee table. I suspected it was numbers, and I wanted to have a look at it. See what we were really dealing with here. "Hey, where'd your mom go?" I asked. If she were out, maybe I could get him to head down to the horses before me, and grab a few minutes alone with that folder.

"Stacy's taking her in to talk to some financial advisor she knows."

"Last-minute thing?"

Lou nodded. "She's a last-minute kind of person."

I didn't know if he meant Stacy or Crystal. I suspected the answer could be both. "But we were supposed to ride all the horses today, and we barely rode two. What if they're not ready for the party?"

"Don't focus on the party," Lou said, impatient. "Like I said before, one party won't change anything."

"So you say. But one party's all we've got. What if they have a great time and leave a really good review on Yelp? Then maybe we get another party booked, and another. It snowballs."

"There's one problem with your snowball theory."

"Yeah?"

"It takes a long time for the snowball to roll into anything even close to an avalanche."

"Well, I don't know a lot about snow, I admit."

"Yeah, neither does my mom." Lou rapped the table with his knuckles. "As a business strategy, it's not the quickest way to get results."

"And we have to be quick?"

"Yeah. We really do."

"Because of money, or—"

"Just trust me." Lou leaned back in his chair and gazed out the sliding door behind me. "There's not a lot of time."

I noticed he didn't say *what* there wasn't a lot of time for. To make the place profitable? To pay an outstanding tax bill? What was Sea Horse Ranch really facing? Stacy wanted me to save the place, but I didn't even know what I was saving it from.

"Why *did* you come back?" I asked suddenly. It was all linked. I knew it was. Lou's absence, his return, his unwillingness to discuss Chicago with his mother—there was something there.

"I told you, I was tired of the cold."

"You gave me a lot of throwaway answers. You said it was too cold. You said you were a fraud. You said—"

"Yeah, I talk too much, but I don't say anything. I get it, I get it —"

"Don't put words in my mouth!" I snapped.

Lou looked at me, surprised.

"I'm sorry. That's—that was an accident. I didn't mean to be rude."

For just a moment, he'd reminded me of Justin. Always deflecting. Always laying the blame on me. Always with the guilt trip. Long before the end, I'd realized I couldn't take it anymore. I'd started blowing up at him, starting band-van fights that embarrassed everyone in our proximity. Except for us.

Lou spilled some more crackers onto the plate between us. "Don't worry about it. I came back because I wanted to help my mom hang onto her dream. This is a good place. It doesn't deserve to get bulldozed and turned into a luxury housing development."

I stared at him. Lou dropped his gaze back to the plate. "Who said anything about bulldozers and houses?" I asked, struggling to hide my impatience.

"This is Florida," Lou said, shrugging. "That's what we're always up against."

But I didn't think it was an off-handed comment, just casually bringing up development.

No, Lou sounded like he knew something. Something he wasn't willing to tell me.

Maybe I was learning to read Lou's face, but that wasn't helping me get any answers out of him. After we'd demolished the hummus and crackers, we went downstairs and started the evening chores. The horses were waiting to be fed, their ears pricked as they watched us plunk down the stairs in rubber boots. The duct tape on mine was starting to pull loose from one heel, trailing in the water. I was going to have to get new boots or work with wet feet. Either way, this definitely wasn't flip-flop weather anymore.

"I can't believe how cool it got after that storm!" I rubbed my arms, happy for the light plaid shirt I'd stashed at the bottom of my backpack. It had been rolled up in a ball for a while and smelled a little musty, but the temperature was somewhere in the lower sixties, with a decent wind off the Gulf side of the island to match.

The breeze ruffled the horses' manes and tails, making them look like they were being blown by fans for a fashion shoot.

Lou was efficient with the farm work, and the horses all seemed to like him. Reggie in particular trailed after him, walking up and down the fence-line in hot pursuit as Lou picked up the palm fronds and tree branches thrown around by the storm. It was pretty cute.

When the horses were inside and eating their dinners, Lou tugged two folding chairs from beneath the barn overhang and set them outside in the golden sunlight. The sun was setting between Marchant and Stacy's houses, and the empty sky was shifting into evening mode. It would be a luminous dusk, I thought happily, settling down beside him. We sat quietly together for a few minutes, watching as Venus appeared in the sky and the deep blues of night began to overtake us, leaving just a border of peach-colored sky along the horizon.

"I've been thinking," Lou said eventually. "You've been a back-up singer, right?"

I stiffened. Something in me didn't want to be pigeonholed that way anymore. I knew how to play instruments—guitar and piano and flute, thanks to some very ambitious music teachers in St. Bart Bay—and I needed to get away from being the support of an act. "I'm a *musician,*" I corrected him. "And a singer. Why do you ask?"

"I don't know. Maybe we could do some stuff together." Lou shrugged a little too elaborately, as if he was working hard to keep the suggestion casual. "I've been kinda bored lately. My ear could use some stretching."

I stared at him. Maybe I was ready to be taken seriously as a musician, but I was a long way from being an indie sensation. This was the voice of *Silvery Star* talking to me right now. I blurted, "You're joking, right?" and immediately regretted it—but hey, sometimes we say exactly what we feel.

"Why do you say that?" Lou turned to face me, the chair creaking beneath him. "You were touring with a band. You obviously have some talent."

"I got them booed off stage and was asked to leave," I reminded him, suddenly determined to downplay my career. Nice to be so good at self-sabotage, Katie. Well done.

"Temporarily. They did come back for you. Remember? I was there for that part."

"That means nothing. Justin would have felt bad if he'd left me for dead in the Keys. That would be bad karma, which he sort of believes in, when it's convenient. And they still needed someone for the Gainesville show." I shook my head. "But just because he asked me back, he knew I was the problem, either way. The people wanted *me* off the stage, not the band. I don't know what I did wrong, but somehow, I earned myself a ticket back to St. Bart Bay last weekend."

"So you have no idea why you got booed?" Lou looked interested. "There must be a reason."

"Sorry." I shook my head. I had theories, but Lou didn't need to hear them. "That's classified information. You're certainly not getting it without several beers, anyway."

Lou grinned, then slapped at his neck. "Well, you're in luck. Or I am. It's mosquito hour. Let's head up to the house and put on some music. I'll liquor you up and you can tell me all about how you failed at your career."

"Perfect," I sighed. "You sure can sweeten up a girl."

Lou took my hand, helping me up from the chair, and the warmth that spread through my stomach at his touch proved that he did, indeed, know how to sweeten up a girl.

✥✥✥✥✥ ✥✥✥✥✥

"Okay. Okay, okay, okay." I held up a hand, pretty sure the floor was quaking beneath my feet. Were there earthquakes in the Keys? Everything held still for a moment, and I felt confident enough to go on. "Here is what happened."

"Yes!" Lou did a very obnoxious fist pump, which almost made me change my mind. But I was several beers and a few shots south of good decisions. The man knew how to get a girl drunk and talking. Tomorrow I'd have to unpack that. Tonight I was spilling my guts.

"Okay," I said again. "So there's this girl. No, woman. We are *women*, not girls."

"Of course."

"There's this *woman*, Cass. As in, Cass Blake." I raised my eyebrows, but Lou just shook his head. "Cass Blake from *Force Five Major?*" I emphasized. "Come on, you've heard of Force Five Major."

"I haven't, and neither has anyone else," Lou told me gently. "Trust me. There was a reason you guys were all playing tiny clubs in college towns."

"Okay, so none of us were exactly in Pitchfork yet. But we were getting there. And Cass does lead vocals for Force Five Major and she's really good. And she's really pretty." I stifled a hiccup.

"I'm sure."

"Like, *really* pretty. Like, hot."

"Like you."

I gave Lou a fish-eyed glare. "Don't patronize me. That's not what this is about. It is not about looks. It is partially about looks, but not only about looks." I lost my train of thought and blinked at him. He was so cute. It was about looks. Everything was.

"I'm sorry." He smiled angelically. "Please tell me the story. Cass Blake is a really pretty singer. Go on."

I tipped back the rest of my beer. I was thirsty. Really thirsty. I needed water. I shook the empty bottle, then put it on the floor. I'd get water in a second. First, I'd tell this awful story. And he'd understand everything.

"So, we're in Key West. Cass and I are backstage and she's like telling me how she wants to do Justin. She told me how lucky I was, really buttering me up, you know? She said she hoped I knew what a catch he was. And I told her, 'Well, too bad you don't know the *real* Justin. What a selfish self-absorbed prick he is.' Because that's what he is, y'know? A selfish, self-absorbed prick."

Lou nodded raptly. "I'm sure he is!" He agreed with me. I knew I liked this guy.

"So she laughs and says she knows. She says I'm a saint to put up with him and she was just talking a lot of crap. So I figured it was nothing."

Lou nodded along. "Sure." He wanted me to go on, which was perfect. I had more. So much more.

"So she goes out, she goes out to the club floor, and I'm sitting back in this little hole they call the green room, like to be funny I guess, and Justin comes slamming in 'cuz he's been mad at me all day, in another one of his really mean moods. And he's asking for my lyric book."

I hesitated and glanced towards my bedroom door, suddenly hungry to see my book, hidden safely beneath the mound of pillows on my bed.

"Why does he want your lyric book?" Lou was leaning forward, really into the story now. Such a good audience. I would tell him anything. Everything. I rubbed my face, trying to clear my swimming vision.

"He always wanted it. He stole it two times—no, three times—and took lines from it. Not my best lines, either. So dumb!" I choked out a laugh. "No taste. Justin's all leather and no brains." I liked this phrasing. I considered it. "All leather, no brains," I repeated, testing the syllables. "Could we rhyme something with brains?"

"We can replace the word *brains* later," Lou suggested. "It doesn't give the right visual. But it's a good concept. I can see where you're going."

"All leather, no *feathers,*" I announced triumphantly.

"No, you're getting farther away from it." Suddenly Lou was next to me, then he was behind me, in the kitchen. I blinked at his rapid movement. I was missing entire sequences of what was going on around me. I needed to eat something.

"What are you doing?"

"Making you a sandwich. You're absolutely wasted, and I feel bad, because I got you this way."

"Oh, okay." I tipped my head back on the couch, suddenly tired. I could sleep while he made me a sandwich, maybe. A li'l nap. Li'l catnap. "We should get a cat," I said.

"Great idea," Lou agreed. "Maybe tomorrow. But back to the story? Justin wanted your lyric book." He was in the kitchen, but of course, the kitchen was very close to the living room. The kitchen was practically in the living room. I liked this house. Lou's voice was low and baritone, like thunder rolling. I liked Lou's voice. The voice said: "Keep going, Katie. Stay with me."

"He wanted my book." I hugged a pillow, remembering. "There was something in it he wanted to steal. For a long time. *My* song. I wouldn't let him have it. I told him to get out and let me prep for the gig. Then we went onstage, and he was purposely heading me off, singing over me, going off in keys I couldn't harmonize with. He made me look like an idiot." I paused, remembering it with sudden clarity. "He made me sound bad *on purpose.*"

"And Cass?" Lou turned, a jar of peanut butter in one hand. "Where was she?"

"At the bar," I grumbled. "Booing the loudest. Does that mean something? I thought we were friends. But she booed."

"She started the booing," Lou suggested.

"No." That was all I could say. Cass had been my friend—as far as I could call one of those rival women on the road my friend. She wanted what I had. She wanted Justin, but she hadn't wanted me to go down in flames like that. Not Cass.

I closed my eyes again, remembering why I didn't get drunk very often—the highs don't last long enough. I was tired and sad now, which wasn't the ending this day deserved. "Let's talk about something else."

Lou was putting a sandwich in my hands. "Eat up, buttercup."

I bit into the sandwich and chewed slowly, feeling as if I'd forgotten how to eat. Lou sat down next to me, a bottle of water in each hand.

I was halfway through the sandwich when I started to feel better. Taken care of. Content. I couldn't remember the last time I'd felt this way. I turned to Lou. He was watching me avidly, and for a moment, I was distracted by the intensity of his gaze. I polished off the sandwich, reached for the bottle of water he held out. Swallowed, smiled.

"Do you really want to make music together?" I asked.

Lou's grin was magnetic. "For a start."

Chapter Eighteen

The next morning bloomed warm and full of sunshine. Too much sunshine, if we're being honest here. My attempts to pre-medicate my way out of a hangover weren't entirely successful, but I was grateful for the painkillers I'd managed to swallow before I crashed into my bed.

Crystal greeted me brightly, fed me dry toast, and told me today we'd ride all the horses. "We'll get them all fixed up for the bachelorettes," she said cheerfully. "No weather in our way today!"

"Oh," I said, chewing my toast carefully so that my teeth didn't accidentally touch and rattle my brain. "How nice." The idea of getting on a horse and bouncing around in the saddle was not at all pleasant.

But it was fun. Toast and sugary coffee got me down the stairs, and once we were riding, the horses were fairly good. Okay, a few were a little rude and spooky, but for the most part they were a quiet bunch, interested mainly in sticking close together and avoiding stepping on Roger, who had ventured off his rock for the day in favor of sitting in the middle of the road. He must have looked like a scary green monster to the horses, who snorted and blew at him as they skirted along the edges of the road. I practiced putting down my heels and sitting deep in the saddle at Crystal's command.

Lou stayed in his room most of the day. Every time we ran upstairs for a quick bathroom break or a snack or a cold bottle of water, I looked at his closed door and wondered what was going on inside. Last night had felt charged, like the air between us was glittering with promise. I'd felt weirdly guilty when Crystal arrived home after midnight, her face drawn, her purse stuffed with paperwork. Like we should have been working as hard as she clearly was, to save the ranch, but instead we'd gotten drunk and flirted really hard in her living room.

But when she had finally come home, she hadn't said anything to us, besides agreeing that yes, she was tired. She went straight to bed and then we crept into our own bedrooms, though not without little surreptitious glances which promised all sorts of future mayhem.

And now today he wasn't even getting up? I was frustrated; I needed to see him, needed to feel that heat between us again and make sure it wasn't just something I'd imagined. I wanted to throw open his door and tug down the covers and—

"I guess Lou's just sleeping all day," Crystal said. We'd come inside for a lengthy break from the sun and a proper lunch. She had that exasperated mother tone in her voice, the one my mom would have used for me when I slept past noon on a perfectly sunny Saturday, or when I refused to 'go outside and do something' in favor of hunkering down in my bedroom with the shades pulled down. Her sigh was definitely right out of the mom playbook. "I wish I knew what that boy planned to do now he's back."

"What did he do in Chicago?" I asked, sensing my chance for some of that elusive backstory I wanted so much. Someone needed to throw me a bone here.

"Oh, you'd have to be a private eye to know for sure." Crystal was pulling hot dogs out of the fridge, her voice muffled by the door. "He keeps all his tricks secret. Let me tell you, though, I *know* he got involved in some shady deals, because he'd suddenly call in the middle of the night and tell me not to give his address out to anyone who called asking, or he'd change his number without any warning. He *said* he was going to work at a theater and go to art school, but I don't think he ever went to more than a few classes. And I don't know that the theater job ever existed."

She put the hot dogs into the toaster oven and started slicing buns with a quick, sure slash of her knife.

I waited hopefully, but she didn't volunteer anything else. I guessed she'd probably told me everything she knew. "Maybe it wasn't that bad," I offered finally. "Sometimes, on the road, I'd find people get real secretive about the silliest things."

"Well, I'm just glad he's back," she said as she put our plates on the table. "Lot less worry having him here in the house. And if we could get the business going, we'd have a job for him, too. Then he wouldn't have to go running off looking for a paycheck again. I'd rather keep him here. He belongs here."

I'd like him to stay, too. "Okay, let's talk about that. What do we *really* need to get the business going?"

"Sand," Crystal answered without hesitation. "Nice white beach sand, like what they got at Half-Moon Beach. If that was spread around here, even just on my half of the island, we'd have enough room to let people go out and splash their horses in the water, do photo shoots, even canter around a little if they knew what they was doin'. We could advertise that, and the pictures would bring people in."

"That sounds doable. We should be able to make a plan to get sand. Would that be enough to run the place long-term?"

Crystal pursed her lips for a moment. "Well, a couple years ago Marchant and Stacy talked about buying that piece of land we use on Little Bucket, maybe fixing up those cottages, turning this place into a real dude ranch, Keys-style. Wouldn't that be neat? We was all going in on it. But I haven't been able to get my share together. I think Stacy and Marchant would still go in with me if I could ever get Sea Horse Ranch to pay enough to cover the investment. Then we'd be set with a real strong business. Totally unique. I think we'd be full every night, if we did that."

"So, if we had the sand, maybe you could do it? Sand equals paying guests equals enough money to invest?"

"Yup," Crystal agreed. "But sand is expensive. And getting it here and dumped and graded and making allowance for erosion..." She shook her head. "I don't know."

We finished our lunch in silence, lost in our thoughts. I imagined Sea Horse Ranch as a working dude ranch, with a new family arriving every few days, learning to feed the horses and clean the pens, staying in little cottages amidst the tangle of jungle on Little Bucket Key, spending some time sunning on the beach every afternoon. Maybe Marchant could teach them to sail, or fish, or even paddle-board—although I doubted Marchant was big on that. Maybe *I* could learn to do it and take on those classes.

I realized I was thinking way, way ahead—jumping all the hurdles in between at one go, as if we had money and had bought the other property and had repaired the cottages. There were probably years of hard work between us and the first guests, if such a plan could actually come to fruition.

Meanwhile, today, in the present, I was aching already, and uncomfortably aware we still had two more horses to ride, and the pens to clean after that. We had to get the place in apple-pie order for the bachelorette party, and with just today and tomorrow to do it, I knew we were going to be working past sunset.

And I could tell we were both feeling our late night. I was yawning. Crystal was yawning. Work or no work, there was no coming back from the lack of sleep, the day in the sun, and the sudden hit of sodium from the hot dogs. So when Crystal sighed and said she needed a nap, I didn't argue. I just went into the bedroom and threw myself atop the rumpled duvet. I was asleep before my head hit the pillow, but my dreams were filled with swirling turquoise waters and gleaming white sand.

❧ ❧

I woke up to several text notifications on my phone and yellow, late-afternoon light reflecting from the water, dancing on the walls. I decided to take in the light first, and gave myself a few moments to admire the turquoise of the sea outside before I committed to whatever was happening in the outside world.

Breathe in, breathe out. I could almost see myself meditating in a place like this. Maybe my brain could slow down for a moment or two—which would be a welcome change from the constant survival mode I'd been operating on for so long.

But whether I found inner peace or not, my phone wasn't going anywhere. It pinged with another message, and I reached for it unwillingly. There'd be no peace as long as my past knew where to find me.

The first text was from Justin. I felt a pit open in my stomach as I clicked the message, which began:

you won't believe the gig we had last night

The rest of the text opened up, white letters exclaiming the rest:

cass sang with us and got two encores. she really nailed heart so true - I think she gets you

I dropped the phone like it was on fire and rubbed my face with my hands, trying to wipe away the sting of the words. Justin knew how to stab me where it would hurt the most. He'd really had *Cass* take my place?

And to bring on Cass, okay, fine, that was just one strategic wound. But not only had Cass gotten up on stage in my place, she'd taken my song—my one and only song which had ever seen the light of day—and apparently knew exactly what to do with it.

Heart So True was my one and only song, the first song I'd written that I considered fit for human consumption. I sang it, the band played it for me. It had been part of the band set list for months. I'd given them that privilege because I'd believed we'd be together forever, and someday we'd record our album and *Heart*

So True would be on it—a song by The Bombers, written and performed by Katie LeBlanc and The Bombers.

I'd never thought some other girl would get up onstage and take my song from me. My only song.

"But it's *not* your only song," I reminded myself. I glanced across the room. My lyric book was on the dresser, a black rectangle containing my deepest self—or the parts of my deepest self I had managed to put into words. And there was more of it now than there had been yesterday. Suddenly, I remembered something from the drunken haze of last night's wee hours: I'd been sitting alongside Lou, listening to him play, and scribbling away. I wondered if I'd written anything coherent. Since I only had the faintest memory of this event, I seriously doubted it.

But even if I hadn't, at least I was writing again. Hell and Dammit Cay (and a lot of alcohol) could be inspirational.

"So there, Justin." I picked up the phone again, flicking ahead instead of answering him.

But the next text was from Cass.

I put the phone down.

Picked it up.

> Justin said he'd tell you but I am going to handle
> female vocals. The Force Five tour schedules sync up
> with the Bombers through July, so it works out.
> Hope that it's cool with you. Good luck in Florida.

I bit my lip. Well, she wasn't asking permission or forgiveness. Had to hand it to Cass there. If she'd orchestrated my departure, as

Lou believed, as I was starting to believe, she was tying her trick up with a bow and showing me that what was done was done.

The last text was from a number I didn't know. I opened it, curious, hoping for better news than the last two I'd gotten.

> I've been mixing what we did last night and it sounds amazing. Get in here.

Lou! I glanced at the time-stamp. He'd sent it half an hour ago.

A full-body tingle took over then. I had only the dimmest idea of what we'd done last night, but if we'd caught even the slightest bit of the magic shimmering in the air between us, it would be amazing. Maybe this was meant to be—maybe I hadn't come to Hell and Dammit Cay to hide from the world, but to find my real destiny. My real partner.

In music, of course.

Although if Lou wanted to take things beyond a musical partnership, I wasn't going to say no...

My phone chimed again.

> Get in here, seriously!!

Inner peace, who needed it? Phone notifications could be my saving grace. I hopped up, ran my brush through my tousled hair, and left the room at light-speed.

Lou was sitting on his bed with a MacBook propped up on a flat pillow, a colossal pair of headphones clamped over his ears. He looked up as I peeked into the room, sliding the headphones back. His smile was welcoming, warm, and made me feel utterly aflame. He exclaimed, "Well, *there* you are! I was giving up hope. I was afraid I'd have to get up and knock on your door like some kind of sociopath."

"Oh, sorry. I was asleep." I closed the door quietly behind me. "And I think your mom still is," I added. "So we have to be quiet."

"She loves an afternoon nap," Lou said indulgently, as if he was talking about a puppy. "But come over here and have a listen."

I glanced curiously around Lou's room as I joined him on the bed. I hadn't been in here before. The light was dim, with the blinds pulled shut against the brilliant day outside, but otherwise, the room was very similar to mine. Light-colored wood furniture, a big mirror over the dresser, the floor tiled with the same terra-cotta as the rest of the house. But he had little photos stuck into the mirror frame, and some posters on the wall: artwork for music festivals, mostly, although there was one small painting of a scantily clad mermaid combing out her hair beside a waterfall. Lou saw my eyes land on the mermaid's shell bra and he chuckled. "I've had Lulu hanging on my wall since I was thirteen. You like her?"

"I've seen weirder fantasy porn," I teased. "If there were elves with armored boobs, I'd be outta here, but the mermaid is fine."

"Lulu isn't porn! She's a muse. Look next to her. She just set down her lyre for a sec."

I squinted at the poster. "Oh, you're right. My bad. I was distracted by her huge tits that are barely covered by her clam shells."

"You're such a perv." Lou's grin was dangerously close to me. I turned and took it all in, admiring the full effect a sunny expression had on his face. Beneath that dark thatch of beard, I suspected there was a baby-face. Probably why he kept it covered. I thought I wouldn't mind him either way; shaved or unshaved, Lou's smile went all the way to his soul.

"I am," I said lightly. "I am *such* a perv."

For a moment, I saw his jaw tighten, and something in his eyes glittered. As that merry smile slipped, the intensity which replaced his light-hearted expression was enough to make me clench my fingernails on the duvet. A hungry sensation awoke in my center, clamoring for attention, and I had to resist the urge to roll onto my side, reach up with one hand, and tug his face close enough to brush an inquiring kiss, and see just where this wild ride was taking me.

A moment later, I wished I hadn't resisted the urge, because he seemed to shake the moment off, turning his attention back to his laptop. Now, I was the only one in the bed who was impossibly turned on.

Completely unfair.

Lou pulled the headphones off his neck and placed them on my head, cupping my ears with the foam padding. They were warm from his neck. I was seeing stars. This was bad.

"Now, listen to this," he told me, and he hit play on the MacBook.

I recognized the song almost immediately. Hearing it brought back full color memories of the night before, and I regained the time I'd lost just like that. Now I remembered: we'd spent the better part of an hour playing with this song. Lou had the melody already, but he'd been struggling with where to take it, what mood it should encapsulate. Boozed-up as I was, I'd gone full autobiographical and suggested this was a lingering, last look at an old life. Lou agreed readily and as he'd fleshed out the track, I'd started singing and jotting down lines I particularly liked.

Now I was listening to a rough draft of what could be a sensational song. My eyes flicked up to his in shock as my vocals wafted over the music, sweeter and more pure than anything I'd ever wailed in The Bombers. He nodded back at me, a satisfied smile on his lips.

"Not bad for something I barely remember," I said when the song ended.

"Seriously?"

"Last night's mostly a blur. I didn't remember we did this until you texted me."

"We had fun."

I looked at him.

He winked. "Nothing too crazy. Okay, listen to the track again."

I listened to our song three times. Then I took off the headphones and stared down at my lap. This didn't feel like the songwriting sessions with The Bombers at all. We'd thrown suggestions and criticisms at each other like lobbed grenades, each person challenging the next to be the one to blow the song up— either into something great, or into smithereens. Justin's lyrics had always skirted shy of the intensely personal, and we had no slow songs to speak of. Even my own *Heart So True* was more a power ballad than anything. There was oneupmanship, and bravado, almost like a contest to see who could be the most critical and biting, as if tearing up mediocre music was the only way to hone it into something good. Our best songs were conceived through battle, and maybe that's why The Bombers had been touring small clubs for so damn long.

I'd never been in any other band. I knew things with Justin and the guys were fairly toxic. But I didn't know how else it could look. Now...

This track, these melodies and lyrics, this was two people being painfully honest through music, and I didn't know what to say next.

Truthfully, I was afraid I'd already said too much. The things I'd sang last night—the feelings I had confessed—an entire lifetime's regret and a spark of soaring new hope were all wrapped up in the words. And it wasn't because I was a stupendous lyricist—don't get me wrong here, this isn't me shouting about what a great writer I am. It was what Lou had done with them, the way the music buoyed the emotions. With his instruments and arrangement, a few simple words became whole feelings.

I shook my head slowly, shocked at what I'd put out into the world. I knew I wanted these things: love, adventure, home. But I didn't know *how much* I wanted them until I heard them on that track.

Maybe working drunk wasn't the worst idea after all.

"Hey." Lou's voice was soft. He put a hand on my shoulder. "You okay?"

I felt a burning in my eyes; I swiped a hand across them, just in case anything threatened to escape. "I'm good," I said finally. I sniffed and turned to Lou with a watery smile. "I just really wish we'd worked in *leather* and *feather*."

He laughed and wrapped his arm around me, tugging me close. "You're so good at writing," he told me, "and then you go running for the rhyming dictionary."

"I'm not that good," I said, pulling at his hand. "I was just drunk and I get maudlin when I'm drunk."

"I don't think so. No false modesty here, please. This is sensational. The only question is, what will we do with it?"

I looked up at him, my forehead rubbing against his beard. "Scratchy," I murmured, and reached my fingers up.

He grabbed them. "Now, now, little miss. My mother is sleeping in the next room, need I remind you."

"Sleeping," I whispered. "I can be *very* quiet."

Lou's eyes smoldered at me as he growled, "Not if I have anything to do with it."

Chapter Nineteen

We stood waiting at the bridge from Little Bucket Key, the three representatives of Sea Horse Ranch. Well, Crystal and I were standing. Lou was trying to pick up Roger, who was sidling away from him, flicking his long tail with irritation. Crystal seemed just as annoyed as the iguana, her eyebrows twitching dangerously as she cast dagger glances at her son. Finally, Roger jumped off the coquina rock and darted into the stones under the bridge.

That seemed to push Crystal, already nervous, over the edge.

"Well, Lou, I hope you're happy!" she snapped. "Roger's part of the island's charm and now we'll be lucky if he comes back out while the customers are here!"

"Jeez." Lou stared at his mother, temporarily reduced to a little boy. "Sorry, Mom. I was just messing around with him." He sidled alongside me and kicked at the white shells littering the roadbed. "Mom's tense," he whispered after a moment's silence.

I shivered; the intimacy of his mouth so close to my ear was almost as thrilling as a caress. It took me back to the afternoon before, sprawled on his bed, as he'd looked at me like a dessert he was ready to tuck into. I was still agonizing over what might have happened. If Crystal hadn't chosen that moment to announce from the other side of the door that she was up from her nap and could use some help finishing up with the horses.

We'd looked at each other and laughed, and if mine sounded a little desperate, well, at least I could take comfort in knowing his had, too. Lou wanted something more from me, and I wanted something more from him. We were getting wrapped up in each other quickly—friendship, making music together, nearly giving in to desire—and even though I knew falling for this guy could make life at Sea Horse Ranch difficult, I wasn't willing to stop it. I wasn't even *capable* of stopping it.

I'd just spent the past year in the back of a van with a guy who barely liked me, stroking his ego in hopes of getting ahead in life. To actually feel something for someone, regardless of what he had or what I wanted in the material realm, was too powerful to ignore.

It took me a moment to screw up the courage to look back at Lou. His azure eyes were twinkling with mischief, tan skin crinkled at the corners. My heart twisted and melted in a puddle of goo, but I had to tamp it all down. For one thing, we had clients coming. For another, Crystal was standing right there, and I didn't want to be obviously drooling over her son. So I settled for hissing, "Be good. The ranch needs this to work out, remember?"

Lou nodded solemnly, but his eyes, still locked on mine, gave away the laughter he was pinning back. Then his cheeks puffed out with the effort. He looked like he was going to burst.

"Stop that," I whispered.

Lou pointed up, covering his mouth with his other hand as a grin broke through.

Cautiously, afraid of what I'd find, I tilted my gaze upwards. I was standing under a palm tree that bent over the road. And hanging from its fibrous bark was a second, smaller—although at this point "smaller" was relative—iguana. A giant green lizard, hanging over my head.

I yelled and jumped away—look, I'm not *afraid* of four-foot-long lizards, but I don't need them just inches from my hair, either. Crystal jumped at my shriek, then she looked around at the iguana, who was blinking at us with a bored expression.

"Well, who are *you?*" Crystal exclaimed, sounding charmed, as if she'd been waiting for a new giant lizard to drop into her life.

"That's a lady-iguana," Lou suggested. "She must be Roger's wife! We'll call her Rogerina."

"Rogerina," Crystal snorted, giving him another motherly glare. "You come up with the worst names—" Her mouth closed as we heard a humming in the distance. Her head snapped around, although the palm trees obscured the neighboring island. "That'll be them crossing the bridge onto Little Bucket. They'll be here in a minute. Everyone straighten up."

We all adopted shoulders-back positions as if we were being inspected for a military parade, even Lou, although he kept turning around, casting longing glances at Rogerina. For her part, the green lizard stayed in the tree, even when the white Hummer with its whooping, shrieking cargo of thirty-somethings on a bender appeared, crossing the tiny bridge to Hell and Dammit Cay before skidding to a halt beside us.

I hated them. Instantly.

Look, I'm used to loud. I've been living on the nightclub-and-festival circuit for the past year. I understand that alcohol makes people louder, and that being sober around drunk people is an excruciating, but necessary, experience in certain lines of work. I also understand that women with careers and difficult modern lives revel in the chance to blow off steam, and that a trip to the Keys with other women—no men, no kids, no problem—can feel like Las Vegas with fewer consequences.

But this wasn't Key West, this wasn't a club, and I wasn't a bartender. This was a quiet, isolated island that had already become my refuge from those places. And I wanted it to *stay* that way, thanks very much.

From the get-go, though, these women weren't going to let me get my wish.

"HORSES!" the driver screamed, leaping out of the Hummer. She was thin as a rail and dressed in clothes I wouldn't have attempted on my most indoor of days: barely there white shorts and a pink halter top which tied at the belly-button, a metallic gold push-up bra peeking from beneath the top button. Her blonde-streaked hair sat in a magically messy bun atop her head. I soon found that she was just like the other four women in the Hummer. It was like a copy machine had churned them out.

"Look at these *horses!*" she shrieked, pointing, as if no one could see them but her.

The horses stared, just as shocked by the noise as I was, and I was willing to swear on oath that Reggie rolled his eyes.

"Hi," Crystal said, putting out a hand to the woman who'd leapt from the truck. "You must be Melia. I'm Crystal." Her voice was already strained.

Crystal hates them, too, I thought.

Melia was nodding enthusiastically and shaking Crystal's hand, but as Crystal started to share vital information—where to park, for example, since they were in the middle of the only road on and off the island—her attention went elsewhere, flicking from me (no interest) to Lou (widened eyes, definite interest) to the iguana still hanging out just above and behind us. "Oh my God!" she shrieked. "Another giant lizard! Randi! Izzy! Look at this *lizard!*"

"Oh my *God!*" the women in the truck echoed. "A *lizard!*"

Lou tipped his head towards me. I sidled a little closer, emboldened by his gesture, but still feeling butterflies in my stomach. Standing so close to him felt like a public statement: *this one's mine.*

And despite the clear attraction between us, the way we clicked when making music or simply doing the barn chores, I had to wonder if we were there. If Lou thought of us as, you know, *us.* Or if it was purely sexual attraction. The question was agonizing, and there was no way to find the answer. We were stuck with these—women.

He murmured in my ear, lips barely moving, "This is the worst, right?"

I nodded. The absolute worst.

And this day was only just getting started.

❧❧❧❧ ❦❦❦❦

Our party plan was a little convoluted. With only six horses to go between four women and three guides, we'd have to take them to the beach on Little Bucket in a couple of groups. Before we got anyone mounted, though, Crystal decided to do photos while everyone was still clean—and before their makeup had time to run. She was pretty wise about matters of sweat, and correct in her assumptions that any bachelorette party would involve a ton of eyeliner and contouring.

So Lou, Crystal, and I led the horses to the shore side of the barn, where we managed to get everyone lined up. Lou was proclaimed photographer, which turned out to be another one of his hidden skills. He took some shots with the horses and women standing against the dazzling turquoise backdrop of the gulf. With the palm trees rising proudly above them and the water shimmering behind, I had to admit, everyone looked pretty tropical and *life's a beach*-y. They certainly couldn't have gotten better beach shots in Cancun or Aruba or anywhere else tourists liked to climb on horses for photos.

And our mustangs, with the wind stirring long forelocks around their dark, soulful eyes, were simply stunning. I was very proud of the work we'd done to clean them up this morning—their coats were shining, their tails blew in the breeze without a single knot. The horses were worthy of any show-ring, I thought. And so quiet! They stood still as the women clutched at the bridles and reins, occasionally twitching a muscle or flicking an ear to shake off a fly.

We mounted them up for a round of horseback photos, and I stepped back to admire Lou's work from behind the camera. While the women hung onto the horses' manes and tried not to shriek every time one shifted their weight, Crystal sidled up alongside me. "I want you and Lou to take out the first group," she murmured.

"Three of them. I'll keep the other two here and out of trouble while you're gone."

"Me and Lou?" I was surprised, and a little dismayed. "But I thought it would be you leading."

"No, you can lead. You know the route well enough now." Crystal nodded at the group. Melia was laughing hysterically from atop Bart, who was handling the situation with his usual laid-back nature. "Lou can stay in back to make sure no one has any trouble balancing. I want to keep an eye on the ones staying here. I'm not leaving you or Lou with these goofs. I like both of you too much for that. And they look like yellers. If anyone gets yelled at, it should be me."

I swallowed back gratitude at this show of affection and tried to acknowledge that Crystal thought my taking them on the ride would be better than staying here. Personally, I had my doubts. There would be whooping, and squealing, and pleas to "gallop" as if any of them had any idea what that really meant. *I* couldn't even gallop a horse, and apparently, I was in charge. But at least on horseback, they'd be stuck in their saddles and sandwiched between Lou's horse and mine. The trail was mostly too narrow to ride two abreast, so they'd be trapped that way, going at my horse's pace and no faster. And I doubted any of them could dismount without help, especially in their tiny shorts. So they'd be contained, anyway, if one of them decided to go rogue and run away across Little Bucket Key.

And once we set off, things seemed to calm down. The women were happy to be on horseback, and the gentle side-to-side motion of the horses soon had them swaying in the saddle with a hypnotic rhythm. Every time I turned around to check, I saw bemused smiles and ethereal expressions. *As good as swinging in a hammock,* I thought. Everyone was feeling the effects of sun, alcohol, and slow movement: they were getting tired. And tired bachelorettes were quiet bachelorettes.

I was finally enjoying myself. This wasn't so bad after all. I focused on the trail ahead, winding through the jungle. We were nearly to the beach.

"Hey, this horse is doing something funny with his ears!"

I'd taken Bart, and now I rose in the saddle, trying to see what the other woman could be talking about. She was on Reggie. I'd had a moment's misgiving when Crystal had mounted the woman on him, but there wasn't any stormy weather predicted. Just sunshine and soft winds.

But when I saw Reggie's behavior, I felt my fingers start to prick with anxiety. He was swinging his head and twitching his ears so rapidly they were almost swiveling.

Maybe just flies, I thought, but there really weren't any, not with this steady afternoon breeze blowing in off the sea. So what could it be? Reggie's super-sensitivity to storms couldn't be the cause. Still, I wheeled around, gazing back over the Gulf, searching the sky for clouds.

Nothing. Just blue, blue, blue.

There was a squeal—I was never really sure if it was a horse or a human—and Bart was tugging wildly at the bit as Reggie went flying past us, his saddle empty.

Everyone started screaming at once.

Chapter Twenty

T he clean-up and apologies took almost as long as the entire party would have taken, had it run according to plan, and the sudden thunderstorm didn't help matters. The whole afternoon turned to wind and rain and lightning before we could even consider getting the second group of women on horseback, forcing Crystal to invite the entire party up to the house, where they crowded the living room and drank the rest of the beer in the fridge, all while looking out at the storm crashing around the island with glowering expressions.

They also took incredible liberties with the place. Jenna, the woman who had been riding Reggie before he dropped her on the ground, actually took a shower in my bathroom without asking. She came out afterwards, wet feet slapping on the tiles, with my towel wrapped around her hair and one of my necklaces swinging on her index finger.

"This is cute," she told the room at large, then turned to me. "Is this yours? Where did you get it?"

I resisted the urge to snatch the necklace away from her. It was just a silver pendant, a sea star with a pearl in its center, but the detailed etching made the creature look almost alive, and I loved it because—despite?—the fact that Justin had given it to me when we were first in love, first on the road, first singing together.

I hadn't worn it since the night he told me to leave the band, but after the afternoon I'd told them to leave without me, I'd dug it out of my bag and left it hanging from the arm of a hunk of white coral which sat on the bathroom counter. I wasn't really sure why, but I liked to look at the sea star's elegant lines, the gleam of the pearl. It wasn't that I was pining after Justin or anything. What? It was pretty. And it seemed to belong on that pale, branching coral.

If it had been a sentimental thing, I probably would have lost it at Jenna's imposition. But Justin wasn't a sweet memory to me anymore. So instead of yanking the chain off the woman's entitled finger, I simply stood, walked over to her, and gently removed it. For a moment, the necklace hung between us in the stormy light, the pearl a moody gray, as if it could reflect the rain hammering down outside. "It was a gift," I told her, as lightly as I could. "I don't know where it came from."

I slipped the necklace into my pocket carefully, hoping I wouldn't twist the chain.

Jenna shrugged and went to throw herself on the couch alongside her friends. I retreated to the kitchen, where Lou watched me with a gleam in his eyes. "A gift, huh," he said, arching one brow eloquently.

"Yes, sometimes people buy things for me. They consider me nice and interesting and worth tokens of affection." I put a cup under the tap and filled it, giving Lou a sidelong glare. "Does that surprise you?"

"You're full of surprises." He shrugged, but his eyes were still lingering on mine. They dipped to my lips, then up again, and I felt a hot thrill in my midsection. Then I thought, *Really, Lou? Now?*

"We have to get rid of them," I muttered. "They can't stay here all day."

"Yeah, we do." His grin was devilish. "If it quits raining, we can send them back to the barn. We'll have a little quiet time then."

Tempting, but not what we needed. "No, you idiot, we have to get rid of them completely. Off the island. Look at your poor mother."

Crystal was sitting at the kitchen table, facing the women sprawled around her living room. She looked relaxed but the tension in her shoulders told me she was ready to hop up and serve them at a moment's notice. She'd done well as a hostess outside, but she had no idea what to do with them now that they were indoors—besides handing them every drink and snack in the house.

"Well, we're stuck with them until the storm lets up," Lou said, shrugging. "It's raining buckets and there's no way they'll agree to drive in this, let alone go down to their car. It's like this storm is getting bigger right over our heads." Thunder crashed, seeming to rise up through the floorboards. He smirked at the natural punctuation to his words. "I made that happen."

"Why? Because you want them to stay?" I cast a glance back at the bachelorette party. The women were looking like they were on the edge of a revolt. "Make it *stop* happening. They're going to trash this place on Yelp, you know. *And* TripAdvisor. Plus, they're going to demand a refund and your mom is going to have to give it to them. So we've lost money and future business on these bimbos."

"Now, don't call names," Lou chided.

"Please don't get high and mighty on me now. I see women like this every day. They come to clubs with their hair in messy knots that took them fifteen minutes to achieve and their heels so high they can't even dance, and they wolf-whistle at the guys in the band and ignore the girls on stage." Or worse, they acted like they thought feminist allies should, shouting things like *"Girl power!"* between songs before doing their best to entice away the male band members after the set. "Trust me, I know their type all too well."

I remembered a gig a few weeks back, before we'd gotten to Key West. We'd been in a Nashville club, playing a set in the middle of the evening. After our time on stage, I wiped myself off and went for a drink at the bar. A woman I recognized from the small crowd sat next to me, and I'd turned eagerly—she'd been giving me such robust support during our set that I almost thought she'd come to hit on me. But she curled her lip at me and her smile was so fake, she nearly bared her teeth. "You better stay out of my way tonight," she hissed at me. *"I'm* going home with Justin."

I'd been so startled by her vicious turn that I hadn't even managed to tell her Justin was going to sleep in the van tonight along with me and the guys; there wasn't a single room in this town at our budget and every couch we knew of was taken. There was no chance she was going home with Justin unless she was planning on taking him back to her place and then bringing him back...and she'd better not count on getting gas money for the trip, either.

As the woman snatched her drink from the bartender and stomped away in her threateningly high boots, I'd felt a weird sense of calm: she hated me because I was on stage, and because I was with Justin, but her hatred couldn't take those things away from me.

Now, though, I felt the precarious truth catching up: if those women across the room hated me, or if they hated Crystal, or simply all of the Florida Keys, they could take my new life down without a thought. I wasn't on the road now. I wasn't flying under the radar now, without an address, in a band that wasn't even close to famous. As a band member, I'd almost been more of an idea than a real person—I floated in and out of towns, mostly ignored and rarely remembered. As a resident of Hell and Dammit Cay, I was investing in something which had permanence—and that very permanence made it delicate, dangerously easy to destroy with a few angry words tapped into a mobile app on the way back to civilization.

Those horses outside, munching hay in their stalls as the rain poured on the roof overhead—Crystal, sitting there at the table, her lined face white with anxiety—Stacy, across the road in her art-hung living room—Marchant, in his blue house with his fluffy cat, dreaming of sailboats—they were all dependent on one another. Hell and Dammit Cay was an ecosystem, like a coral reef, or a rainforest, with vastly different lives which thrived only when everyone thrived.

I wasn't going to let anything disturb this ecosystem. We were going to wow these women. We were going to thrive. We were going to—do something. *Anything.*

I turned to Lou, clutching at his arm. He was clever and seemed good in a crisis. Maybe *he* had an idea. "Listen to me. We have to turn this afternoon around, give them something that they'll feel excited about. Otherwise, they're going to destroy us online."

Lou turned his steady gaze on mine, bringing with it a calmness I wish I could truly absorb. "What did you have in mind? You want me to conjure up a waterspout? Because after that thunder clap, I think I could do it with just a little positive thinking." Wind howled around the kitchen's exhaust fan, as if the storm was trying to push into the house. "See?"

So, Lou wasn't going to be helpful. Fine. I looked around the space almost frantically. Outside, rain dashed itself against the windows and lightning flashed. We were trapped in this house, so our only tools were...

My fingers crept into my pocket, and I clutched the necklace with a sudden intensity. *We* were our only tools.

I looked back at Lou, watching his smile fade as he realized what was coming next. Man, that guy could read me. Like a damned book.

But I'd think about that later.

You're right, Lou.

Aloud, I said, "We can perform for them."

⁂

Lou's expression was about as skeptical as he could get it. I wanted to curl up in a little ball. The embarrassment was *real.* Who was I to ask the hidden figure behind a massively popular but secret recording artist to get out in public and perform with me? Even if the "public" was a couple of drunk thirty-somethings and even if we had been making music together alone just yesterday?

His face told me everything I needed to know: maybe we'd had fun putting some vocals down on tracks in his bedroom, but I was still the woman who had been booed off stage and kicked out of her band in the very recent past.

I clenched my fists and willed myself not to cry, but I could already feel the hot stinging under my eyelids. Dammit, why did women *cry* all the time? Hormones were unfair. It was fine. He didn't think I was good enough? Fine. Fine. *Fine—*

"Let's do it," Lou said.

The room spun a little, but that was just because I looked back at him so quickly, I threw off my own equilibrium. My eyes beat my brain to the punch, leaving me dazed for a moment while my nervous system caught up. "What now?" I breathed as soon as I could say anything.

"You're right. This is our chance to help the ranch. So, we'll pick a couple of easy covers we can do without too much practice, and we'll do your song. *Heart So True.*"

Panic snagged my racing heartbeats. *Anything but that.*

But Lou was already standing up. "Ladies! Mom!" He winked at Crystal. "I have an announcement, friends. There's a long tradition in the Keys of passing a rainy afternoon with music and liquor. We've already got the liquor but we're lacking some music. So it's time for an impromptu performance by—" he looked around the room, his gaze shifting from me to the dark sea roiling outside. I waited, feeling strangely excited by the moment. He was going to announce our band name. Even if we never performed another day, for just a moment, we'd be a duo. And this would be the name I remembered us by.

"Saltwater Express," Lou decided. He nodded as the women stood up and cheered wildly, their squeals and whistles echoing around the open living room. "And now, if you'll excuse us, we have to prepare."

"Saltwater Express?" I asked as soon as the bedroom door was closed. "What does that even mean?"

Lou's grin slipped. "You don't like it?"

"I don't *dislike* it. I just wondered where it came from." I went to the mirror and began to shake out my messy hair. Maybe messy was going to be my look. It would be easier than showing up on stage every night sleek and flat-ironed—I stopped myself, shocked by my line of thinking. Showing up on stage every night? Who did I think I was, a girl in a rock band?

Those days were done.

Lou was pulling out his laptop, typing in some searches. "I just looked at the water and I thought about how fast life is moving and boom, the two words came together."

"An epiphany?" I sat down next to him. He felt warm and strong and pulsing with energy, and I couldn't help but nudge a little closer, so that our legs were pressed together. I wanted to absorb his excitement, share in his passion.

Haha, *yeah, I did.*

Lou pulled his hands through his hair, ruffling the dark waves. "Sure, you could call it that. Or it was just really great word association. Here we go." He pointed at his laptop screen, to a song he'd pulled up. "Do you know this one?"

"I do. Why? Am I doing *all* the singing?"

"I might jump in from time to time. But it's best for a female lead."

"How will I know the arrangements? I might fall behind."

"You'll feel it," Lou promised.

I looked him in the eye and nodded. Oh, I was feeling something, all right. And it wasn't the music.

Lou tapped the keyboard a few more times. He flicked through three different songs. "I'm prepared to do these with my guitar and laptop," he offered, "and then we can finish with *Heart So True*. That's almost twenty minutes right there. And if it hasn't stopped raining by then, we'll just go out and throw ourselves into the sea."

"Deal," I said, even though the idea of performing *Heart So True* with him, in front of other people, set all my senses rocketing again. That song dug deep. I wasn't nearly drunk enough to sing it with Lou's eyes on me.

But there wasn't a choice, either. This was for Hell and Dammit Cay.

We got our gear together, then trooped back into the living room.

Where there were more people than there had been before.

"Marchant," Lou said blankly.

"Stacy," I echoed in the same empty tone.

Marchant tugged a kitchen chair into the living room and wrapped his legs around the back of it, while Stacy settled into an armchair like a queen awaiting a command performance. "This is exciting," she said. "I had a feeling we should hustle over here."

"The storm?" I glanced at the windows and saw that the rain was finally easing up. I realized I hadn't heard any loud thunder in a while.

Maybe my bright idea to perform with Lou had been totally unnecessary.

But no, the bachelorette party was watching us with bright-eyed enthusiasm now, and I knew that a few good songs could change things for Sea Horse Ranch. We just needed some positive reviews. And if we couldn't get them for the equestrian activities, then by God we'd get them for sheer hospitality.

And talent, I thought, glancing at Lou as he set up his laptop stand. They had no idea what kind of famous indie artist they were about to hear. They probably never would.

I stood; Lou perched atop a stool from the kitchen island, hunched over his laptop. A guitar leaned against the wall behind him. I looked around the living room, at the strangers and the friends, and then I cast my eyes towards the big painting of mustangs hanging between the sliding glass doors—a Stacy original, I realized—and waited for my cue as the music began.

Then I opened my mouth and my heart and I started to sing.

It felt so good. I loved singing in front of an audience. I loved touching other people's emotions. As we worked our way through the numbers, I felt a sense of rightness. Even though it was a living room performance, not a club, I knew I was where I supposed to be, doing what I was meant to do.

With the person I was supposed to be doing it with? We worked together in perfect synch. I had never felt such harmony with anyone in The Bombers. Lou made me sound good. I made Lou sound good. And that was pretty spectacular, considering Lou's popularity.

Our covers were innovations; Lou didn't need to follow tabs for other people's songs, he just played with their melodies and put his own spin on everything. I tried to do the same, spilling out the lyrics other songwriters had cried over in my own way. I'd never taken voice lessons beyond middle school choir, and my voice tended to split, hopping the keys at times, but that was considered part of my charm by reviewers—when they bothered to mention me at all—so I embraced my faults in this, if in nothing else.

And I really played this tendency up as we launched into *Heart So True,* letting my voice hop through a soaring chorus and whispered verses, matching the melody set down by Lou, then teasingly leaving it behind for a few breathless beats of freedom.

But the only way to get a song like this right was to dig deep for the emotional underpinnings, the anchors which had stilled my ship while I wrote it, and which I'd eventually have to escape for the song's finale to work. Untrained, raw voices follow the heart, not the mind. So as Lou played the intro, I closed my eyes, swallowed my fear, and pictured home.

Hah! You thought I was going to say Justin, didn't you? And it's a good guess, because Justin broke my heart about sixteen different times and I kept coming back for more, until my heart at last understood some things would never change. But I could never write a song about endless love and forgiven sins with Justin at the heart of it. Because even at the height of my obsession with him, when I was obeying his every whim, just thankful to be in his company, I knew Justin would never be there for me.

His heart was the opposite of true.

That was why it stung so much to know Cass was singing it with him—dedicating it to him—thinking it was *about* him. And, I thought suddenly, the idea blasting through my brain as I tried to prepare for the big finish, it was the reason I needed to record this song myself and lodge my copyright as soon as possible. Otherwise, Justin would publish it with The Bombers, and I'd lose it, and I'd never get over that kind of theft.

For a moment, my eyes fluttered, and then I focused again. The swelling music paused, and at that pause, that stutter, I jumped in. I sang.

The song itself went well. I didn't cry. That was a win. It was in the moments after that I heard it, the words wrapping themselves around my throat.

"Didn't we hear that song in Gainesville a few nights ago?"

"She did a great cover, but she didn't really belt it like that other chick did."

"I mean, they're amateurs. We'll have to tip them well, for sure. It was nice of them to perform for us."

My eyes were burning, and I couldn't look at the women, at Lou, at anything but the tiles at my feet. I was used to being heckled, I was used to being booed. But this was so much worse. They'd heard Justin and Cass sing *my* song. And they thought it was theirs? That they'd done it better?

It was a theft, alright.

As the women stood, gathering their things, I went back into my bedroom. I just managed to close the door before my knees buckled and I sank, sobbing, to the floor, clutching my arms around myself as if I could hold my broken heart together.

Chapter Twenty-One

I overslept the next morning. When I finally staggered out of the guest room, rubbing sleep from my eyes and feeling embarrassed, Crystal was sitting at the kitchen table, head bowed over some documents. Her feet were bare and dirty, which meant she'd been out to feed the horses already. I felt bad for missing the morning chores. Some ranch-hand I was turning out to be.

I didn't bother her, and she didn't look up to say hello. The quiet echoed around me as I poured some coffee into a mug and sat down across from her.

Steam curled around my face. I huddled over the mug, waiting for the coffee to cool. I wasn't hungover, but my foggy head had that feeling—I guess I was just hungover from emotion instead of alcohol.

Last night, I'd stayed in my room until after the party had cleared out, driving their stupid Hummer over the bridge with a roar I could hear even behind my closed door. Then I'd gone downstairs and fed the horses their evening grain alone, before Crystal had a chance to come down and help me. With chores done, and the horses inside their stalls with the screens down, veiling them from the evening's mosquitos, I crept back upstairs, snuck some leftover fried chicken out of the fridge, and closed my door behind me.

Maybe it was cowardly of me to hide inside all evening—especially after the day we'd had, I'd thought at one point, while wiping my greasy fingers on a paper napkin I'd fished from my backpack, everyone could probably use some moral support. Some laughs, some beers, and we'd all be back to normal. But the bruising around my heart was something new, and I felt like I had to nurse it alone.

It wasn't that I was still in love with Justin—I doubted what we'd shared was anything you'd call *real* love, anyway—and it wasn't that I'd written my song, the only song he'd ever approved of, about him. I'd written *Heart So True* about myself, a fable about leaving home but never losing sight of the people I'd grown up with. And no—I know what you're thinking, that it sounds like I wrote a song about how great I am, but it wasn't about that, either.

Heart So True was like a reminder to myself. It was like a letter I read aloud to myself, each night I was on stage, to remember that fame (hah, as if I'd ever attain it) was fleeting and cold, but love would last forever.

No, I don't know what made me so certain of that. I had nothing to go on—well, nothing except the love of my parents, but I *was* pretty sure of that. Otherwise, everlasting love was firmly out of my experience. A few high school boyfriends, a couple of light romances with local guys, then Justin. The heartbreaker I never trusted, the ego I always knew would take center stage, the affair that burned as hot as a firecracker before fizzling out and leaving us with ashes. If anyone thought that my song was about Justin, they were delusional. Or we'd been very convincing.

Still, no matter what other people read into *Heart So True,* it was *mine,* and sharing it with Lou had felt weirdly magical, and while I'd still been flush with the glow of that magic, it had been tarnished by a woman who wrongly attributed it to Cass and Justin. And in that moment, everything I'd done, every bad decision I'd made since the day I'd left home, loomed up so large in my brain I wasn't sure what had happened to the happiness I'd felt just a few moments ago.

Or when I'd feel it again.

So I hid. Because what if I looked at the people I was growing to love, and saw them only as mistakes? I couldn't have faced it.

In the warm sunlight of morning, I could see the truth: Crystal and Lou really mattered to me. They were good things in my life, not problems. Thank goodness for mornings. I could see why I'd spent the past year so deluded and confused; I'd been sleeping through the most clear-minded part of the day.

Now I sipped my coffee, almost cool enough for comfort, and glanced up at Crystal. Her face was still closed and taut, her eyes still skimming over the documents in her hands. The papers had crease marks from being folded in three, having been removed from an envelope. They'd come in the mail? It occurred to me that I had no idea where or when the mail was delivered to the residents of Hell and Dammit Cay. What a simple thing, what a mystery.

At last, her eyes flicked up and met mine. "Thanks for feeding last night," she said. "I was just exhausted from those women."

"No problem. Sorry I left you high and dry this morning."

"Nothing I'm not used to doing alone." Her tone was cool, and I felt myself drawing back in response.

"Is Lou around?" I glanced around the kitchen and living room as if he might appear. I should talk to him about last night. About disappearing like that. It had probably seemed pretty weird to him.

"Left." Crystal's voice was glacial now.

"He...left? Is he coming back this afternoon?"

"Doubtful. He had his backpack with him. I don't know where he was heading," Crystal continued, looking back at her papers, "but I wouldn't expect him home anytime soon."

I stared at her, shocked into silence.

She gave in, putting down the papers. "He does this. That's why Marchant made such a big deal out of him coming home. And why I try not to, even though it breaks my heart every time he leaves."

"I'm so sorry," I murmured, even though I felt more concerned over my heart than Crystal's.

But she just waved a hand at me, dismissing the problem. "I have more to worry about this morning, luckily," she said dryly.

"What's the matter?" I glanced down at the paperwork. "Bad news?"

"Probably the worst, aside from an eminent domain notice." Crystal tossed the papers to me. "They're finally going to develop Little Bucket Key."

❧❧❧❧❧ ❧❧❧❧❧

The words from the documents followed me outside, dancing across my eyes in stern black print. I tried to shush them away, tried to quiet my brain from all the drama crowding inside it, by bringing Reggie from his paddock and saddling him up. In the soft nylon saddle, my bare legs brushing his warm sides, I could almost feel better. Almost remember how I had felt just a few days ago, when Lou was here, when we were preparing for the party, when we knew things were going to be okay if we just worked hard enough.

I hadn't even asked Crystal if we'd gotten our good reviews, but of course it was too early for that. "They're probably still asleep in their hotel room in Key West," I told Reggie, who was picking his way through the grove of shaggy palm trees around Stacy's house. "Hungover, with the blackout shades pulled down."

Reggie flicked his ears and snorted, then found his way to the stony path that led to the island shore. I let him choose his own way. At least if he panicked and ran away again, I'd have a soft landing in the warm waters lapping the narrow shoreline. He stepped into the water and dipped his head playfully, as if he liked the splash. I let him play.

But he deserved a lecture, so I gave it to him while he nodded and pawed at the water. "We need to talk about yesterday," I said. He shook his head. "No, seriously, why did you do that, Reggie? It storms here all the time. You really had to panic about it? Dump a tipsy bachelorette in the dirt? Things were going so well."

Reggie concentrated on pawing the water, splashing us both. I sighed and gave up the lecture. We both knew it wasn't going to change anything. Yesterday was already in the record books.

But in my mind, a different day played out: the ride went perfectly, the women left before the storm started, Lou and I had a nice normal supper with Crystal, he was still here when I woke up at a reasonable hour, he was here right now, sharing this ride with me. He'd be mounted on Trinket, the horse who loved him best. We'd be happy.

I looked around, as if I could make the dream come true. But there was no one.

Well, almost no one.

Literally right out of the clear blue sea appeared Stacy, paddling around the island in a bright orange kayak. She waved an exuberant hello while Reggie snorted and took a few steps back, his ears pricked at the approaching vessel and its passenger. Evidently, women who floated for no good reason were not high on his list of favorite things, either.

I tightened my grip on the reins and added a hunk of mane to my fist for good measure, just in case my horse turned into an equine cannonball. But all Reggie did was stare, ears pricked and head high. Stacy came within a few feet and stopped paddling, letting the kayak bob on the smooth teal waters.

"Nice day for a ride," she observed. "How's Mr. Spooky today?"

"He hasn't dumped me yet. But the day is young." I looked around as if anyone might be able to overhear us, despite the fact that we were standing twelve feet offshore in knee-deep water. "Did you know Lou left?"

Stacy shook her head. "I thought he might. You guys were too good last night."

"What does that mean?"

She shrugged. "Lou doesn't like getting close to people. I saw it happening over the past few days...you two have a connection. That sent him skittering, probably. I'm sorry if that hurts to hear."

"It does, a little." Understatement of the year. I looked down at Reggie's neck, the water sliding beneath it. But I might not be the only reason Lou felt like he had to leave. There was the letter. "And there's something else," I said.

"The letter from the county about Little Bucket? Yeah, I got that, too." Stacy turned in the kayak and looked across the water, to Little Bucket Island peeking from behind Hell and Dammit's shore. "Nothing lasts forever."

She couldn't possibly be so blasé about this. "Well, good things *should*," I blurted. "We should do something."

"Do something?" She gave me a trademark Stacy smile: kind of spacey, kind of wise, like a medium who knew the future but wasn't willing to share her knowledge with anyone. "What are you going to do? Chain yourself to a palm tree? That land belongs to someone, and they've gotten the county to approve new construction. It happens to every island. This is Florida."

"Come on. There has to be some way to stop this." I was getting angry now; Reggie shifted beneath me, his ears flicking uncertainly. I needed to cool it, or I would be about halfway into the water the next time a fish jumped.

Stacy just shook her head, but she at least had the grace to look a little sad. "Don't think I won't help you," she said, dipping her paddle back into the water. "I don't want this to change anymore than you do. And I know people who will be badly hurt by this. But I don't see what anyone can do. Developers run Florida. I can't believe Little Bucket has stayed undeveloped this long. Once that foolish eco-resort failed, it bought us some time, but it couldn't last forever. I guess we thought this far out, so removed from the rest of the islands, maybe we'd make it. But we were fooling ourselves. Everyone wants to build in paradise."

She started to slide the kayak past Reggie. He leaned out to touch her with his muzzle as she went, blowing into her curly hair, wondering how she could float like a duck on the water. Stacy smiled and kissed him on the muzzle, but kept paddling, her kayak silently gliding away from us. Stacy's message was clear: she would float away, letting the tides carry her. Maybe Sea Horse Ranch had sustained her muse for a while, but she'd find another source of inspiration if she had to.

I was upset at how easily she'd give up. I wanted to stay here. I'd just found this place, and it wasn't right that someone could just turn up with a bulldozer and start plowing over everything that made it perfect. And Hell and Dammit Cay would never be the same if they built up Little Bucket.

This lonely little island would be sitting right next to some subdivision of private mansions and million-dollar yachts and towering date palms. The quiet whisper of the sea breeze in the palm trees, the perfect clarity of the water, the fish and rays darting through the seagrass: all of that would be lost to growling engines, thumping stereos, silty water topped by oil slicks.

And what the hell was I supposed to do about it?

I needed Lou. The thought was urgent, and I turned Reggie with a quick flick of the reins, asking him to jog back up the bank and across Stacy's property. As he trotted along, I dug my phone from my pocket. He never should have texted me. I'd saved his phone number, and now he couldn't get away from me. He'd left a trail.

Three rings, chiming across the atmosphere.

And then...

"Hello?" His voice was wary, but I was so amazed he answered, I didn't let it bother me. Everyone had acted like Lou had vanished, but he was just a phone call away? Um, had anyone else tried calling him?

I spoke urgently, before he could make some excuse and hang up. "Lou, listen, they're going to build houses on Little Bucket. Luxury estates, with pools and fences and fountains. Statues of mermaids." I made that sound *really* bad. "The rich people are coming."

"I know," he said. "I went up to the Slutty Mermaid and picked up the mail before I left this morning. They have all the mailboxes around back. Anyway, I saw the letter. I saw it when Mom opened it."

"You *know?* Then where are you going?"

"I had to leave. I can't be there for this."

"And what about me?"

The words were presumptuous; I knew it as soon as they left my lips. But I wanted to know. Reggie shifted beneath me as he turned onto the shell road, his ears pricking at the sight of his home pen and hay. If Little Bucket went under the bulldozer, we'd lose the beach. We'd lose our chance to make enough money to buy sand and build our own beach. We'd lose Sea Horse Ranch. Where would Reggie go? Where would any of them go?

Lou's sigh was heavy. "I'm sorry. For everything. If I led you on...is that a crazy thing to say? I'm sorry, either way. But I can't watch this happen."

"Come back and help me stop it," I insisted.

"No one can stop this," Lou said. "God, don't you know? I started it."

Chapter Twenty-Two

Reggie stopped near Crystal's house, taken in by a patch of grass and my loose fingers on the reins. It was fine. I had the phone pressed against my ear and my heart in my throat. Lou's three-word confession had knocked the wind right out of me.

"You...you *what?*" I managed to choke.

There was a heavy sigh on the other end.

"Lou...come back." I couldn't think what else to say. I swallowed hard, trying to push away the lump in my throat that was holding back my words. "Lou, we can fix this, but I can't do it alone. Or just with your mom. I need you."

The words were raw, and I regretted saying them, but they were true.

I need you.

Who says that to someone they barely know, someone they've spent just a few days with, someone who is practically a stranger to them? But I did. I needed Lou.

On so many levels, but for now, we'd start with saving Little Bucket Key.

He must have heard the urgency, or maybe he realized the enormous emotional weight of that simple little phrase, because the silence suddenly grew weighted. I held my breath. And then he answered.

"I'm already halfway to Miami."

It was said with finality, as if there was no return possible. As if being halfway to the mainland and all its troubles was an excuse enough to abandon the mess left behind. And I remembered leaving home, my mother asking me not to go, the look on her face when I said I couldn't stay, I'd die if I had to stay, and the feeling, as I left, that I could never come back.

But that had just been a feeling. I could go back whenever I wanted. I could hitchhike down U.S. 1 to Key West, get on a plane to New Orleans, and be home in time for dinner. Or at least breakfast tomorrow.

And anyway, times had changed; my mother understood now, we were on fine terms. I wasn't as young as I'd been then; I wasn't as dramatic. A year on the road could change a person.

Now it was time for Lou to get over himself, too. How long had he been running away from home for?

Running away from love?

The word leapt into my brain in large capital letters: *LOVE*. Yeah, of course I was in love with Lou. That was obvious, right? I was crazy about him, head over heels for him. Maybe it was a mistake—no, it was definitely a mistake—but in the end it was just one more complication in this convoluted story I was writing for myself, about running away and finding home and watching it get taken away again.

I debated telling him for one crazy minute, but I knew what happened with guys when a girl threw the love-bomb a little too soon, so that was a no-go. I needed another angle. There had to be a way to make Lou come home. The silence on the line stretched between us. In another moment, he'd probably think the call had dropped and hang up. Would he answer if I called him again?

Reggie pawed impatiently at the stubbly grass he'd been grazing, nearly putting a hoof through the slack reins. I grimaced and tightened them. That would be just great. All I needed to do was break a bridle—or a horse—while I was trying to convince the prodigal son to come home and fix his mess. Like poor Crystal didn't have enough trouble.

"Halfway to Miami means you're only halfway from home," I said finally. The simple route was the best one. "All you have to do is turn around."

"And do what?"

"And talk to me. Tell me what's going on. Help me fix it. I can't lose this place, Lou. Even if you want to leave when it's done—" *Please don't leave when it's done.* "—at least come back and help me save it for *me*. And for your poor mom. And for Marchant and Stacy. This island is perfect just as it is. Help us keep it that way."

"You've gotten pretty possessive of a place where you've only lived for about a week." Lou's tone was gruff.

"I've been around this country three times in the past sixteen months," I told him. "I think I should know when a place is worth saving. Trust me. There's only one Hell and Dammit Cay, and I know we can keep the ranch going if we just have a little more time to fix things."

I heard Lou's breathing on the other end as he thought. Then, finally, a deep breath. "Fine," he said. "Meet me at the Slutty Mermaid in an hour."

I looked down at Reggie, still tugging at the sparse grazing in Crystal's yard. Too bad there wasn't a hitching post at the Slutty Mermaid. I'd have to borrow Crystal's truck, but without arousing her suspicions. I wasn't going to raise her hopes when there was no guarantee Lou would really come back. But I'd figure it out. "Okay," I agreed. "One hour."

❧❧❧❧❧ ❦❦❦❦❦

I've been to dive bars. A *lot* of dive bars. Honestly, I'd been performing for the past year and a half with what was essentially a dive bar band. I know about dark spaces, creaking and sticky floors, and questionable stains on the bars.

Still, I wasn't quite prepared for the level of dark, sticky, and questionable I'd find within the Slutty Mermaid.

And this was the place where the world's best *cinnamon rolls* came from?

Crystal lent me the truck keys without question; I guessed she wasn't really in the mood to look too much into anything, what with the news of the morning and her son going AWOL. So when I parked her rust-bucket truck alongside the line of muddy pickups, Jeeps, and assorted beaters outside the no-name building, at least my vehicle fit in. And, I figured, cut-offs and flip-flops were the uniform for females throughout the Florida Keys. I'd look just fine; I'd fit in with no problem.

I opened the unmarked, windowless door, stood on the edge of an abyss, and realized it didn't matter what I looked like.

No one in there could see me, anyway.

After a moment's confusion, I shut the door behind me and stood there a moment, allowing my eyes to adjust to the room's low light. There *was* a little light; it was just the brilliant Florida sun that made the Slutty Mermaid appear to be a black hole from which no light could escape. The light inside was dim as a cave and came mostly from old neon beer signs; one bright patch escaped from beneath a door which must lead to the kitchen. After a few minutes of determined blinking, I could discern enough around me to make me feel merely as if I was deep underwater, instead of lost in space.

And maybe that was the intent. What with being named for a mermaid and all.

There were booths and pool tables at the far end, but the bar was closest to the door, so I settled onto a vacant bar stool. I could easily spin for a look if the door opened behind me and the silhouette of Lou appeared. I ordered a beer from a deeply tanned man wearing a gold necklace and a faded tank top, the shirt's graphic featuring some fish writhing through a coral reef. I assumed the tanned man worked there—after all, he was behind the bar—and he gave me the beer without a word, but then he went back out to a table with a beer of his own and sat down, to stare into space, which made me wonder what his relationship to the bar actually was.

Five or ten minutes passed without much happening. Then a small gathering of men and women who had been gathered around the pool tables at the far end—playing by feel, I assumed—seemed to all finish their games at once. The group came over to the bar area, and a woman went behind the bar and started pouring beers, while another man in flip-flops began to pound vigorously on the jukebox. Eventually, Alan Jackson joined the party. A little twangy for my taste, but it was better than the deathly silence. Conversation picked up, as if the music covered up a fear of eavesdropping, and the Slutty Mermaid slowly came to life. The woman who had been pouring beers put all the glasses on a tray, then carried them around the counter and placed them in the center of a table. She took a seat alongside the others and picked up a beer, joining in with a noisy toast.

I was still wondering if anyone actually worked here when the door opened.

Heart in my throat, I spun on my barstool—and there he was, hardly more than a dark shape against the white light outside to my eyes, but a shape that was undeniably Lou. I waved my hand, but Lou had to close the door and wait a moment before his own vision adjusted. When he finally saw me, he crossed the floor in three quick strides, throwing himself onto the stool next to me. Even in the half-light, I could see how tired he looked.

"You came," I said, kind of a stupid exclamation, but I'd been starting to think he'd decided to just keep driving, heading off to the mainland, leaving our problems behind.

"Yeah." He leaned over the bar and, with an impressive stretching skill, poured himself a beer from the closest tap.

I raised my eyebrows.

"Locals can self-serve," he explained, settling back down. *"You* have to wait to be served."

"Wait until I change the address on my driver's license. Then we'll see who's a local."

"You're born a local," Lou said. "That's it. Everyone else is a tourist."

"If you're such a local, why do you keep leaving this place in the lurch?"

He sipped his beer before answering. "I see we're jumping right in."

"I don't see the point in skipping around the subject. You came back to explain, right?" I leaned on the bar to demonstrate how ready I was to listen, which was a mistake, because the bar was very, very sticky. Apparently, locals did not have to clean up after their spills.

"Fine." Lou sighed and tipped back his beer glass again. When he put it down, the glass was half-empty. I hoped he wasn't planning on getting right back on the road after this. "It's simple. I got involved with some dumb stuff in Chicago, and one of them was literally land speculation. Selling parcels of unbuildable land. The same way they've been doing in Florida since before the Great Depression. You call people on a list, you make a hard sell, you sell them swamp or mangrove thickets or maybe just a sandbar. The only way to develop it would be to drain it, or bring in loads and loads of fill dirt. Almost no one ever can. So it sits vacant. There are plots like this all over the Keys." He shook his head, clearly embarrassed.

But the embarrassment was what made it okay in my eyes. Lou knew he was in the wrong. However he'd gotten mixed up in his, he regretted it. I could work with regret. It was the refusal to feel bad about hurting people that I couldn't forgive.

"Well, you did tell me you were a fraud," I reminded him. "Go on."

Another tip of the glass. Another sigh. "A few months ago, the guy I was selling for decided to move into legit sales. I guess he wanted a balanced portfolio, but who knows. He was going straight, and there's a lot less profit in that, so he let me go. It was right when the downloads were going through the roof on the Silvery Star record, so suddenly I could pay my rent without defrauding folks. Seemed like a win-win. I was packing up my desk, and we were goofing around in the office, no hard feelings, whatever. And I said, man, if he ever got hold of the empty little islands where I was from, he'd have it made."

I winced. "Oh, Lou."

The glass emptied. Lou put it down, rubbed his eyes. "He says, 'Oh yeah? Where ya from?' So I tell him all about Little Bucket and Cutlass and Hell and Dammit. How they're so lonely and quiet and pristine. Underdeveloped. Undervalued. Because I was proud of being from here, you know? My mom raised me in these islands. I think it's special here. So I showed off a little. Never thinking he'd acquire the deeds. Never thinking he'd literally look up the places I told him about the moment I left the building. But that's what he did."

"How do you know?"

"I called him and asked. This morning, when I saw the news. He told me everything. Not even ashamed. All above-board, he said. His first truly legal land deals, not a whisper of fraud about them. He looked up Little Bucket and Cutlass Cay, he found the owners of the undeveloped parcels, and he started acquiring them. He started before I was out on the street, he said." Lou stared straight ahead for a few moments. Then he hoisted himself up and refilled his glass. "Whoever bought them must have pulled some strings on the county zoning board, or else they were always zoned for big houses and we didn't know. I mean, there are already houses on Little Bucket."

"Not like what they'll build here," I said. "I saw the square footage permitted. Plus dredging for docking their stupid yachts."

"Marchant will hate that," Lou said. "He loves to see a sailboat at anchor in the deeper water offshore. He hates those big diesel monsters that they hoist out of the water to keep them clean."

"If they even built normal houses," I said, "like the ones already there, that would be different. But this isn't that."

"How do we stop this?" Lou asked. "Because I know you think we can, but Katie, this is Florida."

The same reason Stacy gave for giving up without a fight: *this is Florida.*

"Even in Florida, people know a good thing shouldn't be destroyed."

"How do you propose to tell them that Little Bucket shouldn't be destroyed?"

"We have to get the word out somehow," I said.

"Ideas?"

I picked up my beer glass. "None yet," I admitted.

We sat in silence for a while, Lou and I, as the music wailed around us, the pool balls clicked, and the locals of Cutlass Cay poured themselves drinks. Eventually a woman in a black t-shirt came out of the kitchen, the light momentarily blinding us, and asked if we wanted any chicken wings. Lou didn't answer. I said sure—it was now past lunchtime, and he was still drinking cheap beer like it was water. She nodded, gave me a look as if to decide whether I belonged there, then refilled my beer, accepted a five for her trouble, and moseyed back into the kitchen. Her Crocs scuffed on the tile floor.

"The wings are good," Lou said, finally lifting his head to look at me. "I hope you're sharing."

"I'll share if you'll come home," I said. "And help me."

"That's hardball," Lou complained. "But yeah. I'll come home and help."

That was all I could ask for. It wasn't enough, but it was a start.

Chapter Twenty-Three

On our way out of the Slutty Mermaid, mouth still tingling from the wing sauce, I stopped at one of those free newspaper boxes. You know the ones; they have listings for local events, a feature article about someone's home business, and a ton of ads in the back so everyone can sell their old RVs and flatbed trailers and living room sectionals and, in the case of the Keys, their old fishing boats.

As I'd traveled the country, I'd been reading these things from all over the place, and their similarities were remarkable—really illustrating that from Phoenix to Bangor, people's interest in poorly attended local carnivals and selling their backyard junk was pretty much universal. The main differences showed up in the events section, which generally reflected the industry of the area. In Iowa, it was Corn Festivals. In the Keys, it was fishing tournaments.

And music festivals. My fingers tightened on the paper, crumpling the edges, as I looked over the coming attractions in Key West. Another small festival was coming up, its ad filled with fine-print band names that I recognized despite their utter lack of fame. These were people I'd met on the road, traveling the same trails I'd been traveling with The Bombers. Their band names were the titles they gave their stories, strange combinations of words that only meant anything to them: Phoenix Fire Carey, The Marcuses, Flint River South, Billy Jean's Big Reveal.

The life of an afternoon third-stage band was hard, but the dreams were real. For a moment, I wished I was going on that stage. Sure, the Southernmost Lobster Roll and Music Fest wasn't Glastonbury, but it was a step—a very tiny step, and one I wasn't making. Stopping at Hell and Dammit Cay hadn't killed my fantasy of making it as a musician.

Part of me wished I was still in hot pursuit of fame and fortune.

"Someone you know coming to town?" I looked up; Lou was leaning against his truck, arms crossed over his chest.

I shook my head and forced a smile. "Just a lot of familiar names, but no friends," I said. "I know the promoter, though. He's keeping pretty busy, I'd say. Rivers McLean, do you know him?"

"I don't know hardly anyone in Key West," Lou said. "Went to school in Big Pine. Different crowd."

"I think Rivers is originally from Baltimore, anyway." I looked back down at the listings. Rivers had been booking dates up in the Mid-Atlantic earlier last year. His late-winter move to the Keys was what had gotten us here in the first place. To be honest, no one else would have booked us for the Saltwater and Sunsets Festival. We'd done okay with festival sets up north, as long as we were one of the bands somewhere near the bottom of the poster...the fine print. Rivers knew we could take up some time, keep the stage warm for better acts.

The Bombers were small potatoes; Rivers had been kind to us, but we didn't really matter. We could be replaced by just about a million other bands if we couldn't make a gig for some reason.

Lou, on the other hand...Silvery Star was a true sensation. Lou could have headlined a festival like Saltwater and Sunsets. Hell, Lou could headline Pitchfork this year if he really wanted to. A Key West festival would be a step *down* for a name like Silvery Star.

What a weird thought. I looked him over, wondering if there was some way to leverage that kind of potential. Not for me, of course—I mean, I liked Lou, full stop, whether he was famous or not. But for the island.

"Hey," I said suddenly. "If you ever want to come out from Internet hiding, I bet Rivers would book you in a heartbeat."

Lou laughed so quickly, I knew he hadn't even given my words any thought. "Well, *that's* not happening. Come on, let's go back to the ranch."

"Yeah," I agreed, folding the paper and shoving it into my back pocket. Something to think about later. "Let's take out the horses and see what brilliant ideas a good ride gives us, okay?"

⁂

We saddled up Reggie and Trinket almost as soon as we got back to the island, leaving Crystal staring after us as we rode down to the bridge. She was wondering how I'd gotten her son to come back. Probably wondering if I'd gotten him to fall in love with me. Well, Crystal, I was wondering the same thing. But that wasn't the priority right now, either.

Oddly enough.

We passed Roger, who was sitting a few dozen feet away from the fair and lovely Rogerina, and rode the horses over the bridge to Little Bucket. Their hooves clattered on the paved bridge and thumped quietly on the sandy road. We turned off almost immediately, following the trails through the planted jungle and past the dark remnants of the failed eco-resort, the huts with their glass windows looking blankly at us.

"Is that place haunted?" I asked, pushing Reggie alongside Trinket, so that my stirrups bumped against Lou's. The horses touched noses and snorted. "It looks like a ghost hotel."

Lou chuckled. "No one's ever lived there to haunt it," he said. "Little Bucket was a pile of mangroves and scrub before some mainlander moved down and planted all this jungle. The huts are just his mistakes. Nothing sinister about them."

"Couldn't it have worked?" I persisted. "I mean, isn't some kind of meditation and kayaking commune sort of a best-case scenario for all of us? Maybe we should try to get someone to invest in fixing up the resort concept before individual buyers can get their hands on the parcels and put in big-ass houses."

Lou kept his eyes straight ahead. "You know a lot of millionaire investors who want to fix up a failed resort?"

There wasn't much I could say to that. But if he wasn't going to think outside of the box, he wasn't going to be much help, either. I let him ride ahead as we approached the beach, the thick foliage giving way to white sand scattered with vines and low, scrubby native shrubs. A small iguana darted beneath a bush, and Reggie snorted and danced, his small hooves digging into the sand. I gripped the saddle horn with one hand, wondering if Roger and

Rogerina would react if a third iguana crossed the bridge to Hell and Dammit Cay.

As the horses reached the narrow beach, they anticipated a canter and shoved together, pushing my leg against Lou's. He grimaced as if he'd been run into a concrete wall rather than a fairly slim female leg, so I nudged Reggie with my heels and let the reins slip, allowing the little horse to move as quickly as he liked. Reggie tossed his head, his gray mane falling forward over his black-tipped ears as he jumped into a canter, and I rose in my stirrups a little to keep my balance as he bounded across the sand. After a week of riding, I'd managed to remember a lot of what I'd picked up playing with my friends' horses as a kid, and it felt so good: the wind in my hair, the quick movements of Reggie's hooves, the salty small of the water all around us. I wouldn't win any ribbons at a horse show, but I could stay in a saddle without too much danger of tumbling sideways, and that was good enough for me.

The beach being so short, the canter ended too quickly, and Reggie pulled himself up as the water rose up to meet the mangroves which took over the shore. He spun around, looking for Trinket, who was plugging along at a less enthusiastic pace. She might have liked Lou best, but she looked a little offended at having to stretch out into a canter.

As Lou and Trinket slowly lumbered our way, I looked past them, towards the thick jungle we'd left behind. It was time to talk out real, solid ideas to keep this space wild. I didn't want to make Lou feel worse about what he'd done in Chicago, but the fact remained: Little Bucket *couldn't* get plowed over, lined with concrete, and topped with tall houses. There were ways to live with the land, but the developers with their bulldozers and their wedding-cake designs weren't going to do the right thing on their own. So we had to make them.

"Let's ride a little farther," Lou suggested. "The neighbors here don't care." He slid the reins against Trinket's neck and the horse splashed through the shallow water, going around the thicket of mangroves and taking us onto a narrow spit of sand that sat below a few of the hidden houses of Little Bucket. Coconut palms rattled in the breeze, and turquoise water ran smoothly against white sand. Two pelicans floated on the calm sea. It was impossibly tropical.

"Who lives here?" I asked, as the horses slowed and put their heads down to nibble at sea grass. There were faint tracks of white sand running over the scrubby grass that lined the beach, splitting into separate trails as they disappeared into the tall clusters of sea grapes and shrubs I couldn't identify. They must lead to houses, although we couldn't see them at all with that screen of plants in the way. "Do you know any of them? It seems weird that this is the next island over, but it's totally separate from ours."

"I don't know them. I don't even know if Mom knows them. Marchant might, and I think Stacy does. But there's never any visiting between here and our island, as far as I know. They keep to themselves over here. I think it might be a commune?" Lou shrugged. "I just don't know."

A commune! That could have promise. No one who had moved here to form a commune would want a half-dozen mansions at one end of their almost-private island. "We should find out," I said.

"We can ask Stacy," Lou suggested.

Or just knock on doors, I thought, although the gates to these houses were locked, and guarded by cameras. Little island fortresses.

I turned back to the sea and watched the afternoon cumulus clouds drift across the sky, their shadows falling on the open water. In the distance, another low island lifted from the bay, its green hump speckled with the white dots of egrets roosting on mangroves. Even without a generous horticulturist planting them with exotic palms, these scrubby islands in their native forms were works of art. I remembered Key West, the crowds lining up along Mallory Square for the sunset. Everyone who came to Key West wanted to look west, away from solid ground, to the endless sea.

But we needed the land, too. It wasn't just the views of sea that made the Keys special. These little hills of coral and sand mattered. The communities people had made on them mattered. Reggie shifted beneath me as a crab scuttled by, and I stroked his mane soothingly. *I would do anything to save these islands,* I thought, and the idea startled me, because not too long ago I wouldn't have devoted my life to anything but my own dreams.

And how must Lou feel? These islands were his home. He'd betrayed them. I looked at him, his profile stark as he gazed across the sparkling waters. I wondered how far he'd go to save this place.

He must have felt my gaze, because his eyes were suddenly on mine. "You have an idea."

I had the ghost of an idea, not even fully formed yet, but I didn't think he'd go for it. It had been in my head since I'd seen the music festival listing in the local paper. It had gained a little more substance when Lou suggested this might be a commune. But it wasn't there yet. I needed more details.

So I shook my head at him. "No ideas," I said.

But as we turned back towards Hell and Dammit, I began to turn the possibilities over in my head.

It was crazy, but if I could get Lou to agree, we could save these islands.

And even if he didn't go for the idea at first, he'd have to agree eventually, since he'd caused all this.

Right?

Regret could be a powerful motivator. I'd hate to use it against him, but if that was the only option I had, I'd take it.

Crystal had an idea.

"We're going to sabotage the developers," she announced, around a hiccup.

Marchant put a few heaping plates of grouper on the picnic table between us, urging us to eat up, and I thought I saw him shoot a warning glance at Crystal. Something told me these two old hippies were thinking of reliving the glory days of the sixties. And that wasn't going to work out. Don't ask me how I knew. Just a gut feeling.

I would have liked a steadier hand to keep them on the straight and narrow, but Stacy hadn't shown up for dinner. I was sorry not to see her, because I wanted to ask her about the residents of Little Bucket Key. But Lou said when Stacy's curtains were drawn, she wasn't to be disturbed. And every window and door of her house was dark.

"Sabotage is the only way," Crystal continued. "Shows them who's *really* in charge."

"Absolutely not," I said, flashing Crystal a friendly smile to soften the edge of my words. "There will be a better way. We just haven't come up with it yet."

"Beer will help," Marchant announced, putting down a few fresh bottles alongside the grouper. "Drink up, drink up."

"We're going to *sabotage* them," Crystal insisted, snagging a fresh beer. "You can't knock down a jungle when your bulldozer has a flat tire."

"Do bulldozers even have tires?" I asked. "Or just the track things?"

"I don't know," Crystal said. "But they have gas tanks, don't they? Sugar in the tanks! They have steering wheels, right? Dynamite in the cockpit!"

Everyone stilled and looked at Crystal. She made a crooked sort of smile and tipped back her beer.

I'd heard enough for one day. All afternoon and into the evening, she'd been coming up with increasingly unusable plans to stop the developers from surveying and flattening the west end of Little Bucket Key into a series of tidy square tracts for tall, ocean view homes. Now the plans were reaching new heights of desperation and criminal activity. I just hoped it was the beer talking. And that a belly full of Marchant's grouper would shut the beer up.

I walked around the far side of the porch, where the house was blocking the westerly breeze off the sea, and looked over the island. A round moon hung low in the east, its laughing face yellow-gold. It cast a strange light over the palms and the empty horse pens. The barn was dark, the horses inside eating their hay or snoozing on their sides in the clean, deep bedding Lou and I had left for them that evening. I was tempted to go down and visit them, run my fingers along a few soft noses, feel the warmth of hot breath. Bask in the solid, ancient wisdom of resting horses.

"Nice moonrise."

Or I could just let Lou torment me with his presence. "Yeah," I agreed, standing to one side as he came up next to me. "It's going to be bright tonight."

"Perfect for sabotage."

I peered at him. Above his dark beard, his eyes glittered at me. "Very funny," I told him. "But we're going to have to come up with something real, or your mother's going to end up in jail."

"She's just talking. Just drinking and talking."

"Is she? Because she's been going all afternoon. And she was sober when she started. Are you telling me she isn't capable of getting herself into some serious trouble over this?"

Lou hesitated. "Okay, I'm not saying she's totally joking when she suggests dynamiting a bulldozer, but I'm saying it's not likely."

I shook my head. "That's not good enough. I want to solve this before it gets out of hand."

"I don't see how *we* can change anything. There are so many parties involved—the government is in on this, the zoning board, the community board—"

"It's the community," I said, interrupting him. The thought had come to me so many times this afternoon, but the moonlight—and the beer—made it all crystalize. "We have to bring together the community. Starting with Little Bucket's residents, but it's more than that. We have to rally the entire Lower Keys and remind them that if Little Bucket goes, they could all go."

"Oh, and how are we going to do that?"

"A festival," I replied, the words ready now. "We have to put on a festival. Everyone loves a party."

Chapter Twenty-Four

Rivers McLean had his offices upstairs in a pretty Victorian house just off the quieter end of Duval Street, near the Southernmost Point. We stood outside the white house, which had a jazz club on the first floor, and argued quietly.

"This is a mistake," Lou insisted. He'd been saying that since this morning, like a broken record. Ever since I woke him, dragged him out to help me feed the horses before Crystal got up, and reminded him of the promises he'd made last night. "You can't get a guy drunk and then get him to swear he'll help you put on a music festival. That's not fair."

"I know what I'm doing," I said, hands on hips, chin up as far as I could get it. Maybe I wasn't tall, but I had learned stage presence the hard way. "And this is going to work. Rivers is an old friend, so I'll handle him. You just have to do as I say."

"Why should I?"

I tilted my head at Lou, and the fire in his blazing eyes slowly cooled. I didn't want to say, *Because this is all your fault,* but I didn't have to, either.

He knew.

Poor Lou. I tucked his hand into mine and dragged him into the darkness of Southernmost Jazz.

The club was empty except for a cleaner, who was leaning against the bar, tapping into her phone. She ignored us. Our eyes were still dazzled from the brilliant sunlight outside, and I was just trying not to run into any stray bar stools. Lou stumbled over a mop bucket and swore.

"Easy, big guy," I told him, grabbing his arm. "Don't go breaking an ankle. I'm going to need you on stage when this goes down."

"Nothing's going down," Lou grumbled. "This is the very definition of a wild goose chase."

But Rivers was no goose, and I knew exactly where he was. Sitting upstairs, tapping at his laptop, making music into money. And he knew we were coming. I'd called him this morning, made the appointment. It had taken ten minutes for my hands to stop shaking once I'd put my phone down. I'd gone down and wrapped my arms around Reggie's neck, breathing in his warm horse smell, until I felt like I had enough strength to make it all happen. Then I'd gone in, showered, and told Lou it was time to go.

And now here we were.

At the top of the stairs, I paused and took a breath. Lou suddenly tugged me close, as if he wanted comforting. I turned my face up to his. "This is going to work," I whispered, acutely aware of the open door at the end of the short hall. "I promise."

His eyes flicked down to my lips, and we moved together at the same time.

Lou's kiss was soft and searching, almost tentative, but the touch still turned my knees to jelly. I threaded my fingers through his hair and allowed myself this one moment of indulgence. A kiss before battle.

When our lips parted, his eyes locked onto mine. "I'm following your lead, rock star," he promised.

I'm not saying a kiss is a superpower, but I definitely felt stronger as I turned and crossed those last few feet remaining. And when I stepped into Rivers' doorway, the man himself looked up with a broad smile.

"Look who it is! My own little ugly duckling. You flew away from those jokers in The Bombers? They weren't good for you. Come give Papa a hug." He stood up, pushing back his chair, and opened his arms.

I walked around the desk and gave Rivers a hug, smiling to myself. He gave himself all these weird monikers and affectations, like he was some godfather of concerts, but the truth was Rivers was a nice middle-aged dad with a graying beard, who liked to wear suit jackets over jeans, and jeans over flip-flops. He had three kids and a Golden Retriever, for heaven's sake. The guy was not a Nashville music hall kingpin, despite his best efforts to appear that way. When I'd first met him, he was playing Frisbee with his daughters. I'd been singing in what I'd *thought* was a secluded corner of a Baltimore park, trying out some lyrics away from the rest of the guys.

Rivers frequently swore to me that he only started booking The Bombers into his clubs and shows because he knew I had talent and he didn't want it wasted. I wondered if that was still his story, or if he was continuing to put the guys on concert bills without me.

Either way, it didn't matter. We all had to make a living.

"It's good to see you, Rivers," I said as he released me from his bear hug. "Yeah, I left the band." No reason to share that they dumped me. "But, I've got a new partner and I think he's pretty talented."

Lou loomed in the doorway, his lumberjack frame too big for our Victorian surroundings. A gentler time, a smaller people, I supposed. "Hey," he grunted, as Rivers greeted him, and said nothing else.

Was that all he planned on saying? I frowned at him. This was not how the meeting was supposed to go.

Rivers gave Lou an appraising glance, then raised his eyebrows at me. "Who's the thug?"

"He's not a thug," I said, taking a seat in one of the creaking guest chairs as Rivers went back behind his desk. "He's...a cowboy. Right, Lou? We live on his family ranch." My grin was teasing, imploring him to loosen up.

"A ranch!" Rivers looked back at me. "You *have* made some changes!"

"I am *not* a cowboy." Lou joined me in the second chair, but with a scowl etched on his face as if he'd decided to protest the entire proceedings. "I'm a—" He glanced at me, as if for permission. I gave him an encouraging smile. *For Little Bucket Key.* "I'm a musician," he admitted, sounding pained.

"Oh? Have I heard of you?"

Maybe it was Rivers' amused tone which pushed Lou to give up his secret at last? I don't know. But when the words came out, they were fierce and final. "Yeah. I think you probably have. I'm Silvery Star."

Rivers leaned back in his chair. For a moment, he seemed at a loss for words. I felt a little swell of triumph in my chest. How was that for a winning hand? I might have had to slump out of Key West with my tail between my legs, but I'd come back with the year's biggest underground sensation in indie music. I'd unmasked the mysterious Silvery Star. And delivered him to Rivers with a bow on top. I could ask him for the moon now and he'd hand it over.

"Well," Rivers drawled. "Pleased to meet you, Mr. Star."

"You can call me Lou," he replied tensely.

I suddenly realized something was not right here. That Lou wasn't happy about what I'd done. And I felt my triumph begin to sink into sadness. I wasn't here to break this man, or give away his darkest secrets.

But he had to see there was no way around this. I'd dragged him here to create something big, something that could save Little Bucket Key and Sea Horse Ranch and whatever crazy future I was building there. And Lou—I was saving Lou from himself, whether he wanted me to or not. So I cleared my throat. "Rivers," I began. "I have a—"

I paused. The word *request* was on the tip of my tongue. I was here for a favor. But that wasn't the right way to go about this. People came to Rivers for favors all the time. And he granted them, when he felt like it. And he requested favors in return, always.

I didn't want him to feel like he had power over me. Worse, I didn't want him to have power over Lou. I'd brought him here against his will and revealed his secret identity, and yeah, it was all in the name of cleaning up his mess, but that was beside the point.

I couldn't hand Silvery Star over to Rivers McLean as if that privilege was mine to give.

Lou was still in charge of his own destiny, even if he seemed to think otherwise most of the time.

And I had charge of mine, even if it literally never felt that way.

"Rivers," I began again, "I have a proposition for you."

Words mattered.

Rivers looked interested. "Oh, really? I suppose it can't involve anything *too* intriguing, or you wouldn't have brought your bodyguard."

I forced a smile. He was just playing. I hoped. "Let's keep it out of the bedroom, dirty boy. This is about music. The thing you do best?"

"I was hoping I did other things slightly better."

"I guess I'll never know. Because that's not why I'm here." *Keep smiling.* "But this is a *great* idea. You want me to take it to someone else?"

"Not without letting me hear it first." Rivers' smile was pearly; he was ready for his close-up. "Tell me what you've got, baby."

"Okay, here's the pitch." I leaned forward, my elbows on my knees, my hands open by my face. *Star power!* "A lonely island where wild horses play in the surf. A community of artists and eccentrics. A greedy developer who wants to destroy one of the last remaining outposts of the Keys' true bohemian character. And to save it all, a music festival featuring the year's breakout indie performer. A Rivers McLean production." I waggled my fingers to indicate lights on a marquee, fireworks exploding, flashbulbs popping. "What do you think?"

Rivers gave me a thoughtful look. "You want to put on a music festival to save an island? How is that going to work?"

"We raise awareness," I explained. "And a portion of the gate admission raises money for legal battles, if we have to fight them. But mainly it would be about turning public attention to our islands and making people angry that the government is approving this kind of construction. It's the classic argument, you know... corporate destruction versus the heart and soul of the Keys."

"And then you..."

"Buy up the land ourselves?" Lou suggested. I cast him a grateful look.

"To save it," Rivers clarified.

"Correct."

"Or we just get the construction scaled way, way back," I interjected. "In case we don't make millions, which is what I assume the land will sell for now."

"Not quite millions," Lou murmured. "Under a million."

"Either way." I shrugged. "Public outrage is a wonderful tool."

Rivers steepled his fingers. "And your island, it's an island of— what did you say—artists and eccentrics? Is this like a colony? How many eccentrics and artists are we talking, here?"

"Three, on our island," I admitted. "But there are more we don't know." I cast a frustrated look at Lou. "The other island— the one they want to develop—it has some other residents. We just don't know them. They *could* be artists."

"So you know three artists." Rivers sounded skeptical. I was losing him.

"One artist and two eccentrics," I said. Were we bartering something here? "And the horses."

Rivers shook his head. "I'm sorry, Katie, but you gotta do better than that. We need a real pitch. I can see putting on a benefit show to save an...an *enclave,* let's say. Some kind of retreat where crazies hang out and produce art, you get that? People would come out and protest if the big, bad developers tried to take their island. But we're talking three people? Come on, that's beyond a vanity project. No one's gonna step up for three people living on an island. They're going to root *against* them, most likely. They're going to think they're rich and all the jealousy is going to come out."

"The horses," I said pleadingly. "People love horses."

"Honestly, the horses make it worse. People think only the rich have horses. People resent rich folks with horses."

"Trust me, though, we aren't talking about rich people. Not even close."

Rivers spread his hands. "Like I said, you need a better pitch. 'They're kind of weird and not rich,' that's not going to do it."

Lou laughed. I gave him a sharp look. "Even with Silvery Star to headline?"

Rivers glanced at Lou. "I *do* want to work with you, buddy. But this ain't it."

Lou shrugged. "I don't know what to tell ya."

Rivers shook his head. "We're coming back to this conversation, sir. And Katie? I'm sorry. I like the idea. And you know I want this guy. But come back to me when you've dug up some more artists. Or some orphans. A new variety of Key Deer that can only eat plants growing on that island. Something people give a damn about. Okay?"

I slumped in my chair. I couldn't believe we'd lost already.

We stumbled down Duval Street. The strip of restaurants and clubs and t-shirt shops made a racket that was simply an assault on our ears, and the narrow road was filled with exhaust-belching cars and trucks. Tourists crowded the sidewalks, smoking cigars and drinking their lunch from plastic cups. Lou stepped around a guy wearing a parrot on each shoulder, taking selfies with tourists, a credit card machine at his side set up for 'tips,' and led us down a quieter side street lined with pastel-painted Conch cottages, their white picket fences holding back tiny jungles of tropical plants. Lizards darted along the sidewalks and wary cats watched us from porch steps. When we'd left the worst of the traffic noise behind, he leaned against a coconut palm swaying over the street and gave me a tired stare.

"Now what?"

"I don't know," I said. "What do you want me to say?"

"That you have another idea," he admitted, rubbing his beard.

"I didn't know we'd need more than three artists and eccentrics to qualify as being worth saving. I had no idea there was a minimum."

"If only Stacy had built that retreat she'd talked about," Lou murmured.

"What's that now?"

"Oh, a couple years ago, Stacy talked about filling in the bottom half of her house with guest rooms to rent to artists. Marchant and my mom were all for it. But she decided not to, for some reason." Lou shrugged. "It's too bad. Rivers said an artist enclave could work. We just need more artists."

I watched a lizard run up the palm tree's wiry trunk, thinking hard. "Do you think Stacy had a list of artists in mind?"

"I mean, she has a pretty tight circle. Most of them up in Miami, I guess."

That's it, I thought. We needed a better pitch? We needed more artists?

We could find them.

"Lou," I said, putting my hand on his taut arm, "We have to go talk to Stacy."

I didn't care if she'd drawn every curtain in that damn house. This couldn't wait.

Lou dragged for a moment, though, and I turned around, impatient to be going. I saw him looking at me with a hunger that immediately awoke a flock of butterflies in my stomach.

"Come back here," he said, his voice hardly more than a hushed growl.

"Lou," I began, but the words didn't go anywhere. I wanted him to kiss me again, more than anything in the world. The islands could sink beneath the sea, and I'd still want Lou's lips on mine. So I went to him, sliding my hands around the back of his neck as his arms went around me, pulling me close. We kissed beneath the nodding palms, as the tumult of Duval Street crashed a few blocks down and a world away, the sea breeze nudging softly at our skin.

Chapter Twenty-Five

As we drove back up U.S. 1, Lou's hand on my knee, I planned everything I wanted to say to Stacy. If there was really a commune on Little Bucket Key, that could be a huge help —unless they were some kind of really misogynist religion or they were all collecting guns or something, in which case maybe development was for the best.

But I didn't think Armageddon-preppers would live in such pretty pastel houses as the ones I'd glimpsed beyond their walls on the drive through the island, so I was hoping for artists.

Even if they weren't artists, we could certainly find some amongst Stacy's contacts, and we could make Stacy's old idea for an artist community pop up overnight—or if not overnight, at least in the next week. All we needed was some plywood, some paint, some secondhand furniture, and a lot of grit.

We had all of that, I thought grimly, putting my foot down on the gas pedal of Crystal's truck. All of that, and a heaping helping of need to get things right.

We whizzed past the Slutty Mermaid, over the humming bridge, past the distinctive little bucket slid over top of its mailbox post.

An island named for a bucket on a mailbox. This quirky, crazy, beautiful place. I wasn't going to let anything happen to it.

"You're driving too fast," Lou said suddenly.

"I'm in a hurry," I insisted. The bridge was ahead—a few more seconds and we'd be at Stacy's front door. We could get this thing started.

"Slow down, or my mom will kill you."

"Lou, leave me alone!" The truck whirred over the short bridge. On either side of us, the turquoise waters of the Gulf sparkled.

"Watch out!"

Roger!

I was slamming on the brakes, my heart in my throat. "Oh no, did I hit him?"

"I don't know!" Lou got out of the truck, his face stormy. I cowered in my seat while he bent down next to the hood. If I'd hit him, if I'd killed him...

Lou stood slowly. I watched his face fearfully. When it lit up with a big grin, I let out a colossal sigh of relief.

Lou held up Roger, the huge iguana's tail wrapping around his arm. "You didn't hit him. But man, Katie, you drive like a psychopath. Slow down next time, will ya?"

❧❧❧❧❧ ❦❦❦❦❦

Triumph gave way to tragedy pretty quickly. Well—not tragedy, *exactly*. But it sure felt that way.

"What do you mean, Stacy's not here?" I wailed.

Marchant lifted his bushy eyebrows at me. "She had to go to the mainland. Something about her sister again. I'd get another agent, if it was me. That sister of hers always needs her to come to Miami in person to fix things. I wouldn't stand for it. Miami!"

"But I need her. I need to talk to her right this minute." I was about one second from stomping my foot and throwing a temper tantrum.

"Well, I don't know what to tell you. You can try her cell phone."

I looked at Lou. He raised his own eyebrows at me. While slimmer and more elegant than Marchant's fuzzy caterpillars, they managed to express an equal measure of surprise. "Did you, uh, not think of using her cell phone?" he asked.

"I'm getting to it," I snapped, pulling my phone from my pocket. "Hang on. Everyone be quiet."

The phone rang and rang. Finally, just when I was expecting voicemail, Stacy's voice answered.

"What's up, Katie dear?" She sounded wonderfully relaxed. Must be nice. Maybe despite everything Stacy had said about the horses being her inspiration, she already had a Plan B. Maybe she was moving to Miami.

"Stacy, I came back as fast as I could to talk to you. Are you far? Have you gone a long way?"

"I'm just up to Marathon," she said. "Is there a problem?"

"Kind of." I explained in a few short sentences where I'd been that day, the conversation I'd had with Rivers. "If we can provide a reason to save the islands, like this is some eccentric spot that the tourist boards always want to show off in the Keys, I think he'll put on our show. A music festival, just for us."

"But what will a show do? Understand I'm not putting your idea down. I just want to know how it all works."

"The show will get us awareness, and turn public opinion our way, and help us build an emergency fund for legal fees, if it comes to that," I explained. "We'll show them that these islands are worth saving. It'll be a classic heartstrings grab. Trust me. Lawyers will want to represent us. Nearby residents will want to stop the development. Between our share of the gate and donations, we'll be able to put up a fight and find reasons to stop the developers from moving in. There could be a million ways to keep this from happening. We just need the cash to figure it out."

"And you need artists to make the place look like some hive of creative industry," she finished.

"Exactly. So if you could help me get the troops together, and then we can put together some cabins to act as studios or something..." I let the plea in my voice ask the question.

Stacy was quiet for a moment. In the background, I could hear music humming from her car stereo, a sultry Caribbean beat. It thrummed in my ear as I waited, desperately, for her assent.

"Well, I can give you access to my address book," she said finally, and I let out the breath I was holding. "It's in the house. But I can't come back until tomorrow night. I have work to do in Miami, and it can't wait."

"Fine, that's fine." My words tripped over one another. "We'll take whatever we can get."

"Go up to the house and let yourself in—Marchant has a key. In my desk drawer, you'll find a little purple address book. Flip to letter *L*. Then you can call everyone on that list. Tell them your plan and see what they say. See if they can make the trip."

Did I detect a note of amusement in her voice? I couldn't sit around and analyze it. "Thank you, Stacy, *thank you!*" I gave a thumbs-up to Lou and Marchant. "I mean it, thanks a million—"

"You're welcome, dear," she said. "Talk soon."

I looked up from my phone. "Marchant, Stacy says you have a key to her house."

Marchant looked shifty. "Well, I should."

"Marchant!" I shrieked. "Did you lose it?"

"Not that I lost it, dear, it's just that I misplaced it."

I sat down on the ground. "Oh my god."

Lou looked down at me. "You're going to get bit up by fire ants."

"Lou, I literally do not care. The whole world is conspiring against me right now and if I get to crush a few ants between my fingers, that's about the only control I seem to have in my life right now. Ugh! And I forgot to ask Stacy about the Little Bucket people, too. How could I forget?" Everything felt like it was unraveling just as quickly as it had been coming together.

Suddenly Lou was crouching next to me, his face very close to mine. "The *whole world* is conspiring against you? Katie, would it help if I told you that you're not important enough for the whole world to conspire against you?"

I made a face and shoved him, nearly toppling him over. "That's not helpful *at all.*"

"Well, it's the truth. And it can help get you through some sleepless nights, believe me."

I glanced at his face almost shyly, taking in his softening expression. Suddenly, it seemed to me that all our close quarters and flirting had come to nothing because I needed Lou right now, in this moment, to be the closest he'd ever been to me. The Lou I'd written songs with, the Lou I'd ridden horses with. The Lou who had come with me and taken off his mask in front of a concert promoter, giving up his most closely-guarded secret, for me.

And for Hell and Dammit Cay, I reminded myself. For his home, for his mother, for his friends.

But yeah, for me, too.

I wished he would kiss me, but at the same time, I knew I needed Lou for more than just a fling.

I needed this to be real, or nothing.

His lips parted, but it wasn't to lean in and kiss me. It was to say, in a reassuring tone: "Katie, I'm going to help Marchant find the key. And if that doesn't work, we'll pop open a window somehow. Can you just go help my mom with the horses and try to stay calm?"

"I'll try," I promised.

We gazed at one another for a few moments more until Marchant cleared his throat. Lou blinked. "We're going to worry the locals," he murmured, and I laughed despite the tension.

"I think they'll be okay," I suggested. "They like me."

"They do like you," Lou whispered, his breath warm on my ear. "But not as much as I do."

❧❧❧❧❧ ❧❧❧❧❧

While Marchant and Lou searched for Stacy's house key, Crystal and I fed the horses with a grim efficiency. She seemed to have gotten smaller since the letter from the government had come, drooping with depression, and her talk of sabotage was gone. It was as if she'd given up on the islands, and Sea Horse Ranch, overnight. I supposed she was in shock.

An hour passed, and the horses were settled for the night. The lights came on in Marchant's house, but no one shouted from the porch to tell us they'd found the key.

As stars began to twinkle in the deep blue sky, I decided it was time to get a move on. More dire steps must be taken. I would feel bad about breaking one of Stacy's windows, but it was for the greater good. Leaving Crystal to putter around her flowerbeds in the dark, dirt crusting on her knees as she knelt amongst the petunias, I went back to Marchant's house and climbed the stairs.

I was astonished at what I found inside. Not two men tearing apart the house in search of a key, but two men sitting across from one another at the vast dining table, drawing on a ripped-off sheet of butcher's paper.

"What the hell?"

They looked up at me in surprise. Marchant's fat eyebrows came together as he focused on me, then on the slanting moonlight streaming behind me. "What time is it?"

"It's time you got over to Stacy's and let me in," I snapped. "What are you two doing?"

"Drawing up ideas," Lou explained, standing straight with an effort. "I guess we lost track of time."

"Ideas for what?" I crossed the room and looked over the paper. They'd drawn a map of the island, criss-crossed with x's and boxes and circles and cryptic notes written in Marchant's crabby old-man hand. "What is this?"

"An artist's retreat," Marchant said, a note of pride in his voice. "We were going for a convincing look. Pretend it's something that's been here a long time."

"It would be easy to throw up plywood sheets around the bottom of Stacy's house," Lou went on, "but would it look like we'd been here since before the Little Bucket news came out? Probably not. So we decided to pull together something with a little more permanence. Like the eco-resort that was supposed to go in next door, with the bungalows and everything."

"With the bungalows...that are already half-built?" I looked up, a spark of an idea floating before me. "Wait, who owns those? They're not on the development property, are they?"

Lou shrugged. "Not sure. But we could imitate them, fabricate our own..."

"Or we could just take what's over there," I suggested.

"Let's see who owns them first," Marchant said quickly. "Maybe they'll give them to us."

"It's an idea," I agreed, although I liked mine better. The huts were abandoned, after all. And if the jungle around them was surrounded by mansions, an eco-resort was pretty much off the books. But first things first. "Are you guys getting me into Stacy's? What can we use to get in?"

"This," Lou announced, holding up a silver house key.

I stared at him. "You had it this whole time?"

"Well, you were feeding the horses and helping my mom and we got busy—"

I gave Lou a dagger of a look before I snatched the key and ran.

❧❧❧❧ ❦❦❦❦

The address book was exactly where she'd said it would be. I wasn't surprised; Stacy knew her cluttered home perfectly. My fingers were trembling as I turned to *L,* wondering whose name I would find on the page. Some famous artist, maybe. Did I know of any famous artists with a last name starting with L? No, but a better question was probably if I knew any famous artists...and the answer was still no.

I found the page and stared for a moment. There was a long list of names, websites, and numbers. At the top, it said: *Little Bucket Island.*

"Wait," I whispered. "What is this?"

Lou leaned over my shoulder. "Could it be everyone who lives on Little Bucket?"

"You were right," I breathed, realization washing over me. "A commune."

"They're an artist community," Lou said. "Hang on." He took out his phone and started tapping in the websites. One after another, they revealed themselves in splashes of color and light. Our breaths caught in unison.

"So—*everyone* on Little Bucket is an artist?" I asked finally. It was too good to be true.

"It looks that way."

"That explains why they're so standoffish," Marchant declared, startling me—I'd forgotten he was there. "Artists don't like nobody but other artists."

"And why they didn't want the eco-resort to succeed," Lou said. "They wanted to be left alone."

"But this development is too big, backed with too much money," I said. "They can't just chase them out by being mean."

"Nope," Lou agreed. "They have to chase them out by admitting who they are and joining forces with us."

"So we're going to organize the artists." I smiled, hardly able to believe our fortune was turning around at last. "This could be good."

Lou wrapped his arm around me, tugging me against him. "This is going to work."

Chapter Twenty-Six

"I'll call them," I said, still staring at the list of entries in the address book. "Or send them emails? We can send them emails. They'd probably prefer that. No one likes a cold call from a stranger."

Lou shook his head. "We don't have time for emails."

I looked up at him, studying his face. Slowly, I traced a finger through a deep line carving itself between his eyes. His skin was hot beneath my touch.

He wrapped firm fingers around my wrist, his eyes dancing with amusement. "Are you trying to distract me?"

"You just looked so worried. I didn't mean to..." I sighed as he pressed his lips to my neck. "Okay, I don't think we have time for *that,* either," I laughed as I recovered.

"You're right," he told me, voice grumbly. "But we can get there that much more quickly if we hustle through this job."

"Fine," I said. "You want to go fast? Let's go over there. We can meet the neighbors in person."

"We should ride over," Lou suggested. "People love horses. They've probably been sitting over there wishing they knew their neighbor with the horses for years now."

"Or maybe we'll invite them over to meet the horses," I reflected, imagining the damage Reggie or Trinket might inflict on those lush, tropical gardens I'd glimpsed through the gaps in their high stone walls and wooden fences. I didn't think letting a horse trample their flowers was the best introduction, no matter how cute they were. "We better walk."

"In the morning, then," Lou said. "One thing I know about people who live behind walls—you don't show up at night."

I missed the horses once we were on Little Bucket Key, ready to start meeting the neighbors.

It just wasn't easy to knock on that first door. I could have used a buffer. A horse would be such a nice conversation starter, as Lou had suggested.

Even though we'd already gone through the artists' websites and determined that most of the people on the Little Bucket list appeared to be normal, functioning members of society—albeit ones who had decided to go off the radar for personal reasons—it was frightening to open the gates in those high walls, and walk up the garden paths behind them. The tropical plants, green and bursting with blooms, nodded all around us, half-hiding the houses behind them. When they appeared, nearly all the houses were on stilts—like the ones on Hell and Dammit Cay—and that made things even worse. Climbing the stairs, aware of the blank windows above us, the possibility we were being stared at, judged.

Figuring it was easier to work our way home, we walked all the way to the humming bridge, then turned back and started at the very first house on the island. It was a two-story villa of bright blue and white. The front door was on the first floor, but thick clumps of umbrella tree hid most of the facade. I smiled weakly for the security camera above us as Lou knocked on the front door.

Steps inside came almost instantly.

Then the door opened and a red-haired woman of some undetermined middle age was leaning out, looking us over curiously. She was wearing a vanilla scent and a bikini top, with a patterned sarong wrapped around her hips. Smoke curled from a joint held in two long, delicate fingers. Behind her, soft piano music played from an unseen speaker. Her smile was slow, curving, as if she knew us. There was a glamour to her that made me feel very shabby in my pink flip-flops, sleeveless top, and flowered skort.

"Yeah?" she asked, forgoing a more normal hello.

"Hi—we're friends of Stacy's," Lou said, and I bit back a nervous grin, pretty sure it would look like I was baring my teeth at her.

"Stacy?" The woman peered around us hopefully. "Is she here?"

"No—uh—she said we should talk." Lou hesitated, then added, "We're neighbors? From Hell and Dammit Cay."

Her smile didn't waver. "Well, come on in!" she said, stepping back, and I wondered if everyone from Hell and Dammit had been welcome here, all this time, and no one had known but Stacy.

We were settled onto sofas on the back patio, overlooking the water and a small round swimming pool, while our hostess introduced herself. Her name was Daphne Barr, and she was a mixed materials artist. "And sometimes a watercolorist, and sometimes a sculptor, and sometimes an essayist," she explained, offering us a pungent tea. "Today's a writing day. I was just taking a little break when you knocked."

Lou refused; I took some, to be polite, and nearly choked on the rich herbal brew. I had the distinct impression I was drinking some of the fat green leaves brushing against the house's windows. "Oh," I said. "This is—um—interesting.

"Sorry, I don't keep any Lipton in the house," Daphne said, and she sounded genuinely apologetic that she didn't have any plebeian tea for me. "But I could get you a ginger ale? It's made with fresh ginger. Very spicy. Or maybe you'd prefer spring water."

She was actually stumbling a little in her words, trying to think of what would make me happy, and that was when I realized these people weren't going to be scary monsters just because they were hidden behind high walls.

They were simply artists trying to be left alone to do their work, and we could help them keep that solitude. Recruiting them to help stop the development was not going to be hard. We were all on the same team.

"I suppose you know about the development coming," I began.

"Yes, we got the letter—I mean, *I* did," Daphne said, flicking through some envelopes on the coffee table. "I assume everyone on the island did. I talked to George—that's George Shipstead, the Jamaican collage artist? No?" She didn't seem annoyed when we shook our heads apologetically. "Let's just say George has some big exhibitions under his belt. A lot about sugar and colonialism. Anyway. I talked to George just last night and I gotta admit, the conversation mostly ran towards finding somewhere else to live. These places have really appreciated in value."

"Well, you can't *leave,*" I breathed, horrified at the idea. I was kind of obsessed with my surroundings right now; Daphne's home, like Stacy's, was an inspirational clutter of art and fine old furniture. The open doors of the living room showed off dark wood accenting white tile, while shadows from the thick umbrella trees danced across our legs, and the water sparkled just beyond the pool deck. "You're never going to find another place like this. I mean, come on, you're just going to buy another island with this kind of privacy, start all over again? That would take millions!"

Daphne gave me a steady look for a moment, a look which led me to believe maybe they *had* millions. Well, I didn't know. What kind of money did artists make? Maybe they were all loaded. These *were* really nice houses, even if they'd built them back before the island was worth anything to millionaires with yachts and bad taste.

"No, you're right," she said eventually. "Recreating what we've got here on Little Bucket would be a colossal pain in the ass."

If that was how she wanted to see it, as an inconvenience, I would accept that.

"And then there's the spirit of the place," Daphne went on, her eyes flicking to the water. "That certainly will be hard to recreate. Some of us have lived here for more than twenty years. Working on our projects. There's an energy in the ground from all of this creation, you know? And there's the environment to consider, of course. New construction will be so invasive. And the history. Did you know Little Bucket was a pirate's hideout in the nineteenth century? There's a little inlet on the north side, close to Karim's house—Karim Butler, you'll love him—and it was a known hiding spot where pirates could find harbor and hide from the Navy ships sailing out of Key West. We've gone down and dug around the mangroves tons of times, trying to find chests of gold, but of course, nothing yet. We keep trying. Karim is dying to get his hands on some doubloons."

"That's the kind of history you'd be protecting," Lou said, giving me a glance that said, *Rich people are crazy.*

"So, what do you want us to do?"

Once we'd laid out our plan, Daphne laughed, made a drink in a plastic cup, and escorted us to George's house. An hour later, the two of them took us to Karim's. Two hours later, we were eating lunch from Karim's hand-fired plates, decorated in blue waves that I knew would make Marchant sigh with envy.

By the time dusk had fallen over Little Bucket Key, we had a party of six artists on board with our plan. And a buzz coupled with a contact high that was making it tougher and tougher to sketch out said plan for newcomers.

But everyone we'd gathered seemed to love the idea of building a little artist's village on Hell and Dammit Cay. There was hot debate flying past my head at one point, something about where to put the galleries, but then Lou reminded everyone that to start, we just needed studio space.

"It has to look as though you do your best work on Hell and Dammit," he explained. "Like you are out in the open, surrounded by nature and water and all that jazz, and it inspires you to create like nothing else. We can include both islands as the concept of an artist retreat...it just means you have to be more open about the fact that you guys live here on Little Bucket, and love working on Hell and Dammit. It has to be real in that sense, not just a bunch of huts where you show up now and then."

"It can't be built on fraud," I said, realizing where he was going. "We want to make something real."

Lou smiled at me gratefully, and I squeezed his hand as the artists considered our words.

Daphne was the first to speak. "Yes. I see what you're saying. And it's time, I think. We've been so insulated here, I think we're all getting a little too pretentious for our britches. George, that last piece you did, with the metal spikes on the palm tree? I'm sorry, but we both know it just didn't *land*. And Karim?"

Karim held up one hand. "Don't even mention last autumn to me," he said in his rich voice.

Daphne shook her head at us. "Karim will tell you about autumn in L.A. when he's ready."

"Never," Karim assured us.

"Art show gone bad," Daphne stage-whispered.

"Whatever!" Karim said. "You're saying we should join the community, get out more? Fine. Let's open a roadside stand along U.S. 1 and sell our work like the guys in Mallory Square. That's what you want?"

"Maybe," Daphne said, winking at him. "I hadn't thought about it yet."

George and a few of the others were laughing, taking the edge off Karim's tension. Daphne turned back to us. "I think we have a lot to talk about. Leave the rest to me, and I'll talk to you in the morning, okay, guys?"

"Sounds good," Lou said. "Let's meet by the bridge at, say, ten o'clock?"

"Why so late?" I asked as we walked home, the white road seeming to glow in the blue dusk. "We could get started by eight and really hit the ground running."

"They're artists," Lou laughed. "You've seen Stacy's lights on at two o'clock in the morning, right? I've never met an artist who didn't stay up all night and sleep as late as possible. Even if they want to catch the sunrise for a painting or something. They'll stay up all night to avoid getting up early."

"That's a silly stereotype!" I gave him a swat on the arm.

Or I tried to.

I ended up smacking him on the ass instead. Lou stopped, laughing, and pulled me against him. "Hey! You're high as a kite, little lounge singer."

"I am not," I huffed. "But even if I was, maybe I just wanted to give your ass a nice pat. Did you ever think of that?"

"Well, maybe I want to pat *your* ass," he growled, his voice rumbling in his chest.

"Well, I guess you should."

Lou maneuvered me onto a coquina rock guarding the entrance to the Hell and Dammit bridge and leaned over me. His long, leisurely kiss seemed to explore every bit of my lips and mouth, and I wrapped my arms around his neck, hair gathered up in one gripping fist. He was so firm and strong and *real*, a person who somehow felt dependable and kind just by touch. Or maybe I was just impossibly turned on. Heat ignited in my center as he deepened the kiss, turning my insides liquid with a rush of desire.

When he lifted his head, I stood still for a moment, my chin nearly touching his chest. I could feel the heat of him there before I even opened my eyes. His hands still gripped my arms, and for a moment I considered pressing back, going straight for that second kiss. We could stay out here all evening, I thought drowsily, under that luminous night sky, under that golden moon, with the water lapping against the rocks—

Then a mosquito whined in my left ear.

I shook my head quickly, my hair slapping the bug away, but Lou was letting go of me then, swinging his hands around his own head.

The Keys struck again. It could be hard to be romantic in a place that was so relentlessly *alive*.

"I think time just ran out," I giggled, flicking a mosquito away from Lou's forehead. "It's mosquito hour."

"Let's run home before we get eaten alive," Lou growled, taking my hand. "Maybe we can continue this conversation in your bedroom."

And I wasn't much for running in flip-flops, but for Lou, I gave it my best shot.

Chapter Twenty-Seven

The artists of Little Bucket worked quickly.

Maybe it was Daphne's leadership, or Stacy's influence—once she returned, she stepped right in and started working. In any case, over the course of two days, they had numerous meetings to draw up plans for the Hell and Dammit Artist Colony, drank copious amounts of wine, and feasted on not one but two grouper dinners hosted by Marchant on his deck, with everyone shrieking about the spicy Dammit Salt and working their way through several cases of beer and wine.

It felt like a successful way to meet the neighbors, even if we weren't trying to create a visible artist's colony out of what had been a completely invisible one, as fast as possible.

The owner of the eco-resort was uncovered through someone's address book and from a distance he okayed the very cheap sale of the huts once meant for an eco-resort. The horses watched in astonishment as we commandeered all the pickups between the two islands to haul over the dismantled segments of the huts.

"Hut" wasn't the most appropriate term; they had been built to be basic little bungalows but with good materials, luxurious simplicity, catering to wealthy northerners looking for a chance to feel like soulful sun-worshipers. A kind-eyed, tan-skinned artist named Peter took charge of the move, saying he understood the wood and wouldn't let any harm come to it. Daphne assured us that Peter worked with wood *all the time,* and he would treat the fittings of the huts with utmost respect. Which was to say, it took a little longer than we'd expected to get the huts broken down and brought over in segments to be reconstructed on Hell and Dammit, but the job was done to perfection, and the wood really did seem happy. Peter handed out buckets of stain and sealant, and once we'd painted them up, the wood glowed in the sunlight.

After a week of long and hectic days, we had a pop-up artist colony that would be the envy of any quirky island going for eccentric status. The huts were the centerpiece, tiny studio spaces where each artist could set up their mediums of choice. But scattered across Stacy's previously empty acre of land, woven in and out of the palm trees which popped out of the weedy ground like giant toadstools, we built something which was half renaissance fair, half eco-resort, and all fun.

Marchant knew where to find old maritime props and pieces which could make any village into a crazy-cakes land of whimsy, so there were pieces of ship throughout the winding trails we laid in crushed shell between the huts and the road. Queen Tom, an oil painter/performance artist, brought over heaps and heaps of flowers from the gardens of Little Bucket and set to work landscaping around the huts. There was a minor disagreement when George discovered that Queen Tom had dug out George's new traveller palm that he'd just bought on the mainland and had planted by his front door, but Queen Tom was unrepentant, saying that the needs of the islands outweighed George's need for a fancy palm tree, and anyway George's garden didn't have room for the size that palm would grow to. Queen Tom prevailed, and the traveller palm stayed on Hell and Dammit.

By sunset on the eighth day of construction, a cool wind was blowing from the north and rain was tiptoeing across the water. Lou and I were feeding the horses as the artists headed home for showers, promising to come back for a celebration dinner. Marchant already had the fire going in the grill, and the smoke was spreading in a lazy haze across the island.

"This place changed overnight," Lou observed as we let the horses gallop into the barn.

"It really did. I can't believe there's been an artist colony here all along. When I decided to sell the idea to Rivers, I was just grasping at straws. But maybe I felt the vibe in the air."

"The vibe," Lou snorted. "You've been hanging out with Daphne too much."

"She's cool," I protested, maybe a little too much, because I suspected he was right. I'd been hanging on to Daphne whenever I saw her, following her around like a little kid who spotted a superhero hidden in plain sight. I couldn't help it; Daphne was smart and strong and sultry—she felt like the kind of person I'd like to be, if I could just get myself together. I wanted to learn from her. But of course, that was way too much to say to Lou, so I settled for telling him, "I guess she's kind of like Stacy. They both have a spooky earth mama thing going on. It's fun to be around."

"I guess I don't notice it as much in Stacy, because I've known her since I was a kid. But phew," Lou started letting down the screens as the horses dug into their dinners. "It's crazy that she had this secret from me for all this time. Seems like they could have done more to protect Little Bucket themselves, you know? But I guess this is the best case for them, moving the studios onto Hell and Dammit. Since my mom has already got the ranch going, and wants to get tourists out here."

I busied myself putting down the screens on my end of the barn. The horses inside were chowing down, teeth grinding against their buckets. Once they finished eating, the island would fall silent, with only the sounds of birds and the wind rustling in the palm trees. The patter of rain on the hard-packed sand around the houses and barn. At least for a little while, until the artist colony came back for supper.

There would be more noise here if this plan worked. That part was hard to swallow: giving up the silence and the true peace of Hell and Dammit Cay to allow others in. Because, of course, tourists were part of the plan. Combining the artist's village we'd built with Sea Horse Ranch—letting the artists sell work directly at festivals we put on, staging regular weekend events to bring people in and, once they were here, to put them on horses and take their photos—would change the place we were trying to save.

It was really a win-win, of course, because the money spent here would let the ranch stay in business, and hopefully convince the zoning board not to give Little Bucket over to the millionaires just yet—we couldn't sell this place as a tranquil retreat if it was right next door to towering mansions or something—but it would be a shift. This wasn't just our island anymore—we'd changed it already, bringing in the artists. Stacy's property was completely transformed, no longer just a house on stilts above a grove of shaggy Sabal palms. Change was good, but change *hurt*.

Lou picked up the empty grain buckets and walked them down to the feed room. I trailed him, feeling a delicate shade of blue. "Lou, we're doing the right thing, aren't we?"

I saw his shoulders shift as he laughed to himself. "I think it's too late to ask that question."

"But—I mean—" I stumbled on the words I couldn't quite figure out for myself. I leaned on the feed room door as he stacked the buckets neatly on their shelf. "Nothing here will ever be the same."

"It wasn't going to be the same, anyway," he said gently, turning to face me. His eyes were shifty; they darted from my eyes to the dusky paddocks, as if he couldn't keep meeting my eyes for more than a few seconds.

I knew what it was about; I reached out and took his hand. "I'm sorry," I said softly. "I didn't mean to make you feel bad."

"I still can't believe I screwed up so spectacularly, that's all." His fingers tightened on mine. "I took a place my closest friends and family loved and I set it up for destruction."

"But it's like everyone here says, the developers are always coming in Florida. It was a matter of time."

The rain fell a little harder, pattering on the barn's tin roof, and all at once, a chorus of tree frogs began to sing, their symphony rising above the rainfall until the combination was nearly deafening.

That was fine; we didn't need to talk. I stepped all the way into the feed room and tucked myself up against Lou's shoulder, wrapping my arms around him until I felt his chin drop to my head, accepting the comfort—and forgiveness—I could offer.

"So what's next?" Stacy asked, walking past us along the flattened grass between the bungalows. "In your great plan?"

I brushed a rivulet of sweat from my forehead. The rain had passed in the night, but the island was resting under a thick, humid blanket of gray clouds which were in no hurry to pull away. I had a feeling spring was already behind us, while it was just starting up north.

"I have to go back and see Rivers," I said. "Put the festival together."

"While you're doing that, I'll lay down some rules for how it's going to work moving forward," Stacy told me. "We'll put together a calendar, dates when this place is open for business, that kind of thing. We're going to need a plan. Because if you want to throw a festival celebrating the artist colony at Hell and Dammit, you're going to have to welcome folks back, again and again. Everyone knew that, right?"

Lou nodded. "The others figured that out in about two minutes. They're a smart group. Everyone saw this as the perfect opportunity to build up buzz about their work and cut out some of the middlemen galleries they've been selling through. A few times a year, anyway."

Stacy paused at the foot of her stairs. "You built us a whole new world in three days," she said to us. "I'm not saying we were asking for a new world...but I know that's how they usually happen. Out of necessity." She took another look around the colony we'd built at the base of her home, shook her head, and grinned. "I think we're going to have some real fun here."

Then she went up the stairs, the long tail of her skirt swaying.

I looked at Lou. "I think we've nailed step one, honestly. The place looks great and everyone's on board."

"You go work on step two, then. Unless you want my help?"

I shook my head, wishing I could accept it. His back-up would be wonderful. "I do want it, but I think I need to deal with Rivers alone on this. Just a feeling I've got. You don't mind, do you?"

Lou smiled, tugging me close. "I don't mind," he told me, "as long as you don't sell any of my rights off in the heat of the moment. Don't promise him any albums or anything."

I laughed. "You're safe. I wouldn't trust anyone in the music business at this point. Not after what happened with my work," I added, thinking of Cass, out there singing my song.

"We'll have to figure that out later, too," he said.

A pause stretched between us. I thought about my song, my lost career. I didn't know what Lou thought about it, not really. Hell, I didn't know what *I* thought about it. Finally, I straightened and turned around, ready to head back to the ranch. "What are you going to do while I'm gone?" I asked as he fell into stride beside me.

"Teach Roger not to hang out in the road," Lou said. "That dummy's going to get himself run over with all the extra traffic this festival is going to bring in."

Chapter Twenty-Eight

R ivers didn't want to meet me a second time in his office; instead, he gave me the name of a cafe down Simonton Street. I borrowed Crystal's truck and drove down, parking it with some difficulty in the Key West parking garage (its enduring graffiti, over the years, was a cursive *"They paved paradise and put up a parking lot,"* and it couldn't have been more correct) before walking down the palm-lined streets, dodging tourists and the occasional chicken. Key West was a study in contrasts: beautiful and peaceful on side streets, chaotic and smelly on the main drags. I was never sure if I should love it here or hate it, and I thought a lot of locals felt the same way.

The stately Victorian house where the cafe was located was beautiful, offering a check-mark in the 'love it' column. On a wraparound porch, beneath gingerbread-mermaid detailing and a crystal chandelier whimsically hung with pinwheels, Rivers sat and sipped green tea. Iced, of course; the sunny morning was wickedly hot and sticky, with a layer of humidity I now knew wasn't going away as the day—or the year—progressed.

As I approached his table, Rivers lifted his hand and gestured to the wicker chair across from him. He was cooly elegant in short sleeves and linen trousers; I'd pulled on a sundress and was glad I'd made a little effort to look nice. He smiled and said, "Nice to have you back, Katie. Did you figure out your little island's quirk? The thing you can sell to the world?"

"You better believe it," I said. I pulled up the camera roll on my phone and slid it across the table to him. "We've built a permanent installation for the Little Bucket Key and Hell and Dammit Cay artist community."

"The *what* now?" Rivers flicked through the pictures, his eyebrows raising. "I didn't even know such a thing existed. Little Bucket Key is full of artists? Why didn't you bring it up before?"

"We didn't know either," I confessed. "We thought they were just very secretive neighbors. It turns out behind their walls they were all artists living in a kind of commune."

"Very secretive neighbors!" Rivers burst into laughter. "Oh my god. You were always an innocent, Katie. Makes me nervous to think the folks you've fallen in with are, too. I can't imagine what strange trails you're going to lead them down.

"Well, people keep to themselves in the islands," I countered. I didn't even try to touch his sidelining of me as an *innocent*. Whatever. Let him think that. Maybe I was, but it didn't affect my knowledge and know-how for what I was proposing. I'd spent the past year and a half touring clubs and playing festivals. I knew what we could do with just a little support from Rivers' huge music machine. "I'm from the bayou, you know. I understand places like this."

Rivers cocked an eyebrow and said nothing.

I pressed on. "So, are you ready to work with me? I brought the quirk to make the islands stand out. I've got the cause now. And I've still got Silvery Star—which is an exclusive, might I remind you? No one else is getting him."

Rivers pushed my phone back across the table, his steely eyes meeting mine. There was a shrewd twist to his smile. I'd seen this expression before. Rivers liked my idea, and now he was just calculating the profits. A rush of relief expanded in my chest as he spoke. "Well, so you have. And you know I want him. Good for you, bringing such a solid hand to the table. Let's be really frank with each other now, Katie. What do you want from me? Give me all the details."

"I want a regionally sized outdoor gig," I said, going for it. "It should bring in some people from the mainland, some fans will fly in, but it won't be like, a national-sized festival. Silvery Star will headline, so I'll need crowd control, security, stage, sound system, and three local bands for support. And promotion—notices in the south Florida papers, website, paid ads from your company's social media channels."

"So, nothing big," Rivers said dryly. "Just a full-on show, put together in what, two months' time? No, I suppose you want it faster than that. This weekend, maybe?"

"Come on, Rivers. I don't want it this weekend, but this is your *business*. You have everything you need at hand. You *could* put it on this weekend if you wanted to." A server wandered over and looked me over. I asked for a cold brew. I needed the pleasant security of that cold cup in my hand, the bitter thrill of caffeine hitting my tongue and rushing through my bloodstream, urging me on. "Tell me you'll do it."

"This is the kind of thing that generally takes months to put on," Rivers pointed out, and fairly, too. "But I know you don't have that kind of time. Be honest. When do you want it?"

I looked through the porch railings, watching a black and white cat stalk a lizard through the ferns lining the cafe's front walk. The cat was patient, but not patient enough; when the cat pounced, the lizard ran down the sidewalk, safely out of reach. The cat looked disappointed.

I could identify with the cat's dilemma. Impatience was bad for every hunter, but I didn't have much time. "We have one month," I said. "Let's put it on Memorial Day weekend. You can find a spot, right?"

Rivers gave me a long, hard stare. Then he shrugged. "For Silvery Star, I'll do it. There's nothing available here, and we can't do it on Hell and Dammit, but there are plenty of random clearings between Key West and Sugarloaf where we could put something on. *Stop* making that face at me! This will be bigger than you think, Katie. You can't do it on your island."

"But the point is to make people fall in love with Hell and Dammit," I argued. "So they'll write letters and fight for it. You don't think it has to be there?" Although at the same time, I recognized he was right. Two thousand people trampling down the grass of Hell and Dammit, startling the horses—what a mess. Would that many people even fit on the island? I realized I hadn't thought the venue part through properly.

Well, that was why I came to a professional for help, right? We all had our specialties.

"We'll arrange tours," Rivers said, typing into his phone. "I'll get some tractors and trams or something to bring people in from the highway. A second admission fee, proceeds to benefit the artist's colony. Leave it to me."

"Is there anything else I can do?" I accepted my coffee from the server and put it to my lips immediately, desperate for the cold comfort. Suddenly I felt very afraid; I'd staked everything on this moment, on Rivers saying he'd do the job.

"Just trust me, Katie," Rivers said, shaking his head with a wry smile. "You're giving me Silvery Star in his first ever live performance? For that, I'll save your island."

❧❧❧❧ ❧❧❧❧

The emails started flying in a few days later—the contracts, the proposals (which were more like commands than suggestions). I signed papers until my hand ached, and I listened to the rough-cut demos of three dozen local bands, looking for the ones which would support Lou and me the best. Rivers insisted we couldn't push too much electronica, or we'd scare away the older crowd that always swarmed the Keys—*This isn't a mini Electric Daisy Carnival,* he wrote, irritation clearly dripping from his text, when I suggested a band with too much synth and not enough guitar— and he pushed instead for more acoustics, more folk, more Margaritaville-style music. When I texted back that this would in no way prepare the crowd for Silvery Star, he simply stated that the older people would leave before eight o'clock, leaving only the youngsters who wanted to vibe out to electronica.

"Do you think he's right?" I asked Lou anxiously, but Lou was next to no help with the festival preparation. He closeted himself with Marchant and the artists instead, fiddling with the structures they'd built, working with his hands and ignoring music completely, as if he wasn't about to headline a show which Rivers predicted would draw five thousand people.

Five *thousand.* The number was huge; it took me aback when he first promised it. But he found a venue between Cutlass Cay and Key West, an open-air field on a sprawling chunk of rather desolate island where we could stick a stage, food trucks, stalls for our artists, and plenty of propaganda about the proposed destruction of Little Bucket Key and, by extension, Hell and Dammit Cay. There was even a corral planned, for pony rides on the quietest of our horses, and cowboy-style photo-ops. Crystal was cheerfully gearing up for an uptick in bookings for rides, and I'd seen her pricing out a sand delivery, admiring images of shimmering white beaches on her tablet. The sight spurred me on. I was determined to get Crystal her beach, give Sea Horse Ranch its chance.

The possibility that this festival would change everything, boosting everyone's fortunes in one fell swoop—it was intoxicating, it was incredible, it was terrifying. Because it wasn't like I would just surprise them one day with a saved island, a boost in bookings, and a brand-new beach. The buildup was what was killing me; all the time to wonder what would happen if this failed.

In my uncertainty, I wished Lou would come and help me, make me feel better. I lay awake at night and wished he'd give up his bedroom and come visit mine. But Lou withdrew from me. Probably it was nerves; my little plan was putting him on stage for the first time, and that was going to be frightening for him. But I missed the touches we'd shared throughout the day, the meaningful looks, the long, slow make-out sessions we'd begun to indulge in behind the barn at night, hidden from the rest of the island's view. Now he barely spoke to me, barely met my eyes across a dinner table or over a conversation about contracts, and shut his door on me at night.

I understood it. But I couldn't believe how alone I felt in the midst of rescuing this perfect little island. The timing of Lou's retreat was brutal.

In search of some peace, I started riding every morning, right after we fed breakfast and turned the horses back out in their pens. I mostly rode Reggie, finding something about the little horse that appealed to me. I was growing stronger and more sure in the saddle, and I got up earlier and earlier, craving the time spent on horseback even as the days grew longer and hotter.

The month of May was spoiling for summer storms, restless clouds billowing over the Gulf. In the far distance I could see them piling up over the mountains of Cuba, tropical downpours building on the distant island's sizzling inland heat. It was too early for a hurricane threat, but I still checked the forecasts religiously each morning, fearing that a festival at the end of May was asking for trouble, but aware it was the soonest we could pull so many threads together into a solid piece of cloth, and the latest we could go without risking bulldozers on Little Bucket.

At least on horseback, my problems were not so insurmountable; with Reggie or one of the other horses lifting me up, and the incomparable view of the sea between a horse's pricked ears, I felt strong and capable and able to make hard decisions. So I did, tugging out my phone and dictating the answers I'd send to Rivers' endless questions, to the artists planning the best way to sell their work without the usual barrier of agents and galleries between them and the public, to Marchant and Crystal, who were trying to grapple with how the improvement of Hell and Dammit Cay would affect their daily lives.

Only Stacy didn't need me; Stacy sat atop her house on stilts and made things appear. I didn't know how—a website, a mailing list, social media channels, calendars, careful plans for the art festivals we'd hold here. She didn't tell me what she was doing; her work simply came into being, fully rendered and open for business, and I was beyond grateful for her silent mastery of the mysteries of the Internet, of marketing. The entire artist's colony was grateful, in fact. If they'd had a presidency, Stacy would have been unanimously elected their leader. She turned their quiet commune into a hive of industry; they all worked harder and, some said, smarter, with the promise of the coming concert and the art festivals on the way.

The date crept closer and closer, the days speeding up as they went, until one morning I was sitting on Reggie, gazing across the water, and realized that the week had arrived.

The festival was in just seven days.

Chapter Twenty-Nine

"This is where it all happens, Katie."

I glanced at Rivers. Silhouetted against the early morning sun, he was a dashing figure, even with those eternal flip-flops. A man who made things happen. A man respected in the music world. I was lucky to know him. I wished he quit reminding me about that, though.

I also wished Lou was with me, but Lou was coming to the festival grounds later on, with the artists. He was helping pack their vans and trucks—he and Marchant had appointed themselves the official valets of the artist's colony.

That left me to drive down to the festival site alone, in Crystal's truck, the Navajo blanket on the seat scratchy against my bare legs. I had my backpack in the cab, with my change of clothes for my set with Lou tonight. We hadn't practiced a single note in the past week, and even though I knew that what we could make was pure magic even when just jamming together, I was still uneasy about the lack of rehearsals. Why did he have to be so difficult about this? Everything was lining up for Lou. Even his friend who had worked on the original album had bowed out completely, leaving the Silvery Star name to him. This was Lou's chance to be a star. Why was he refusing the fame the world wanted to lavish on him?

And the world *did* love him. At least, the indie music world did. Tickets to the evening music set at Rivers' *Lower Keys Music and Art Fest: Save Our Island* had sold out in seconds. The afternoon art festival admissions had been slower to sell, but once the AARP discovered the festival and ran a paragraph in their magazine, it was all over. Hotels in Key West were already full for the holiday weekend, but now their guests had a new destination. We would have a lot of blue hair wandering the festival grounds today, and it wouldn't be attached to punks.

"That's who buys our art," Stacy explained when I'd shared my concerns about the older demographic coming to the art festival portion of the day. "Young people like art, but they can't afford it, or else they don't have anywhere to put it. Older people have money and houses with plenty of wall space. Trust me, everyone's going to be glad the tickets went the way they did. It's a festival for everyone, not just one group of people. Which is the way the Keys should be," she added thoughtfully. "Open to everyone who wants to love and have fun."

And so everyone was glad. Everyone was ready. Everyone except for me and Lou.

But it would be fine. *I* would be fine. Even if we weren't at the top of our game tonight, no one was actually coming to see me. They were coming for Silvery Star. I was back-up, once again. I could live with it—for now. At least Lou never made me feel small about it.

And I knew that Lou could get on that stage looming over there, bomb completely, and still not disappoint a single fan. I'd seen acts like his before. Fandoms like his before. The allure of Silvery Star was, for a brief shining moment in music history, invincible. That was the real value of staying anonymous and refusing to play live. The worst set in the world was still a treat no one else had ever experienced.

Rivers was walking ahead of me, his flip-flops sinking into the short wet grass of the field. Dew drops sparkled on every blade of grass; there wouldn't be a single patch of sod left tonight. Not when all the coming feet were done tramping over it. "This is going to be quite a scene in just a few hours," he said with satisfaction. "I'm glad you came to me, Katie." He turned, eyebrows lifting in that way he had. "And what do you plan to do next?"

He didn't really mean me. I was sure of that. This was about Lou. "I don't think we have any plans," I said carefully. I couldn't commit him to anything. He was like quicksilver, Lou; one wrong move, and I'd scare him off.

I couldn't bear to think of him leaving again. I needed him to stay on Hell and Dammit Cay, with me. Sure, it meant living with his mother...but there was that empty house. The fourth house. Could we fix it up? I took a moment to imagine living in a house like Crystal's, Marchant's, and Stacy's. With Lou. Making music. Riding horses. Could there be a better version of life?

Rivers was building empires of his own, lost in his thoughts. Aloud, he said, "There needs to be a next step. Make sure Lou understands that, okay? I'm ready to make you guys a national tour. Maybe more. The summer festivals are booked, but I can find you some autumn spots if you want to hit the road."

I laughed ruefully. He could offer us Buckingham Palace, and Lou would still say no. Unless something changed in him while onstage tonight. "There's no way Lou will agree to that."

"And what about you?"

That's when I realized it: Rivers didn't understand that I wasn't part of Silvery Star, and that everything I did tonight on that stage would be a guest spot. He thought I was part of Lou's greatness and, more jarringly, he thought I could convince Lou we should take our star act on the road. I opened my mouth to tell him how wrong he was.

And then I closed it.

What about you? he'd asked.

Was that question a chance? Was it an opening? Was it an invitation? I thought about the life I'd given up, the dreams I'd had. Still there.

Just dormant.

Just waiting.

I was sure I couldn't have it all—couldn't have the island and Lou *and* be a touring musical sensation—but I didn't want to discount having it all out of hand, either. Maybe, in time...

"I don't know," I hedged. "I don't have any solo work to promote."

Rivers shrugged elaborately. "That can be remedied. Buying some studio time is the least of my concerns, if that's what's slowing you down. Let me know, Katie. Soon. I'd like to act on the momentum we're going to build tonight."

I watched him set off across the field again, his sure stride as he moved to inspect the miles of cable, the towers of metal. He knew this business inside out; Rivers' expertise was what allowed him to work from a Victorian house on the most far-flung island in the continental United States. Rivers' clout was what let him make his own rules under a tropical sun while the other promoters slummed it in New York and Los Angeles and Nashville and Chicago.

If Rivers wanted to back me, I had a career ready-made and waiting.

Talk about temptation.

Behind me, a truck door slammed. I didn't have to turn to know it was Lou, arriving with his first delivery of paintings and sculpture. And I wasn't ready to look at his closed, withdrawn face. So I just stood there in that field, as the sun rose over the Florida Keys, and wondered what on earth I was going to do after today.

❧❧❧❧❧❧ ❧❧❧❧❧❧

Fried food sizzling. The coconut smell of sunblock. A million pairs of flip-flops. Mirrored mosaics flashing in the sunlight. A sea breeze tangy with salt. I listened to the Jimmy Buffett cover band jamming their enthusiastic way through *Volcano* and savored, for as long as I could keep my mind centered, the sweet pleasures of the Keys.

Of course, it was Memorial Day weekend in the tropics, so the fried food wasn't the only thing sizzling. I'd had to find shade beneath one of the many canopies Rivers' concert production company had set up, with myriad mister fans blowing cool, damp air onto my bare shoulders. At my side, a literal bucket of lemonade. In my hand, a rapidly melting coconut paleta. In my head, the lyrics to *Heart So True*. My song about leaving home and coming home. My song which escaped my own comprehension. I thought it meant one thing, then another. Today, I had no idea what it meant. When I sang it tonight, would I know? Would it give me a clue where I was going next?

Marchant appeared and sat next to me, his breath coming fast, his face red. "It's scorching out here today," he gasped, and I stuck my paleta in my mouth so I could use both hands to pass the lemonade bucket.

"I feel bad dragging you Conchs out of the shade on a summer's day," I joked, once my mouth was free again. "No one melting, I hope?"

"Hey, we're the only ones who know better than to be out in the sun all day," Marchant countered. "Only *tourists* go wandering around in this heat."

"Well, the tourists spend money," I reminded him. "So, every once in a while, I guess we gotta risk heat stroke long enough to take their cash."

Marchant grinned at me around the straw of my lemonade, but said nothing. He also let me keep the word 'we' without further discussion. Hey, I wasn't saying I would ever be a native Conch, but couldn't I at least slowly nudge my way into honorary status?

We sat companionably for a while, watching the crowds move amongst the art stalls, watching the drunk women take off their tops for the Jimmy Buffett cover band. In the Keys, it took surprisingly little to get certain middle-aged women to remove their shirts—a couple of margaritas, a couple of choruses of *Cheeseburger in Paradise*. There was something different about the Keys, it was often said, but more and more I was beginning to suspect the "something different" was more about the way tourists behaved when they got here than about the Conchs who lived here year round.

Or maybe I was just getting used to the locals. I glanced at Marchant; in the space of a few minutes in the shade, he had fallen asleep, his head tipped back against the wooden pillar bracing the canopy, his mouth wide open. I took back my bucket of lemonade and finished it, slurping around the remaining ice cubes. I wished there was something stronger in it. But if I started drinking now, I wouldn't stop. And it was too hot to consider going onstage while anything less than fully hydrated.

Onstage. This was the biggest crowd I'd ever faced. I looked around at all the strange faces, wishing Lou was at my side—just as I'd been doing all day. All week. For the past month. Maybe I'd made up everything I'd thought there was between Lou and me. Maybe that burst of affection, those stolen kisses behind the barn, hadn't really been anything at all. Maybe he wouldn't come back to me after this. It was painful to think I'd lost him so quickly. And all to save his island.

Maybe he'd stay with me, maybe it was nothing but nerves. But it had been weeks since we'd kissed, or even laughed together over some private joke, and I was afraid it was over. I was afraid he would leave. Head north. Find himself some new trouble.

I wanted to convince Lou that I was all the trouble he needed. We could stay together on Hell and Dammit Cay. Make music. Make love.

But first, we had to get through today.

Stacy wandered past, looking dreamy. I waved, and she turned her head, smiling as she saw me. "You keeping busy?" she asked, eyeballing Marchant.

"Just baby-sitting Marchant. If I leave him while he's sleeping with his mouth wide open like that, some kid might pop something in his mouth."

Stacy snorted. "He'd love that."

"Maybe so, but I think the stuff on the street is purer these days than anything our Marchant is used to."

"You're not kidding. Tell you what, I'll sit with our Captain Snoozles for a while. You go on over to the corral and help Crystal with the horses. I think she could use a familiar face."

I didn't want to drag reluctant horses in circles while children sat on their backs, screaming for their parents, but I supposed the entire situation was basically my fault, so I went over to the corral. It was partially shaded by some palm trees—that is to say, the shade was pretty spotty. Poor Crystal was red in the face from heat and frustration, and I felt bad for leaving her to do pony rides alone. "Let me take over," I said, taking Trinket's lead-rope from her hand.

"Thanks." Crystal wiped a hand across her sweaty brow. "Lou was helping, then he disappeared again."

"He was?" I held the lead a little too tightly and Trinket tossed her head in protest. The small girl on her back squealed. "Relax," I told the kid. "You're fine."

"Yeah. I don't know where he got to." Crystal gave me a level look. "I think he got stage fright, poor boy."

"Oh, no. I might have to go find him before we get too close to set time, then. Talk him down a little."

"Just walk these guys long enough for me to get some lunch," Crystal said. "Then I'll come back and you can go find him."

I agreed and started walking Trinket around the corral. Screaming kids, fearful grandparents, smiling for the camera: it was as bad as I'd expected. Well, whatever life I was cut out for, it wasn't a life as a carnie walking ponies in circles. At least I knew *that* much.

❧ ❧

By the time I got away to start searching for Lou, the sun was slipping towards the slanting gold of late afternoon. I didn't mean to take so long, it just ended up that way. People wanted my help, horses got riled up and needed settled, Marchant woke up and came over, wanting to tell me about a dream he'd had involving a boat and a horse, and then it was past four o'clock. We went on at seven-thirty, so there was plenty of time to find Lou and make sure he was okay...but the schedule still felt tight.

The crowds were shifting now, the younger people arriving, the older crowd drifting towards their cars. They'd drive back to Key West, or the rental homes along the Lower Keys, to eat grouper or pink shrimp for supper and drink a few margaritas or beers before watching the sunset and hoping to see the green flash. All the while I'd be here, stressing about our set.

"I'm going to find Lou," I told Marchant. "You're good, right?"

"I'm good," Marchant assured me. "Break a leg!"

I hoped not. I took off through the artist's stalls, waving hurried hellos to the people who had become my friends over the past month. I couldn't tell them that I didn't want to see any of them now; I only wanted to see Lou. But he wasn't with any of the artists, and he wasn't by the food trucks, and he wasn't near the beer tent. I stood still for a helpless moment, surrounded by throngs of sunburned people, trying to gather my thoughts.

"Katie?"

I turned, my heart sinking. There he was. Not Lou—God, I wish it was Lou.

It was Justin.

He looked as beautiful as ever, and my heart stuttered a little, as if my insides were staggered by the idea of his gorgeous face. But I knew more about him now. I knew the bitterness behind those good looks.

He didn't belong here, in these sunny islands where having a good time was the local trade. I had a sudden rush of fear: someone like Justin could ruin everything.

"Katie," he repeating, smiling—a smile that didn't reach his eyes. "Hi, you."

"What are you *doing* here?"

The words came out more sharply than I'd intended and I was instantly embarrassed, my southern upbringing shocked at the way I'd greeted an old friend—an old *boyfriend,* no less. But I couldn't help it. I didn't want to see Justin. Not now, not when I was so rumpled up and scared and conflicted and—

His face was sympathetic. "Katie, you look so freaked out! I'm not here to cause any trouble. I just wanted to see Silvery Star in person. What are you doing here? Same thing, I guess."

Of course. My name wasn't on the billing. I was performing with Lou, but there was no *special guest* on the concert poster.

No one knew who I was, no one knew about me at all.

"Yeah," I said. "I just want to see Silvery Star."

"Well, let's watch together! I'd much rather hang out with you than all by myself."

I cocked my head. "You're alone?" Justin was *never* alone. He surrounded himself with people who adored him. Even with just a small band to back him up, a cocky, sexy frontman can gather groupies. Lord knew Justin was both of those things, and then some. He usually had a trail of swooning women wherever he went.

"I mean—the band is somewhere here, but I decided to look around by myself, and I'd rather hang out with you than them." Justin laughed, showing me all his pearly teeth. "I'm with them all the time. I haven't seen you in months."

And I'm better off for it, I thought. "Yeah," I said, shrugging. I could be casual with him, even if my heart was going a mile a minute. "It's been awhile, right?" *Since you told me to get off the stage. Since you humiliated me in front of a crowd, as I did my job. Since you sided with Cass and broke my heart.*

"There's something I want to talk to you about, anyway," Justin went on. He put his hands into his pockets and managed to look as sheepish as a little boy asking the girl next door to go on a bike ride. "Come on, get a beer with me?"

I looked around, hoping Lou would materialize and save me, as he had so many times before. Nothing. I was on my own here. And maybe that was for the best. I wanted the truth from Justin. I wanted to know why he'd really kicked me out of the band, then come back for me. This was my chance; it might never come again.

"Well?" Justin cocked his head, dark hair falling over one eye. He was a devil. He was a handsome, wicked man. And who ever refused an invitation from a guy like that?

"Okay," I agreed at last. "One beer."

Chapter Thirty

The craft beer tent was clever, set up to look like a fish camp saloon with hanging buoys and nets. A rough wooden bar ran the length of the tent, and a few hired salts from the Lower Keys were slinging plastic cups to thirsty festival goers. When we entered, I noticed immediately that the age had lowered considerably from earlier this afternoon; everyone in the tent seemed to be around our age, and there were more than a few feathers sticking up from the women's messy buns.

"God," I muttered to myself. "The Coachella crowd showed up."

Justin ordered our drinks while I sat down in a free seat near the end of the bar. It was a nice place; the breeze was blowing inside, fluttering the loose hair away from my face. When Justin handed me my beer I drank deep, anxious for the feeling of calm the alcohol would give me, however briefly.

"Feel better?" He grinned at me.

I rolled my eyes. "What did you want to talk about, Justin? I have things to do."

"Oh? Why would that be?"

I cursed inwardly. Of course, I would give away almost immediately that I was involved with the festival. "I'm here with some vendors," I said, hoping to cover it up.

"Ah. Well, I wish them good luck." Justin hoisted his cup in a toast. "But you belong onstage, my dear, not out there hawking dreamcatchers."

This was so far from a dreamcatcher crowd, I didn't even know where to begin telling him he was wrong. But I let it slide. Anything to speed up this conversation. "Either way, Justin. What's up?"

"I'll make it simple," he said. As if he'd ever made anything simple. Justin lived for unnecessary complications and drama. "I want to break up the band and cut an album with you. Just the two of us. And then go on the road with you. I want you back, Katie. But this time, I want all of you."

Okay. This time, he did make it simple. So simple, he'd completely ruined my brain. I gaped at him, unable to comprehend his words. Break up The Bombers? For *me?*

Justin grinned. "Speechless? Well, I guess that's better than throwing your drink in my face."

That's what I should be doing, I thought, but my hand wouldn't move. "Why are you saying this?" I croaked, finding my voice with difficulty.

"Why? That's your question?" Justin flashed his pearly whites at me. He'd had them whitened *again,* the self-satisfied codfish. "Because you're a talented, beautiful, incredible woman, Katie. And I treated you badly, and I want to make it up to you."

I felt a sudden twist of revulsion. Justin was going to put himself first in this, as in everything. If I went with him, I'd never be more than his back-up. And he'd make sure everyone knew it. "Treated me badly?" I laughed bitterly. "You left me in Key West! You *abandoned* me!"

"We left you at a paid-for hotel room, and we came back for you," Justin said, his tone extremely reasonable. "You didn't call, and we thought you could use some alone time after that show. You're the one who went hitchhiking up the highway. *You're* the one who left!"

"That's not how it happened." So like him, to rewrite history. "I had no idea you stayed another day, for one thing, and you told me I was done with the band, for another. You can't just change things to suit your narrative, Justin."

"Katie, that's exactly how it happened." Justin leaned forward. Somehow, despite the heat and his black clothes, he managed to smell absolutely delicious. As usual. "You were distraught after that show. And in hindsight, yes, I can see that leaving you alone was the wrong thing to do. I guess I thought you'd get some sun, enjoy the pool, relax a little...but I should have told you that was exactly what I wanted you do with the time."

A flare of anger ignited in my chest. "Because I need to be told exactly what to do?"

His whisper raised goosebumps on my arms. "Yes, Katie. You do. You need to be told *exactly* what to do."

I swallowed hard. Because he knew what he was doing.

One whisper from that husky voice, and suddenly it was all coming back to me, the nights sitting close together in the van, the days wrapped around one another, the promises and whispers in the wings as we waited for our call to go onstage. Justin had always been so beautifully in control, and I had always been so happy, so relieved, so *desperate* to do exactly what he told me to do.

The anger burst into excitement, and my physical reaction to his whisper was horrifying to my good sense...but my good sense was shutting down. I looked from side to side, as if just one more time, Lou might come forward and save me. But he didn't.

And then Justin's hand was on my arm, his fingers tugging at my skin. Cajoling, then *commanding*. "Come with me, Katie," he whispered.

My lips parted; my breath was coming fast. I was under his spell, and in just a few short seconds, a few quick syllables, I didn't care. I was his.

Justin's.

He pulled me behind the craft beer tent; there was nothing at our back but the lapping waters of the Gulf, tumbling over chunks of coquina stone. An orange-billed ibis poked through the water, looking for snails and minding his own business. Justin sat me down on one of the rocks and leaned forward, planting a hot, urgent kiss on my lips.

I kissed him back, my hands snaking around his neck until he caught them and held them, gripping me by the wrists. He was pressing down hard and I felt a sudden surge of fear—*real* fear, not the sexy kind that's really just lust in a masquerade mask. Seated beneath him, his fingers grinding against my bones, I was suddenly aware of the empty space behind me, the dark water rippling endlessly through the tumble of rocks. If I wanted to get away from him, there was nowhere to go but backwards, beneath the calm, relentless lapping of the careless open water.

I tried to pull away, to gain enough space to tell him he was hurting me, but he went after me, his lips hard on mine, and all I could do was whimper.

Finally he stopped, straightening, his breath coming hard and fast. "Let's find a place," he said.

"No," I said, pulling back against his iron grip. "We aren't going to do that. Not here," I added, afraid of the fierce look in his eyes, but he knew I meant *not ever,* and his face darkened.

"You've changed," he growled. "I think you need a little reminder of what's good for you."

"This isn't good for me," I told him. "We used to play at being rough, Justin, but now you're hurting me. So knock it off." I gave another tug and this time he let go. I flung my hands behind me to catch myself before I fell into the water, scraping my palms painfully against the rough coquina. I winced as he stood over me, afraid for the first time that Justin might do something violent.

He just laughed and turned away.

I watched him start to walk away from me, handsome in his black jeans and black shirt, his boots and his tattoos. He took what he wanted; he sauntered off in a snit when he couldn't have it. I realized Justin was more of an asshole than I'd ever given him credit for, and that was really saying something. "You're a dick," I called after him, just to make sure he knew how I felt.

He didn't bother turning around. "You're a hack," he replied cooly. "Good luck ever making it in music."

I sat on the coquina stone for a while after he'd gone, the ibis hunting around me, pressing his long curved beak into the water and flinging up small snails. I sat there until my back ached and my hands were sore with the effort of pressing into the jagged shell face of the rock, and then, when I was finally thinking of getting up, I saw Lou coming around the corner.

He stopped short, staring at me.

I sighed. "*Now* you show up."

⁂

"I've just been keeping a low profile," he said, looking away from me.

We were in the trailer behind the stage that was provided for the talent. Rivers had only shelled out for one, despite his keen interest in Silvery Star, so we'd had to wait until the last warm-up band was onstage before we could enjoy the air conditioning and what was left of the refreshments. I picked up a bag of barbecue potato chips and shook it, looking at the crumbs within.

"For a month?" I asked, digging out some of the sad chips. "I've had to do all this by myself. I'm not qualified to put on a music festival."

"Oh, like I am?" Lou shook his head. "I handled the artists, anyway. They're the ones everyone has to love, the ones everyone has to save. We're just the wedding band."

I looked away; he was right. We brought in the ticket sales and the notoriety, but that didn't make us the belles of the ball at all. No one had come to save the home of Silvery Star, reclusive recording artist. And certainly not to do anything for me.

"Well, what's important is that all of these people want to stop the construction on Little Bucket," I said. "And the artists are making money. And the festivals will bring bookings to Sea Horse Ranch. What we do isn't even relevant, I guess."

"That's right," Lou agreed, but I thought his chin jutted as he said it, and that his eyes looked a little rebellious afterwards.

"Can we just rehearse one song, please?" I asked after a half hour of sitting in sullen silence, listening to the bass of the band outside, and the hum of the air conditioner.

"Which one?" He asked. As if he had to ask.

"You know it's *Heart So True,*" I snapped. "You know that song makes me nervous. I just want to be sure I'm ready."

"Fine," he retorted. "You and this damn song. I wish you'd never written the damn thing."

"So do I," I muttered. "Believe me. It's caused me more heartache than any song should have a right to."

"Speaking of rights," Lou said, pulling out his keyboard. "Are we going to owe royalties when Justin hears us performing it?"

I wheeled around. "Justin?"

"I saw him in the crowd."

"Oh." I knew he hadn't seen us together, of course he hadn't, and still relief flooded over me, making my nerves tingle with a burst of adrenaline. "Yeah. He's here. But he doesn't own this song, no matter what he says."

"How do you know?"

I smiled—a genuine one this time. "I copyrighted it myself. Last month."

"Good job," Lou told me. "Okay. Let's sing your song."

Chapter Thirty-One

Thunder rumbled as we stepped out of the trailer, and a cold gust of wind whipped my skirt up. I shrieked and pushed it down. Really, Florida? I saw storm clouds rearing up in the sky and thought I was going to lose my mind. "Oh no! You have to be kidding me with this! We're about to go on and it's going to *storm?*"

Lou looked grimly at the gray clouds amassing to the south. "Maybe it will stay out to sea," he said. "All we can do is get set up and try to play through it."

"What if there's lightning? Rivers will tell them to shut us down. He can't be held liable if someone gets struck." I thought of all the artists out there, their beautiful work dangling in the elements. "And the vendor village will have to close."

"I'm sure they've made their money for the day," Lou said, shrugging. "And the fact is, so have we. This show is rain or shine. No one's getting a refund, even if lightning shuts it down."

I stared at Lou, unable to comprehend how he could be so cool and collected in the face of this oncoming disaster. And he was wrong to be so dismissive about refunds. People weren't going to support us if we skipped out on them. No one was going to stand up for Little Bucket Key if they were angry at Silvery Star for abandoning them to a thunderstorm. We would squander all the goodwill we'd worked so hard for. Even if we made the money we needed to challenge the development, the entire day would be a loss when it came to community opinion.

"You're thinking too hard," he told me. "Come on, let's get up there."

It was hard to set up our gear with that sea of people watching us. No one knew who we were; they were waiting for someone special, the one and only Silvery Star, and we were just two roadies to them. That and the approaching storm were enough to take the very worst of the pressure off; but I was still a little leery of the crowd. It had been a long time since I'd been in front of any gathering larger than what could wedge into a club, and I'd certainly never been the headliner; never been on a festival stage as the sun was going down.

I finished my set-up before Lou, and to distract myself, I gazed over the crowd to the corral where the horses were. Crystal had let them wander loose inside, just keeping out one horse for photo ops, and they were grooming each other, scratching away the itches of the day while the wind whipped through their long manes and tails. I remembered the peace and freedom these horses brought into my life. Tranquility and calm when I needed it most. I tried to channel that feeling now, and it worked...a little.

"Okay, let's pop offstage now and let the crowd get worked up," Lou told me, and we hustled back into the wings of the stage. It wasn't a very large space, but it was enough room for a couple of folding chairs and a cooler. I dug out a Diet Coke; I'd felt like I'd already had enough alcohol to last a week. Lou sat across from me and opened a water.

We looked at each other as the crowd began to shout and whistle and stomp. *"Silvery Star, Silvery Star, Silvery Star!"*

It was the first time I'd ever heard a chanting crowd before I went onstage. No one got too worked up over The Bombers. Maybe I wasn't the star here, but it felt pretty wild anyway, knowing people were waiting for us, getting impatient enough to chant.

Lou just drank his water and stared at nothing. The silence between us seemed as loud as the crowd's roar.

"So, we're really doing this," I said finally, anxious for anything at all to break the quiet.

Thunder rumbled. If I'd just waited, the storm could've done it for me, and I wouldn't have had to say something so stupid and meaningless.

But Lou just grinned. "Maybe, yeah. If the weather lets us. Are you ready for instant stardom?"

I thought I was, actually. Still, I was just the back-up singer. Again. At least Lou didn't make me feel replaceable. I felt like I had to make something clear—I knew the crowd was here for *him*. "Listen, if they get tired of me out there and just want you solo—"

"Won't happen."

"It could." I remembered my last gig. "Trust me, I have been booed before."

"That was premeditated," Lou reminded me. "Someone *caused* that to happen."

"I'm just saying, don't let me sink your ship."

"Hey." Lou leaned forward, put a finger under my chin. "Don't think you're not the wind in my sails, miss."

For the second time that day, I felt a thrill rush through me. But this one was different—it was warm and uplifting, like I could soar through the air. Our eyes locked on each other's, and I leaned forward, too.

Lou's lips parted ever so slightly, and just like that, I had him back.

When the rain hit the stage, it was coming down sideways, but the crowd didn't care. They went on screaming, shouting, stamping. They wanted Silvery Star. They wanted Lou.

Too bad, I had him. Right where I wanted him, wrapped in my arms.

We'd abandoned the folding chairs; they were kicked away, falling backwards as we leapt for one another, our legs straightening, our hands wrapping around each other's necks and arms and backs. We were curled around one another, an s-curve of sensuality, finally giving in to everything which had sizzled between us while he'd been dealing with his nerves or whatever it had been. A month since those first kisses, then nothing! Had it been so long? It had been forever. I had been searching for this moment forever. I was starved for him.

Lightning flashed against our closed eyelids, thunder rumbled the boards beneath our feet, and rain lashed against our legs, but I wasn't afraid of the storm and I didn't care what happened out there in the festival grounds—for just these special, stolen moments, I was wrapped up in Lou, and he was wrapped up in me.

Finally, it was the absence of sound that got our attention. Our lips broke contact, and Lou looked around, blinking. "Did something happen?" he asked, his voice guttural, as if he hadn't spoken in a long, long time.

I looked around as well, and it registered that the clouds were parting and a golden light was sifting into the cramped wing. "I think the storm passed."

"That's great, but what about the crowd?"

I turned towards the stage and gasped, just as a great roar of laughter went up from the crowd. "Lou, your mother has a *horse* on stage!"

❧❧❧❧❧ ❧❧❧❧❧

Crystal had never told us she had a magic act with Reggie. "My secret," she laughed later. "Because it's embarrassing! Marchant always teased me about it. But the weather was passing, and you weren't coming out, so I walked over to the wing to see what was up. I saw you two were having some sort of moment and I didn't want to bother you. So I looked at Reggie and he looked at me, and I said, well, guess it's our time to shine."

"But why did you have Reggie?" Lou asked helplessly. We were sitting on the empty stage, gazing out at the dark festival. Once Crystal had finished her magic show, our set had been a hit; *Heart So True* had made at least three dozen girls in the first few rows cry, and Rivers had promised that he wasn't done hounding me about putting together a record. Justin was nowhere to be seen. I doubted he'd even stayed to see Silvery Star. Justin had always been a little afraid of thunderstorms, although he'd never have admitted it.

"Oh, he just seemed like he wanted a walk," Crystal said with a little shrug. "And I taught him to climb stairs, so it was easy getting him on stage. Getting down was a little harder. He jumped the last three steps."

"Friends, I'm gonna have to ask you to leave." The security guard who had asked us to leave on three previous circuits of the field was now looking a little put out. "Go home. *Please.* So I can go home."

"Oh, all right." Crystal hopped down from the stage and picked up Reggie's lead rope. "I suppose it's late."

"Ma'am, it's midnight. Shouldn't your horses be in bed?"

I snorted with laughter. "They certainly should be, sir."

We took Reggie back to the corral, where one horse was still waiting, eating hay and looking put-upon; Marchant had already taken back the other two and returned the trailer earlier in the evening. They loaded up willingly and we piled into the truck. My thigh was pressed against Lou's, and he smiled before he wrapped his arm around my shoulder and pulled me close.

I let my head drop onto his shoulder, where it fit as snugly as a puzzle piece finding its mate.

Chapter Thirty-Two

Stacy planned the first art festival for the following weekend. "And then we'll do two a month for the summer," she decreed. "Until we see how much traffic we get."

We couldn't handle much traffic at first, so she didn't advertise it beyond the social media and newsletter channels she'd built up before the music festival. Still, RSVPs were pouring in, all the trail ride slots were booked, and Lou was trying to teach Roger and Rogerina to hang out on the rocks farther down the bank, away from the bridge and the road. He didn't want any more close calls like the time I'd almost run over Roger.

"Crickets," he called to Roger, who was sunning himself on the big rock alongside the road. "Nice, juicy crickets!"

"Training an iguana is harder than they tell you," I observed, sitting down next to Lou.

"I'm not giving up. Once he figures out there are crickets down here, we'll be in business."

"Maybe you should teach him the word cricket, first."

Lou gave me a thoughtful glance. "You know, you might be on to something."

While my foolish boyfriend was trying to train an iguana, I was trying to keep up with Crystal, and ignoring constant calls and texts from Rivers. Neither task was easy; in their own ways, both were keenly tenacious people. Crystal wanted the barns and pens spruced up, the tack spotless, and the horses trimmed up and looking spiffy before their first full weekend of trail rides.

"We won't have any trouble getting these people to leave reviews," she told me. "So everything has to be perfect."

I was happy to pitch in and took on the new list of chores she presented to me, mucking pens and trimming manes and painting fence. It kept my mind off my phone, which was kept on silent now. But the messages transcribed themselves right onto my screen.

Katie, we've got to get together. You said we'd talk about an album. Get to my office pronto and let's hash it out.

Had I said that? I couldn't remember. It sounded like something idiotic I'd say to get a guy off my back. I had a bad habit of doing that. I was trying to break the cycle, though, so I didn't answer. Didn't call him back. After all, what did Rivers want, but to take me away from here? To lead me up on the mountaintop and show me everything that could be mine, if I gave up Sea Horse Ranch, and Hell and Dammit Cay, and Lou.

I couldn't let that happen. But I knew myself well enough to know he could convince me. So the phone stayed on silent.

Lou and I rode the horses on Friday night, taking them out two by two for one more dry run of the Little Bucket beach route. By now the trail had been thoroughly trampled flat, and there was no fear of horses tripping on vines or spooking at scary-looking roots. They knew the trail inside out, right down to the splash in the water along the narrow beach. No excuses.

I rode Reggie on our last ride, braced for the worst because there was a distant storm lighting up the evening, zigzags of electricity flickering through its towering heights. He didn't seem to have any sillies in him, though, bowing his head and mouthing the bit like a dressage horse. Beside us, Lou's horse walked and trotted just as decorously. "I think we're ready," I said, as we stood them up on the beach and gazed towards the storm.

Lou gathered the reins in one hand and reached for me. I gave him my hand, thrilling at his touch. I wondered when that excitement would wear off. I would remember it forever, I told myself, even when we were used to each other, when the first bloom was gone.

"I'm thankful for this," Lou said. "For everything. For *you.*"

My heart was thumping in my chest. Reggie felt it and shifted, tugging at the reins.

"You saved this island. I know, I know it's not done yet, I know there are a million things to do. But the first steps, that's all you. And they're huge first steps. There's no way developers are going to get their way with Little Bucket." Lou's gaze held mine like a magnet. "You did that."

"I set things in motion," I admitted. "But you worked just as hard. The artist's colony, all that building and organization...this was a group effort. If anyone saved Little Bucket, it's *us.*"

He nodded. "Just as long as you know you spearheaded it. That nothing would have happened without you."

I nodded in return. I wasn't sure it was true, but I could be gracious about a heartfelt compliment. "So what's next?" I asked after a moment. "We have the first art festival. We keep building community support..."

"I think we should release a song," Lou said, shocking me.

"A *song?*"

"A Silvery Star-Katie LeBlanc duet. Rivers will give us the studio space and produce it."

"Have you been talking to Rivers?"

"No, but I know he's been calling you. I know you don't want to do a solo record with him, for whatever reason."

I couldn't tell him why I wouldn't, so I just nodded again.

"So I think that we should do a song together. If that's okay with you. And it will raise money for our efforts to save Little Bucket. Do you want to?"

Reggie shifted again, and this time our fingers parted as the horses pulled apart, but the separation didn't mean anything. I circled my horse, listening as his hooves splashed in the water. From far away, thunder grumbled over the open sea.

"Let's do it," I decided. "Let's do a song together."

Lou smiled. "Katie, you're going to be a star."

I was almost afraid he was right.

But luckily, I knew Lou liked me too much for me to take him really seriously. He was just flattering me. "We'll see," I said, and then I touched Reggie's sides gently with my heels, sending him leaping into a canter.

I didn't have to look back to know Lou was hot on my heels.

Bonus Story

Stay on Hell and Dammit Cay a little while longer!

Look for a second book in the Sea Horse Ranch series later in 2022. While you're waiting, enjoy a bonus epilogue! You'll get a sneak peek at how things are going for Katie, Lou, and everyone else on Hell and Dammit Cay. Just visit my website at nataliekreinert.com/bonus-content to download your bonus story.

And thanks so much for joining me on this adventure in the Florida Keys!

Acknowledgments

When I had a sudden idea about writing a love story based in the Florida Keys, I was so excited I wrote three chapters and posted the beginning to my Facebook group on the very first day. Something about my imaginary paradise of Hell and Dammit Cay simply captivated me, and I couldn't let it go until I'd written all of Katie and Lou's story.

I am so appreciative of the members of my Patreon, and the readers who enjoyed the first version of this story on Kindle Vella. Although it's definitely against all the marketing advice to publish a book without having a plan for a series, the enthusiastic reception *Sea Horse Ranch* received with early readers told me that even if it takes me a while to come up with a sequel, the book is wanted right now. So I took it out of the imaginary drawer where books in revision sit, cleaned it up, and here we are!

Thanks to everyone who helped me with early reading, feedback, and typo control. I must especially thank Susan Cover, June Monteleone, and Becca B. for their lightning-fast proofreading! You're amazing!

And I would be lost without my Patreon group, who support me at every step of the writing process. Thank you, once again, for helping me bring another new world to life! Some of you have been with me from the very start of my Patreon, and I'm incredibly grateful for your input on every novel I write.

You can join us at patreon.com/nataliekreinert.

My Patrons include: Tayla Travella, Gretchen Fieser, JoAnn Flejszar, Nancy Neid, Elizabeth Espinosa, Renee Knowles, Libby Henderson, Maureen VanDerStad, Genevieve Dempre, Jean Miller, Susan Cover, Sherron Meinert, Leslie Yazurlo, Nicola Beisel, Mel Policicchio, Harry Burgh, Alyssa, Kathlynn Angie-Buss, Amelia Heath, Katy McFarland, Peggy Dvorsky, Christine Komis, Annika Kostrabula, Thoma Jolette Parker, Karen Carrubba, Emma Gooden, Silvana Ricapito, Risa Ryland, Sarine Laurin, Di Hannel, Jennifer, Dana Probert, Heather Walker, Cyndy Searfoss, Kaylee Amons, Mary Vargas, Kathie Lacasse, Rachael Rosenthal, Orpu, Diana Aitch, Liz Greene, Zoe Bills, Cheryl Bavister, Sarah Seavey, Megan Devine, Mara Shatat, Tricia Jordan, Brinn Dimmler, Lindsay Moore, Princess Jenny, Caitlin Harrison, Rhonda Lane, C. Sperry, Heather Voltz, and Kim Keller.

I hope to see you all back at Hell and Dammit Cay really soon!

About the Author

I currently live in Central Florida, where I write fiction and freelance for a variety of publications. I mostly write about theme parks, travel, and horses! I've been writing professionally for more than a decade, and yes...I prefer writing fiction to anything else. In the past I've worked professionally in many aspects of the equestrian world, including grooming for top eventers, training off-track Thoroughbreds, galloping racehorses, working in mounted law enforcement, on breeding farms, and more!

Visit my website at nataliekreinert.com to keep up with the latest news and read occasional blog posts and book reviews. For installments of upcoming fiction and exclusive stories, visit my Patreon page and learn how you can become a subscriber!

For more:

- Facebook: facebook.com/nataliekellerreinert

- Group: facebook.com/groups/societyofweirdhorsegirls

- Bookbub: bookbub.com/profile/natalie-keller-reinert

- Twitter: twitter.com/nataliegallops

- Instagram: instagram.com/nataliekreinert

- Email: natalie@nataliekreinert.com